CRANFORD

Elizabeth Gaskell

COLLINS
CLASSICS

Harper Press
An imprint of HarperCollins*Publishers*
77–85 Fulham Palace Road
Hammersmith
London W6 8JB

This edition published 2011

A catalogue record for this book is available from the British Library

ISBN-13: 978-0-00-742031-5

Printed and bound in Great Britain by Clays Ltd, St Ives plc

Life & Times section by Gerard Cheshire
Classic Literature: Words and Phrases adapted from
Collins English Dictionary
Typesetting in Kalix by Palimpsest Book Production Limited,
Falkirk, Stirlingshire

10 9 8 7 6 5 4 3 2 1

History of Collins

In 1819, millworker William Collins from *Glasgow*, Scotland, set up a company for printing and publishing pamphlets, sermons, hymn books and prayer books. That company was Collins and was to mark the birth of HarperCollins Publishers as we know it today. The long tradition of Collins dictionary publishing can be traced back to the first dictionary William published in 1824, *Greek and English Lexicon*. Indeed, from 1840 onwards, he began to produce illustrated dictionaries and even obtained a licence to print and publish the Bible.

Soon after, William published the first Collins novel, *Ready Reckoner*, however it was the time of the Long Depression, where harvests were poor, prices were high, potato crops had failed and violence was erupting in Europe. As a result, many factories across the country were forced to close down and William chose to retire in 1846, partly due to the hardships he was facing.

Aged 30, William's son, William II took over the business. A keen humanitarian with a warm heart and a generous spirit, William II was truly 'Victorian' in his outlook. He introduced new, up-to-date steam presses and published affordable editions of Shakespeare's works and *Pilgrim's Progres*s, making them available to the masses for the first time. A new demand for educational books meant that success came with the publication of travel books, scientific books, encyclopaedias and dictionaries. This demand to be educated led to the later publication of atlases and Collins also held the monopoly on scripture writing at the time.

In the 1860s Collins began to expand and diversify and the idea of 'books for the millions' was developed. Affordable editions of classical literature were published and in 1903 Collins introduced 10 titles in their Collins Handy Illustrated Pocket Novels. These proved so popular that a few years later this had increased to an output of 50 volumes, selling nearly half a million in their year of publication. In the same year, The Everyman's Library was also instituted, with the idea of publishing an affordable library of the most important classical works, biographies, religious and philosophical treatments, plays, poems, travel and adventure. This series eclipsed all competition at the time and the introduction of paperback books in the 1950s helped to open that market and marked a high point in the industry.

HarperCollins is and has always been a champion of the classics and the current Collins Classics series follows in this tradition – publishing classical literature that is affordable and available to all. Beautifully packaged, highly collectible and intended to be reread and enjoyed at every opportunity.

Life & Times

About the Author

Elizabeth Gaskell was raised by her aunt in a village in Cheshire, England, where she rubbed shoulders with a broad cross-section of society. This exposure to diverse and varied sectors of society is reflected in her literature, especially when measured against the works of her literary predecessors – writers such as Jane Austen who had been preoccupied with writing stories about the English upper class. Gaskell chose to write about the working class and the emerging middle class, with particular attention paid to the role of women in society.

Gaskell and her husband belonged to a branch of Christianity called Unitarianism, which sees its god as being one entity as opposed to being three (Father, Son and Holy Spirit). An extension of this was a doctrine to understand and accept other faiths, which also meant an egalitarian view on society. Gaskell therefore found it easy to observe the behaviour and speech of people from different walks of life, as she bore no prejudice. This meant that her characterization was faithful and accurate in its detail, thereby lending her stories a genuine air of realism. She even used dialectical and vernacular language in her dialogue to bring her characters to life, which was considered an unorthodox approach to writing at the time.

About *Cranford* and the Victorian Era

Cranford is a string of short stories rather than a novel involving a group of people within a small community. The book is made up of a series of sub-plots and could be described as a 19th-century soap opera, as the stories were initially serialized. The collection was first published in 1851.

The central character and narrator of *Cranford* is Mary Smith, who is acquainted with everyone else in the stories. She belongs to a social circle of 'Cranford ladies'. The tales revolve around these women as they gossip and pass judgment on the comings and goings of others in the community. As it is set in the Victorian era, the ladies hold some rather reserved ideas about etiquette and correctness, but Gaskell uses this to comic effect. None of the women belong to the upper class, however they strive to imitate them with their own snobbery and self importance. The warmth and charm of Gaskell's writing, however, shows genuine affection for these characters as she attempts to celebrate the day-to-day minutiae of village life

Today, *Cranford* is regarded by historians as valuable documentation of everyday life in rural Victorian England, not least because other writers at the time were focusing on more highbrow topics. Gaskell's novel provides a detailed insight into the lives and minds of ordinary people of that period and highlights the fact that human character and behaviour remain constant, regardless of class or era. The villagers concerns are more parochial than panoramic, because they care most about the things that affect them directly. For these reasons, *Cranford* tends not to be viewed as a literary masterpiece, but is more generally regarded by critics as a fine example of storytelling at its best.

Gaskell wrote a number of other novels, but *Cranford* always remained her favourite work. Through her characters and setting she managed to address some worthy themes relating to the class structure and distribution of wealth in England during the Industrial Revolution without forcing the big issues. These themes were subtly woven into the fabric of *Cranford*, and reveal themselves only to very analytical readers. There is a pervading sense of humanitarianism throughout Gaskell's writing, which has made her own reputation as an author and the value of her works gain popularity and interest over the years.

Cranford, the novel, has been adapted successfully to British television and a number of her other short stories have been incorporated to produce the series *Cranford* and *Return to Cranford*. They include *The Last Generation in England* (1849), *Mr. Harrison's*

Confessions (1851) and *My Lady Ludlow* (1858). Whether modern-day readers would prefer society to be bound by the convention that existed in Gaskell's day, or alternatively are relieved that we are no longer limited by such values, her stories remain as popular today as when they were first published.

CRANFORD

CONTENTS

CHAPTER 1

Our Society

In the first place, Cranford is in possession of the Amazons; all the holders of houses above a certain rent are women. If a married couple come to settle in the town, somehow the gentleman disappears; he is either fairly frightened to death by being the only man in the Cranford evening parties, or he is accounted for by being with his regiment, his ship, or closely engaged in business all the week in the great neighbouring commercial town of Drumble, distant only twenty miles on a railroad. In short, whatever does become of the gentlemen, they are not at Cranford. What could they do if they were there? The surgeon has his round of thirty miles, and sleeps at Cranford; but every man cannot be a surgeon. For keeping the trim gardens full of choice flowers without a weed to speck them; for frightening away little boys who look wistfully at the said flowers through the railings; for rushing out at the geese that occasionally venture into the gardens if the gates are left open; for deciding all questions of literature and politics without troubling themselves with unnecessary reasons or arguments; for obtaining clear and correct knowledge of everybody's affairs in the parish; for keeping their neat maid-servants in admirable order; for kindness (somewhat dictatorial) to the poor, and real tender good offices to each other whenever they are in distress— the ladies of Cranford are quite sufficient. "A man," as one of them observed to me once, "is *so* in the way in the house!" Although the ladies of Cranford know all each other's proceedings, they are exceedingly indifferent to each other's opinions. Indeed, as each has her own individuality, not to say eccentricity, pretty strongly developed, nothing is so easy as verbal retaliation; but, somehow, good-will reigns among them to a considerable degree.

The Cranford ladies have only an occasional little quarrel, spirited out in a few peppery words and angry jerks of the head; just enough to prevent the even tenor of their lives from becoming too flat. Their dress is very independent of fashion; as they observe, "What does it signify how we dress here at Cranford, where everybody knows us?" And if they go from home, their reason is equally cogent, "What does it signify how we dress here, where nobody knows us?" The materials of their clothes are, in general, good and plain, and most of them are nearly as scrupulous as Miss Tyler, of cleanly memory; but I will answer for it, the last gigot, the last tight and scanty petticoat in wear in England, was seen in Cranford—and seen without a smile.

I can testify to a magnificent family red silk umbrella, under which a gentle little spinster, left alone of many brothers and sisters, used to patter to church on rainy days. Have you any red silk umbrellas in London? We had a tradition of the first that had ever been seen in Cranford; and the little boys mobbed it, and called it "a stick in petticoats." It might have been the very red silk one I have described, held by a strong father over a troop of little ones; the poor little lady—the survivor of all—could scarcely carry it.

Then there were rules and regulations for visiting and calls; and they were announced to any young people who might be staying in the town, with all the solemnity with which the old Manx laws were read once a year on the Tinwald Mount.

"Our friends have sent to inquire how you are after your journey to-night, my dear" (fifteen miles in a gentleman's carriage). "They will give you some rest to-morrow; but the next day, I have no doubt, they will call; so be at liberty after twelve—from twelve to three are our calling hours."

Then, after they had called:

"It is the third day; I dare say your mamma has told you, my dear, never to let more than three days elapse between receiving a call and returning it; and also, that you are never to stay longer than a quarter of an hour."

"But am I to look at my watch? How am I to find out when a quarter of an hour has passed?"

"You must keep thinking about the time, my dear, and not allow yourself to forget it in conversation."

As everybody had this rule in their minds, whether they received or paid a call, of course no absorbing subject was ever spoken about. We kept ourselves to short sentences of small talk, and were punctual to our time.

I imagine that a few of the gentlefolks of Cranford were poor, and had some difficulty in making both ends meet; but they were like the Spartans, and concealed their smart under a smiling face. We none of us spoke of money, because that subject savoured of commerce and trade, and though some might be poor, we were all aristocratic. The Cranfordians had that kindly *esprit de corps* which made them overlook all deficiencies in success when some among them tried to conceal their poverty. When Mrs. Forrester, for instance, gave a party in her baby-house of a dwelling, and the little maiden disturbed the ladies on the sofa by a request that she might get the tea-tray out from underneath, every one took this novel proceeding as the most natural thing in the world, and talked on about household forms and ceremonies as if we all believed that our hostess had a regular servants' hall, second table, with housekeeper and steward, instead of the one little charity-school maiden, whose short ruddy arms could never have been strong enough to carry the tray upstairs, if she had not been assisted in private by her mistress, who now sat in state, pretending not to know what cakes were sent up, though she knew, and we knew, and she knew that we knew, and we knew that she knew that we knew, she had been busy all the morning making tea-bread and sponge-cakes.

There were one or two consequences arising from this general but unacknowledged poverty, and this very much acknowledged gentility, which were not amiss, and which might be introduced into many circles of society to their great improvement. For instance, the inhabitants of Cranford kept early hours, and clattered home in their pattens, under the guidance of a lantern-bearer, about nine o'clock at night; and the whole town was abed and asleep by half-past ten. Moreover, it was considered "vulgar" (a tremendous word in Cranford) to give anything expensive, in the way of eatable or drinkable, at the evening entertainments. Wafer bread-and-butter and sponge-biscuits were all that the Honourable Mrs. Jamieson gave; and she was sister-in-law to the late Earl of Glenmire, although she did practise such "elegant economy."

"Elegant economy!" How naturally one falls back into the phraseology of Cranford! There, economy was always "elegant," and money-spending always "vulgar and ostentatious"; a sort of sour-grapeism which made us very peaceful and satisfied. I never shall forget the dismay felt when a certain Captain Brown came to live at Cranford, and openly spoke about his being poor—not in a whisper to an intimate friend, the doors and windows being previously closed, but in the public street! in a loud military voice! alleging his poverty as a reason for not taking a particular house. The ladies of Cranford were already rather moaning over the invasion of their territories by a man and a gentleman. He was a half-pay captain, and had obtained some situation on a neighbouring railroad, which had been vehemently petitioned against by the little town; and if, in addition to his masculine gender, and his connection with the obnoxious railroad, he was so brazen as to talk of being poor—why, then, indeed, he must be sent to Coventry. Death was as true and as common as poverty; yet people never spoke about that loud out in the streets. It was a word not to be mentioned to ears polite. We had tacitly agreed to ignore that any with whom we associated on terms of visiting equality could ever be prevented by poverty from doing anything that they wished. If he walked to or from a party, it was because the night was *so* fine, or the air *so* refreshing, not because sedan-chairs were expensive. If we wore prints, instead of summer silks, it was because we preferred a washing material; and so on, till we blinded ourselves to the vulgar fact that we were, all of us, people of very moderate means. Of course, then, we did not know what to make of a man who could speak of poverty as if it was not a disgrace. Yet, somehow, Captain Brown made himself respected in Cranford, and was called upon, in spite of all resolutions to the contrary. I was surprised to hear his opinions quoted as authority at a visit which I paid to Cranford about a year after he had settled in the town. My own friends had been among the bitterest opponents of any proposal to visit the captain and his daughters only twelve months before; and now he was even admitted in the tabooed hours before twelve. True, it was to discover the cause of a smoking chimney before the fire was lighted; but still Captain Brown walked upstairs, nothing daunted, spoke in a voice too large for the room, and joked quite in the way of a tame man about the house. He had been blind to all the small slights, and omissions of trivial ceremonies, with which he had been received. He had been friendly, though the Cranford ladies had been cool; he had answered small sarcastic compliments in good faith; and with his manly frankness had overpowered all the shrinking which met him as a man who was not ashamed to be poor. And, at last, his excellent masculine common sense, and his facility in devising expedients to overcome domestic dilemmas, had gained him an extraordinary place as authority among the Cranford ladies. He himself went on in his course, as unaware of his popularity as he had been of the reverse; and I am sure he was startled one day when he found his advice so highly esteemed as to make some counsel which he had given in jest to be taken in sober, serious earnest.

It was on this subject: an old lady had an Alderney cow, which she looked upon as a daughter. You could not pay the short quarter-of-an-hour call without being told of the wonderful milk or wonderful intelligence of this animal. The whole town knew, and kindly regarded Miss Betsy Barker's Alderney; therefore great was the sympathy and regret when, in an unguarded moment, the poor cow tumbled into a lime-pit. She moaned so loudly that she was soon heard and rescued; but, mean while, the poor beast had lost most of her hair, and came out looking naked, cold, and miserable, in a bare skin. Everybody pitied the animal, though a few could not restrain their smiles at her droll appearance. Miss Betsy Barker absolutely cried with sorrow and dismay; and it was said she thought of trying a bath of oil. This remedy, perhaps, was recommended by some one of the number whose advice she asked; but the proposal, if ever it was made, was knocked on the head by Captain Brown's decided "Get her a flannel waistcoat and flannel drawers, ma'am, if you wish to keep her alive. But my advice is, kill the poor creature at once."

Miss Betsy Barker dried her eyes, and thanked the captain heartily; she set to work, and by and by all the town turned out to see the Alderney meekly going to her pasture, clad in dark grey flannel. I have watched her myself many a time. Do you ever see cows dressed in gray flannel in London?

Captain Brown had taken a small house on the outskirts of the town, where he lived with his two daughters. He must have been upwards of sixty at the time of the first visit I paid to Cranford after I had left it as a residence. But he had a wiry, well-trained, elastic figure, a stiff military throw-back of his head, and a springing step, which made him appear much younger than he was. His eldest daughter looked almost as old as himself, and betrayed the fact that his real was more than his apparent age. Miss Brown must have been forty; she had a sickly, pained, careworn expression on her face, and looked as if the gaiety of youth had long faded out of sight. Even when young she must have been plain and hard-featured. Miss Jessie Brown was ten years younger than her sister, and twenty shades prettier. Her face was round and dimpled. Miss Jenkyns once said, in a passion against Captain Brown (the cause of which I will tell you presently), that "she thought it was time for Miss Jessie to leave off her dimples, and not always to be trying to look like a child." It was true there was something childlike in her face; and there will be, I think, till she dies, though she should live to a hundred. Her eyes were large, blue, wondering eyes, looking straight at you; her nose was unformed and snub, and her lips were red and dewy; she wore her hair, too, in little rows of curls, which heightened this appearance. I do not know whether she was pretty or not; but I liked her face, and so did everybody, and I do not think she could help her dimples. She had something of her father's jauntiness of gait and manner; and any female observer might detect a slight difference in the attire of the two sisters—that of Miss Jessie being about two pounds per annum more expensive than Miss Brown's. Two pounds was a large sum in Captain Brown's annual disbursements.

Such was the impression made upon me by the Brown family when I first saw them all together in Cranford Church. The Captain I had met before—on the occasion of the smoky chimney, which he had cured by some simple alteration in the flue. In church, he held his double eyeglass to his eyes during the Morning Hymn, and then lifted up his head erect and sang out loud and joyfully. He made the responses louder than the clerk—an old man with a piping feeble voice, who, I think, felt aggrieved at the Captain's sonorous bass, and quavered higher and higher in consequence.

On coming out of church, the brisk Captain paid the most gallant attention to his two daughters. He nodded and smiled to his acquaintances; but he shook hands with none until he had helped Miss Brown to unfurl her umbrella, had relieved her of her prayer-book, and had waited patiently till she, with trembling, nervous hands, had taken up her gown to walk through the wet roads.

I wondered what the Cranford ladies did with Captain Brown at their parties. We had often rejoiced, in former days, that there was no gentleman to be attended to, and to find conversation for, at the card-parties. We had congratulated ourselves upon the snugness of the evenings; and, in our love for gentility, and distaste of mankind, we had almost persuaded ourselves that to be a man was to be "vulgar"; so that when I found my friend and hostess, Miss Jenkyns, was going to have a party in my honour, and that Captain and the Misses Brown were invited, I wondered much what would be the course of the evening. Card-tables, with green baize tops, were set out by daylight, just as usual; it was the third week in November, so the evenings closed in about four. Candles and clean packs of cards were arranged on each table. The fire was made up; the neat maid-servant had received her last directions; and there we stood, dressed in our best, each with a candle-lighter in our hands, ready to dart at the candles as soon as the first knock came. Parties in Cranford were solemn festivities, making the ladies feel gravely elated as they sat together in their best dresses. As soon as three had arrived, we sat down to "Preference," I being the unlucky fourth. The next four comers were put down immediately to another table; and presently the tea-trays, which I had seen set out in the storeroom as I passed in the morning, were placed each on the middle of a card-table. The china was delicate egg-shell; the old-fashioned silver glittered with polishing; but the eatables were of the slightest description. While the trays were yet on the tables, Captain and the Misses Brown came in; and I could see that, somehow or other, the Captain was a favourite with all the ladies present. Ruffled brows were smoothed, sharp voices lowered at his approach. Miss Brown looked ill, and depressed almost to gloom. Miss Jessie smiled as usual, and seemed nearly as popular as her father. He immediately and quietly assumed the man's place in the room; attended to every one's wants, lessened the pretty maid-servant's labour by waiting on empty cups and bread-and-butterless ladies; and yet did it all in so easy and dignified a manner, and so much as if it were a matter of course for the strong to attend to the weak, that he was a true man throughout. He played for threepenny points with as grave an interest as if they had been pounds; and yet, in all his attention to strangers, he had an eye on his suffering daughter—for suffering I was sure she was, though to many eyes she might only appear to be irritable. Miss Jessie could not play cards; but she talked to the sitters-out, who, before her coming, had been rather inclined to be cross. She sang, too, to an old cracked piano, which I think had been a spinet in its youth. Miss Jessie sang "Jock o' Hazeldean" a little out of tune; but we were none of us musical, though Miss Jenkyns beat time, out of time, by way of appearing to be so.

It was very good of Miss Jenkyns to do this; for I had seen that, a little before, she had been a good deal annoyed by Miss Jessie Brown's unguarded admission (*à propos* of Shetland wool) that she had an uncle, her mother's brother, who was a shopkeeper in Edinburgh. Miss Jenkyns tried to drown this confession by a terrible cough—for the Honourable Mrs. Jamieson was sitting at the card-table nearest Miss Jessie, and what would she say or think if she found out she was in the same room with a shopkeeper's niece! But Miss Jessie Brown (who had no tact, as we all agreed the next morning) *would* repeat the information, and assure Miss Pole she could easily get her the identical Shetland wool required, "through my uncle, who has the best assortment of Shetland goods of any one in Edinbro'." It was to take the taste of this out of our mouths, and the sound of this out of our ears, that Miss Jenkyns proposed music; so I say again, it was very good of her to beat time to the song.

When the trays reappeared with biscuits and wine, punctually at a quarter to nine, there was conversation, comparing of cards, and talking over tricks; but by and by Captain Brown sported a bit of literature.

"Have you seen any numbers of *The Pickwick Papers?*" said he (they were then publishing in parts). "Capital thing!"

Now, Miss Jenkyns was daughter of a deceased rector of Cranford; and, on the strength of a number of manuscript sermons, and a pretty good library of divinity, considered herself literary, and looked upon any conversation about books as a challenge to her. So she answered and said, "Yes, she had seen them; indeed, she might say she had read them"

"And what do you think of them?" exclaimed Captain Brown. "Aren't they famously good?"

So urged, Miss Jenkyns could not but speak.

"I must say, I don't think they are by any means equal to Dr. Johnson. Still, perhaps, the author is young. Let him persevere, and who knows what he may become if he will take the great doctor for his model?" This was evidently too much for Captain Brown to take placidly; and I saw the words on the tip of his tongue before Miss Jenkyns had finished her sentence.

"It is quite a different sort of thing, my dear madam—" he began.

"I am quite aware of that," returned she. "And I make allowances, Captain Brown."

"Just allow me to read you a scene out of this month's number," pleaded he. "I had it only this morning, and I don't think the company can have read it yet."

"As you please," said she, settling herself with an air of resignation. He read the account of the "swarry" which Sam

Weller gave at Bath. Some of us laughed heartily. *I* did not dare, because I was staying in the house. Miss Jenkyns sat in patient gravity. When it was ended, she turned to me, and said with mild dignity:

"Fetch me 'Rasselas,' my dear, out of the book room."

When I brought it to her, she turned to Captain Brown,

"Now allow *me* to read you a scene, and then the present company can judge between your favourite, Mr. Boz, and Dr. Johnson."

She read one of the conversations between Rasselas and Imlac, in a high-pitched majestic voice; and when she had ended, she said, "I imagine I am now justified in my preference of Dr. Johnson as a writer of fiction." The Captain screwed his lips up, and drummed on the table, but he did not speak. She thought she would give a finishing blow or two.

"I consider it vulgar, and below the dignity of literature, to publish in numbers."

"How was *The Rambler* published, ma'am?" asked Captain Brown in a low voice, which I think Miss Jenkyns could not have heard.

"Dr. Johnson's style is a model for young beginners. My father recommended it to me when I began to write letters—I have formed my own style upon it; I recommend it to your favourite."

"I should be very sorry for him to exchange his style for any such pompous writing," said Captain Brown.

Miss Jenkyns felt this as a personal affront, in a way of which the captain had not dreamed. Epistolary writing she and her friends considered as her forte. Many a copy of many a letter have I seen written and corrected on the slate, before she "seized the half-hour just previous to post-time to assure" her friends of this or of that; and Dr. Johnson was, as she said, her model in these compositions. She drew herself up with dignity, and only replied to Captain Brown's last remark by saying, with marked emphasis on every syllable, "I prefer Dr. Johnston to Mr. Boz."

It is said—I won't vouch for the fact—that Captain Brown was heard to say, *sotto voce*, "D—n Dr. Johnson!" If he did, he was penitent afterwards, as he showed by going to stand near Miss Jenkyns's armchair, and endeavouring to beguile her into conversation on some more pleasing subject. But she was inexorable. The next day she made the remark I have mentioned about Miss Jessie's dimples.

CHAPTER 2

The Captain

It was impossible to live a month at Cranford and not know the daily habits of each resident; and long before my visit was ended I knew much concerning the whole Brown trio. There was nothing new to be discovered respecting their poverty; for they had spoken simply and openly about that from the very first. They made no mystery of the necessity for their being economical. All that remained to be discovered was the Captain's infinite kindness of heart, and the various modes in which, unconsciously to himself, he manifested it. Some little anecdotes were talked about for some time after they occurred. As we did not read much, and as all the ladies were pretty well suited with servants, there was a dearth of subjects for conversation. We therefore discussed the circumstances of the Captain taking a poor old woman's dinner out of her hands one very slippery Sunday. He had met her returning from the bake house as he came from church, and noticed her precarious footing; and, with the grave dignity with which he did everything, he relieved her of her burden, and steered along the street by her side, carrying her baked mutton and potatoes safely home. This was thought very eccentric; and it was rather expected that he would pay a round of calls on the Monday morning to explain and apologise to the Cranford sense of propriety; but he did no such thing: and then it was decided that he was ashamed, and was keeping out of sight. In a kindly pity for him, we began to say, "After all, the Sunday morning's occurrence showed great goodness of heart," and it was resolved that he should be comforted on his next appearance amongst us; but, lo! he came down upon us, untouched by any sense of shame, speaking loud and bass as ever, his head thrown back, his wig as jaunty and well-curled as usual, and we were obliged to conclude he had forgotten all about Sunday.

Miss Pole and Miss Jessie Brown had set up a kind of intimacy on the strength of the Shetland wool and the new knitting stitches; so it happened that when I went to visit Miss Pole I saw more of the Browns than I had done while staying with Miss Jenkyns, who had never got over what she called Captain Brown's disparaging remarks upon Dr. Johnson as a writer of light and agreeable fiction. I found that Miss Brown was seriously ill of some lingering, incurable complaint, the pain occasioned by which gave the uneasy expression to her face that I had taken for unmitigated crossness. Cross, too, she was, at times, when the nervous irritability occasioned by her disease became past endurance. Miss Jessie bore with her at these times even more patiently than she did with the bitter self-upbraidings by which they were invariably succeeded. Miss Brown used to accuse herself, not merely of hasty and irritable temper, but also of being the cause why her father and sister were obliged to pinch, in order to allow her the small luxuries which were necessaries in her condition. She would so fain have made sacrifices for them, and have lightened their cares, that the original generosity of her disposition added acerbity to her temper. All this was borne by Miss Jessie and her father with more than placidity—with absolute tenderness. I forgave Miss Jessie her singing out of tune, and her juvenility of dress, when I saw her at home. I came to perceive that Captain Brown's dark Brutus wig and padded coat (alas! too often threadbare) were remnants of the military smartness of his youth, which he now wore unconsciously. He was a man of infinite resources, gained in his barrack experience. As he confessed, no one could black his boots to please him except himself; but, indeed, he was not above saving the little maid-servant's labours in every way—knowing, most likely, that his daughter's illness made the place a hard one.

He endeavoured to make peace with Miss Jenkyns soon after the memorable dispute I have named, by a present of a wooden fire-shovel (his own making), having heard her say how much the grating of an iron one annoyed her. She received the present with cool gratitude, and thanked him formally. When he was gone, she bade me put it away in the lumber-room; feeling, probably, that no present from a man who preferred Mr. Boz to Dr. Johnson could be less jarring than an iron fire-shovel.

Such was the state of things when I left Cranford and went to Drumble. I had, however, several correspondents, who kept me *au fait* as to the proceedings of the dear little town. There was Miss Pole, who was becoming as much absorbed in crochet as she had been once in knitting, and the burden of whose letter was something like, "But don't you forget the white worsted at Flint's" of the old song; for at the end of every sentence of news came a fresh direction as to some crochet commission which I was to execute for her. Miss Matilda Jenkyns (who did not mind being called Miss Matty when Miss Jenkyns was not by) wrote nice, kind, rambling letters, now and then venturing into an opinion of her own; but suddenly pulling herself up, and either begging me not to name what she had said, as Deborah thought differently, and *she* knew; or else putting in a postscript to the effect that, since writing the above, she had been talking over the subject with Deborah, and was quite convinced that, etc.—(here probably followed a recantation of every opinion she had given in the letter). Then came Miss Jenkyns—Deborah, as she liked Miss Matty to call her, her father having once said that the Hebrew name ought to be so pronounced. I secretly think she took the Hebrew prophetess for a model in character; and, indeed, she was not unlike the stern prophetess in some ways, making allowance, of course, for modern customs and difference in dress. Miss Jenkyns wore a cravat, and a little bonnet like a jockey-cap, and altogether had the appearance of a strong-minded woman; although she would have despised the modern idea of women being equal to men. Equal, indeed! she knew they were superior. But to return to her letters. Everything in them was stately and grand like herself. I have been looking them over (dear Miss Jenkyns, how I honoured her!), and I will give an extract, more especially because it relates to our friend Captain Brown:—

"The Honourable Mrs. Jamieson has only just quitted me; and, in the course of conversation, she communicated to me the intelligence that she had yesterday received a call from her revered husband's quondam friend, Lord Mauleverer. You will not easily conjecture what brought his lordship within the precincts of our little town. It was to see Captain Brown, with whom, it appears, his lordship was acquainted in the 'plumed wars,' and who had the privilege of averting destruction from his lordship's head when some great peril was impending over it, off the misnomered Cape of Good Hope. You know our friend the Honourable Mrs. Jamieson's deficiency in the spirit of innocent curiosity; and you will therefore not be so much surprised when I tell you she was quite unable to disclose to me the exact nature of the peril in question. I was anxious, I confess, to ascertain in what manner Captain Brown, with his limited establishment, could receive so distinguished a guest; and I discovered that his lordship retired to rest, and, let us hope, to refreshing slumbers, at the Angel

Hotel; but shared the Brunonian meals during the two days that he honoured Cranford with his august presence. Mrs. Johnson, our civil butcher's wife, informs me that Miss Jessie purchased a leg of lamb; but, besides this, I can hear of no preparation whatever to give a suitable reception to so distinguished a visitor. Perhaps they entertained him with 'the feast of reason and the flow of soul'; and to us, who are acquainted with Captain Brown's sad want of relish for 'the pure wells of English undefiled,' it may be matter for congratulation that he has had the opportunity of improving his taste by holding converse with an elegant and refined member of the British aristocracy. But from some mundane failings who is altogether free?"

Miss Pole and Miss Matty wrote to me by the same post. Such a piece of news as Lord Mauleverer's visit was not to be lost on the Cranford letter-writers: they made the most of it. Miss Matty humbly apologised for writing at the same time as her sister, who was so much more capable than she to describe the honour done to Cranford; but, in spite of a little bad spelling, Miss Matty's account gave me the best idea of the commotion occasioned by his lordship's visit, after it had occurred; for, except the people at the Angel, the Browns, Mrs. Jamieson, and a little lad his lordship had sworn at for driving a dirty hoop against the aristocratic legs, I could not hear any one with whom his lordship had held conversation.

My next visit to Cranford was in the summer. There had been neither births, deaths, nor marriages since I was there last. Everybody lived in the same house, and wore pretty nearly the same well-preserved, old-fashioned clothes. The greatest event was that the Misses Jenkyns had purchased a new carpet for the drawing-room. Oh, the busy work Miss Matty and I had in chasing the sunbeams, as they fell in an afternoon right down on this carpet through the blindless window! We spread newspapers over the places, and sat down to our book or our work; and, lo! in a quarter of an hour the sun had moved, and was blazing away on a fresh spot; and down again we went on our knees to alter the position of the newspapers. We were very busy, too, one whole morning, before Miss Jenkyns gave her party, in following her directions, and in cutting out and stitching together pieces of newspaper, so as to form little paths to every chair set for the expected visitors, lest their shoes might dirty or defile the purity of the carpet. Do you make paper paths for every guest to walk upon in London?

Captain Brown and Miss Jenkyns were not very cordial to each other. The literary dispute, of which I had seen the beginning, was a "raw," the slightest touch on which made them wince. It was the only difference of opinion they had ever had; but that difference was enough. Miss Jenkyns could not refrain from talking *at* Captain Brown; and, though he did not reply, he drummed with his fingers, which action she felt and resented as very disparaging to Dr. Johnson. He was rather ostentatious in his preference of the writings of Mr. Boz; would walk through the streets so absorbed in them that he all but ran against Miss Jenkyns; and though his apologies were earnest and sincere, and though he did not, in fact, do more than startle her and himself, she owned to me she had rather he had knocked her down, if he had only been reading a higher style of literature. The poor, brave captain! he looked older, and more worn, and his clothes were very threadbare. But he seemed as bright and cheerful as ever, unless he was asked about his daughter's health.

"She suffers a great deal, and she must suffer more; we do what we can to alleviate her pain; God's will be done!" He took off his hat at these last words. I found, from Miss Matty, that everything had been done, in fact. A medical man, of high repute in that country neighbourhood, had been sent for, and every injunction he had given was attended to, regardless of expense. Miss Matty was sure they denied themselves many things in order to make the invalid comfortable; but they never spoke about it; and as for Miss Jessie!—"I really think she's an angel," said poor Miss Matty, quite overcome. "To see her way of bearing with Miss Brown's crossness, and the bright face she puts on after she's been sitting up a whole night and scolded above half of it, is quite beautiful. Yet she looks as neat and as ready to welcome the Captain at breakfast-time as if she had been asleep in the queen's bed all night. My dear! you could never laugh at her prim little curls or her pink bows again if you saw her as I have done." I could only feel very penitent, and greet Miss Jessie with double respect when I met her next. She looked faded and pinched; and her lips began to quiver, as if she was very weak, when she spoke of her sister. But she brightened, and sent back the tears that were glittering in her pretty eyes, as she said—

"But, to be sure, what a town Cranford is for kindness! I don't suppose any one has a better dinner than usual cooked, but the best part of all comes in a little covered basin for my sister. The poor people will leave their earliest vegetables at our door for her. They speak short and gruff, as if they were ashamed of it; but I am sure it often goes to my heart to see their thoughtfulness." The tears now came back and overflowed; but after a minute or two she began to scold herself, and ended by going away the same cheerful Miss Jessie as ever.

"But why does not this Lord Mauleverer do something for the man who saved his life?" said I.

"Why, you see, unless Captain Brown has some reason for it, he never speaks about being poor; and he walked along by his lordship, looking as happy and cheerful as a prince; and as they never called attention to their dinner by apologies, and as Miss Brown was better that day, and all seemed bright, I dare say his lordship never knew how much care there was in the background. He did send game in the winter pretty often, but now he is gone abroad."

I had often occasion to notice the use that was made of fragments and small opportunities in Cranford; the rose-leaves that were gathered ere they fell to make into a pot-pourri for some one who had no garden; the little bundles of lavender flowers sent to strew the drawers of some town-dweller, or to burn in the chamber of some invalid. Things that many would despise, and actions which it seemed scarcely worth while to perform, were all attended to in Cranford. Miss Jenkyns stuck an apple full of cloves, to be heated and smell pleasantly in Miss Brown's room; and as she put in each clove she uttered a Johnsonian sentence. Indeed, she never could think of the Browns without talking Johnson; and, as they were seldom absent from her thoughts just then, I heard many a rolling three-piled sentence.

Captain Brown called one day to thank Miss Jenkyns for many little kindnesses, which I did not know until then that she had rendered. He had suddenly become like an old man; his deep bass voice had a quavering in it, his eyes looked dim, and the lines on his face were deep. He did not—could not—speak cheerfully of his daughter's state, but he talked with manly, pious resignation, and not much. Twice over he said, "What Jessie has been to us, God only knows!" and after the second time, he got up hastily, shook hands all round without speaking and left the room.

That afternoon we perceived little groups in the street, all listening with faces aghast to some tale or other. Miss Jenkyns wondered what could be the matter, for some time before she took the undignified step of sending Jenny out to inquire.

Jenny came back with a white face of terror. "Oh, ma'am! oh, Miss Jenkyns, ma'am! Captain Brown is killed by them nasty cruel railroads!" and she burst into tears. She, along with many others, had experienced the poor Captain's kindness.

"How?—where?—where? Good God! Jenny, don't waste time in crying, but tell us something." Miss Matty rushed out into the street at once, and collared the man who was telling the tale.

"Come in—come to my sister at once, Miss Jenkyns, the rector's daughter. Oh, man, man! say it is not true," she cried, as she brought the affrighted carter, sleeking down his hair, into the drawing-room, where he stood with his wet boots on the new carpet, and no one regarded it.

"Please, mum, it is true. I seed it myself," and he shuddered at the recollection. "The captain was a-reading some new book as he was deep in, a-waiting for the down train; and there was a little lass as wanted to come to its mammy, and gave its sister the slip, and came toddling across the line. And he looked up sudden at the sound of the train coming, and seed the child, and he darted on the line and cotched it up, and his foot slipped, and the train came over him in no time. O Lord, Lord! Mum, it's quite true—and they've come over to tell his daughters. The child's safe, though, with only a bang on its shoulder as he threw it to its mammy. Poor captain would be glad of that, mum, wouldn't he? God bless him!" The great rough carter puckered up his manly face, and turned away to hide his tears. I turned to Miss Jenkyns. She looked very ill, as if she were going to faint, and signed to me to open the window.

"Matilda, bring me my bonnet. I must go to those girls. God pardon me, if ever I have spoken contemptuously to the Captain!"

Miss Jenkyns arrayed herself to go out, telling Miss Matilda to give the man a glass of wine. While she was away, Miss Matty and I huddled over the fire talking in a low and awestruck voice. I know we cried quietly all the time.

Miss Jenkyns came home in a silent mood, and we durst not ask her many questions. She told us that Miss Jessie had fainted, and that she and Miss Pole had had some difficulty in bringing her round; but that, as soon as she recovered, she begged one of them to go and sit with her sister.

"Mr. Hoggins says she cannot live many days, and she shall be spared this shock," said Miss Jessie, shivering with feelings to which she dared not give way.

"But how can you manage, my dear?" asked Miss Jenkyns; "you cannot bear up; she must see your tears."

"God will help me—I will not give way—she was asleep when the news came; she may be asleep yet. She would be so utterly miserable, not merely at my father's death, but to think of what would become of me; she is so good to me." She looked up earnestly in their faces with her soft true eyes, and Miss Pole told Miss Jenkyns afterwards she could hardly bear it, knowing, as she did, how Miss Brown treated her sister.

However, it was settled according to Miss Jessie's wish. Miss Brown was to be told her father had been summoned to take a short journey on railway business. They had managed it in some way—Miss Jenkyns could not exactly say how. Miss Pole was to stop with Miss Jessie. Mrs. Jamieson had sent to inquire. And this was all we heard that night; and a sorrowful night it was. The next day a full account of the fatal accident was in the county paper which Miss Jenkyns took in. Her eyes were very weak, she said, and she asked me to read it. When I came to the "gallant gentleman was deeply engaged in the perusal of a number of *Pickwick*, which he had just received," Miss Jenkyns shook her head long and solemnly, and then sighed out, "Poor, dear, infatuated man!"

The corpse was to be taken from the station to the parish church, there to be interred. Miss Jessie had set her heart on following it to the grave; and no dissuasives could alter her resolve. Her restraint upon herself made her almost obstinate; she resisted all Miss Pole's entreaties and Miss Jenkyns's advice. At last Miss Jenkyns gave up the point; and, after a silence which I feared portended some deep displeasure against Miss Jessie, Miss Jenkyns said she should accompany the latter to the funeral.

"It is not fit for you to go alone. It would be against both propriety and humanity were I to allow it."

Miss Jessie seemed as if she did not half like this arrangement; but her obstinacy, if she had any, had been exhausted in her determination to go to the interment. She longed, poor thing, I have no doubt, to cry alone over the grave of the dear father to whom she had been all in all, and to give way, for one little half-hour, uninterrupted by sympathy and unobserved by friendship. But it was not to be. That afternoon Miss Jenkyns sent out for a yard of black crape, and employed herself busily in trimming the little black silk bonnet I have spoken about. When it was finished she put it on, and looked at us for approbation—admiration she despised. I was full of sorrow, but, by one of those whimsical thoughts which come unbidden into our heads, in times of deepest grief, I no sooner saw the bonnet than I was reminded of a helmet; and in that hybrid bonnet, half helmet, half jockey-cap, did Miss Jenkyns attend Captain Brown's funeral, and, I believe, supported Miss Jessie with a tender, indulgent firmness which was invaluable, allowing her to weep her passionate fill before they left.

Miss Pole, Miss Matty, and I, meanwhile, attended to Miss Brown; and hard work we found it to relieve her querulous and never-ending complaints. But if we were so weary and dispirited, what must Miss Jessie have been! Yet she came back almost calm, as if she had gained a new strength. She put off her mourning dress, and came in, looking pale and gentle, thanking us each with a soft, long pressure of the hand. She could even smile—a faint, sweet, wintry smile—as if to reassure us of her power to endure; but her look made our eyes fill suddenly with tears, more than if she had cried outright.

It was settled that Miss Pole was to remain with her all the watching livelong night; and that Miss Matty and I were to return in the morning to relieve them, and give Miss Jessie the opportunity for a few hours of sleep. But when the morning came, Miss Jenkyns appeared at the breakfast-table, equipped in her helmet-bonnet, and ordered Miss Matty to stay at home, as she meant to go and help to nurse. She was evidently in a state of great friendly excitement, which she showed by eating her breakfast standing, and scolding the household all round.

No nursing—no energetic, strong-minded woman could help Miss Brown now. There was that in the room as we entered which was stronger than us all, and made us shrink into solemn, awestruck helplessness. Miss Brown was dying. We hardly knew her voice, it was so devoid of the complaining tone we had always associated with it. Miss Jessie told me afterwards that it, and her face too, were just what they had been formerly, when her mother's death left her the young anxious head of the family, of whom only Miss Jessie survived.

She was conscious of her sister's presence, though not, I think, of ours. We stood a little behind the curtain: Miss Jessie knelt with her face near her sister's, in order to catch the last soft, awful whispers.

"O Jessie! Jessie! How selfish I have been! God forgive me for letting you sacrifice yourself for me as you did! I have so loved you—and yet I have thought only of myself. God forgive me!"

"Hush, love! hush!" said Miss Jessie, sobbing.

"And my father! my dear, dear father! I will not complain now, if God will give me strength to be patient. But, oh, Jessie! tell my father how I longed and yearned to see him at last, and to ask his forgiveness. He can never know now how I loved him—oh! if I might but tell him, before I die! What a life of sorrow his has been, and I have done so little to cheer him!"

A light came into Miss Jessie's face. "Would it comfort you, dearest, to think that he does know?—would it comfort you, love, to know that his cares, his sorrows—" Her voice quivered, but she steadied it into calmness: "Mary! he has gone before you to the place where the weary are at rest. He knows now how you loved him."

A strange look, which was not distress, came over Miss Brown's face. She did not speak for some time, but then we saw her lips form the words, rather than heard the sound—"Father, mother, Harry, Archy;"—then, as if it were a new idea throwing a filmy shadow over her darkened mind—"But you will be alone, Jessie!"

Miss Jessie had been feeling this all during the silence, I think; for the tears rolled down her cheeks like rain, at these words, and she could not answer at first. Then she put her hands together tight, and lifted them up, and said—but not to us—

"Though He slay me, yet will I trust in Him."

In a few moments more Miss Brown lay calm and still—never to sorrow or murmur more.

After this second funeral, Miss Jenkyns insisted that Miss Jessie should come to stay with her rather than go back to the desolate house, which, in fact, we learned from Miss Jessie, must now be given up, as she had not wherewithal to maintain it. She had something above twenty pounds a year, besides the interest of the money for which the furniture would sell; but she could not live upon that; and so we talked over her qualifications for earning money.

"I can sew neatly," said she, "and I like nursing. I think, too, I could manage a house, if any one would try me as housekeeper; or I would go into a shop, as saleswoman, if they would have patience with me at first."

Miss Jenkyns declared, in an angry voice, that she should do no such thing; and talked to herself about "some people having no idea of their rank as a Captain's daughter," nearly an hour afterwards, when she brought Miss Jessie up a basin of delicately-made arrowroot, and stood over her like a dragoon until the last spoonful was finished; then she disappeared. Miss Jessie began to tell me some more of the plans which had suggested themselves to her, and insensibly fell into talking of the days that were past and gone, and interested me so much I neither know nor heeded how time passed. We were both startled when Miss Jenkyns reappeared, and caught us crying. I was afraid lest she would be displeased, as she often said that crying hindered digestion, and I knew she wanted Miss Jessie to get strong; but, instead, she looked queer and excited, and fidgeted round us without saying anything. At last she spoke. "I have been so much startled—no, I've not been at all startled—don't mind me, my dear Miss Jessie—I've been very much surprised—in fact, I've had a caller, whom you knew once, my dear Miss Jessie—"

Miss Jessie went very white, then flushed scarlet, and looked eagerly at Miss Jenkyns.

"A gentleman, my dear, who wants to know if you would see him."

"Is it?—it is not"—stammered out Miss Jessie—and got no further.

"This is his card," said Miss Jenkyns, giving it to Miss Jessie; and while her head was bent over it, Miss Jenkyns went through a series of winks and odd faces to me, and formed her lips into a long sentence of which, of course, I could not understand a word.

"May he come up?" asked Miss Jenkyns, at last.

"Oh, yes! certainly!" said Miss Jessie, as much as to say, this is your house, you may show any visitor where you like. She took up some knitting of Miss Matty's and began to be very busy, though I could see how she trembled all over.

Miss Jenkyns rang the bell, and told the servant who

answered it to show Major Gordon upstairs; and, presently, in walked a tall, fine, frank-looking man of forty or upwards. He shook hands with Miss Jessie; but he could not see her eyes, she kept them so fixed on the ground. Miss Jenkyns asked me if I would come and help her to tie up the preserves in the store-room; and, though Miss Jessie plucked at my gown, and even looked up at me with begging eye, I durst not refuse to go where Miss Jenkyns asked. Instead of tying up preserves in the store-room, however, we went to talk in the dining-room; and there Miss Jenkyns told me what Major Gordon had told her; how he had served in the same regiment with Captain Brown, and had become acquainted with Miss Jessie, then a sweet-looking, blooming girl of eighteen; how the acquaintance had grown into love on his part, though it had been some years before he had spoken; how, on becoming possessed, through the will of an uncle, of a good estate in Scotland, he had offered and been refused, though with so much agitation and evident distress that he was sure she was not indifferent to him; and how he had discovered that the obstacle was the fell disease which was, even then, too surely threatening her sister. She had mentioned that the surgeons foretold intense suffering; and there was no one but herself to nurse her poor Mary, or cheer and comfort her father during the time of illness. They had had long discussions; and on her refusal to pledge herself to him as his wife when all should be over, he had grown angry, and broken off entirely, and gone abroad, believing that she was a cold-hearted person whom he would do well to forget. He had been travelling in the East, and was on his return home when, at Rome, he saw the account of Captain Brown's death in *Galignani*.

Just then Miss Matty, who had been out all the morning, and had only lately returned to the house, burst in with a face of dismay and outraged propriety.

"Oh, goodness me!" she said. "Deborah, there's a

gentleman sitting in the drawing-room with his arm round Miss Jessie's waist!" Miss Matty's eyes looked large with terror.

Miss Jenkyns snubbed her down in an instant.

"The most proper place in the world for his arm to be in. Go away, Matilda, and mind your own business." This, from her sister who had hitherto been a model of feminine decorum, was a blow for poor Miss Matty, and with a double shock she left the room.

The last time I ever saw poor Miss Jenkyns was many years after this. Mrs. Gordon had kept up a warm and affectionate intercourse with all at Cranford. Miss Jenkyns, Miss Matty, and Miss Pole had all been to visit her, and returned with wonderful accounts of her house, her husband, her dress, and her looks. For, with happiness, something of her early bloom returned; she had been a year or two younger than we had taken her for. Her eyes were always lovely, and, as Mrs. Gordon, her dimples were not out of place. At the time to which I have referred, when I last saw Miss Jenkyns, that lady was old and feeble, and had lost something of her strong mind. Little Flora Gordon was staying with the Misses Jenkyns, and when I came in she was reading aloud to Miss Jenkyns, who lay feeble and changed on the sofa. Flora put down the *Rambler* when I came in.

"Ah!" said Miss Jenkyns, "you find me changed, my dear. I can't see as I used to do. If Flora were not here to read to me, I hardly know how I should get through the day. Did you ever read the *Rambler*? It's a wonderful book— wonderful! and the most improving reading for Flora" (which I dare say it would have been if she could have read half the words without spelling, and could have understood the meaning of a third), "better than that strange old book, with the queer name, poor Captain Brown was killed for reading—that book by Mr. Boz, you know—'Old Poz'; when

I was a girl—but that's a long time ago—I acted Lucy in 'Old Poz.'" She babbled on long enough for Flora to get a good long spell at the "Christmas Carol," which Miss Matty had left on the table.

CHAPTER 3

A Love Affair of Long Ago

I thought that probably my connection with Cranford would
cease after Miss Jenkyns's death; at least, that it would have
to be kept up by correspondence, which bears much the
same relation to personal intercourse that the books of dried
plants I sometimes see ("Hortus Siccus," I think they call
the thing) do to the living and fresh flowers in the lanes and
meadows. I was pleasantly surprised, therefore, by receiving
a letter from Miss Pole (who had always come in for a supple-
mentary week after my annual visit to Miss Jenkyns)
proposing that I should go and stay with her; and then, in
a couple of days after my acceptance, came a note from Miss
Matty, in which, in a rather circuitous and very humble
manner, she told me how much pleasure I should confer if
I could spend a week or two with her, either before or after
I had been at Miss Pole's; "for," she said, "since my dear
sister's death, I am well aware I have no attractions to offer;
it is only to the kindness of my friends that I can owe their
company."

Of course I promised to come to dear Miss Matty as
soon as I had ended my visit to Miss Pole; and the day after
my arrival at Cranford I went to see her, much wondering
what the house would be like without Miss Jenkyns, and
rather dreading the changed aspect of things. Miss Matty

began to cry as soon as she saw me. She was evidently nervous from having anticipated my call. I comforted her as well as I could; and I found the best consolation I could give was the honest praise that came from my heart as I spoke of the deceased. Miss Matty slowly shook her head over each virtue as it was named and attributed to her sister; and at last she could not restrain the tears which had long been silently flowing, but hid her face behind her handkerchief and sobbed aloud.

"Dear Miss Matty," said I, taking her hand—for indeed I did not know in what way to tell her how sorry I was for her, left deserted in the world. She put down her handkerchief and said—

"My dear, I'd rather you did not call me Matty. *She* did not like it; but I did many a thing she did not like, I'm afraid—and now she's gone! If you please, my love, will you call me Matilda?"

I promised faithfully, and began to practise the new name with Miss Pole that very day; and, by degrees, Miss Matilda's feeling on the subject was known through Cranford, and we all tried to drop the more familiar name, but with so little success that by and by we gave up the attempt.

My visit to Miss Pole was very quiet. Miss Jenkyns had so long taken the lead in Cranford that, now she was gone, they hardly knew how to give a party. The Honourable Mrs. Jamieson, to whom Miss Jenkyns herself had always yielded the post of honour, was fat and inert, and very much at the mercy of her old servants. If they chose that she should give a party, they reminded her of the necessity for so doing: if not, she let it alone. There was all the more time for me to hear old-world stories from Miss Pole, while she sat knitting, and I making my father's shirts. I always took a quantity of plain sewing to Cranford; for, as we did not read much, or walk much, I found it a capital time to get through my work. One of Miss Pole's stories related to a shadow of a love affair that was dimly perceived or suspected long years before.

Presently the time arrived when I was to remove to Miss Matilda's house. I found her timid and anxious about the arrangements for my comfort. Many a time, while I was unpacking, did she come backwards and forwards to stir the fire, which burned all the worse for being so frequently poked.

"Have you drawers enough, dear?" asked she. "I don't know exactly how my sister used to arrange them. She had capital methods. I am sure she would have trained a servant in a week to make a better fire than this, and Fanny has been with me four months."

This subject of servants was a standing grievance, and I could not wonder much at it; for if gentlemen were scarce, and almost unheard of in the "genteel society" of Cranford, they or their counterparts—handsome young men—abounded in the lower classes. The pretty, neat servant-maids had their choice of desirable "followers"; and their mistresses, without having the sort of mysterious dread of men and matrimony that Miss Matilda had, might well feel a little anxious lest the heads of their comely maids should be turned by the joiner, or the butcher, or the gardener, who were obliged, by their callings, to come to the house, and who, as ill-luck would have it, were generally handsome and unmarried. Fanny's lovers, if she had any—and Miss Matilda suspected her of so many flirtations that, if she had not been very pretty, I should have doubted her having one—were a constant anxiety to her mistress. She was forbidden, by the articles of her engagement, to have "followers"; and though she had answered, innocently enough, doubling up the hem of her apron as she spoke, "Please, ma'am, I never had more than one at a time," Miss Matty prohibited that one. But a vision of a man seemed to haunt the kitchen. Fanny assured me that it was all fancy, or else I should have said myself that I had seen a man's coat-tails whisk into the scullery once, when I went on an errand into the store-room at night; and another evening, when, our watches having stopped, I went to look at the clock, there was a very odd appearance, singularly like a young man squeezed up between the clock and the back of the open kitchen-door; and I thought Fanny snatched up the candle very hastily, so as to throw the shadow on the clock face, while she very positively told me the time half an hour too early, as we found out afterwards by the church clock. But I did not add to Miss Matty's anxieties by naming my suspicions, especially as Fanny said to me, the next day, that it was such a queer kitchen for having odd shadows about it, she really was almost afraid to stay; "for, you know, miss," she added, "I don't see a creature from six o'clock tea, till missus rings the bell for prayers at ten."

However, it so fell out that Fanny had to leave; and Miss Matilda begged me to stay and "settle her" with the new maid; to which I consented, after I had heard from my father that he did not want me at home. The new servant was a rough, honest-looking country girl, who had only lived in a farm-place before; but I liked her looks when she came to be hired; and I promised Miss Matilda to put her in the ways of the house. The said ways were religiously such as Miss Matilda thought her sister would approve. Many a domestic rule and regulation had been a subject of plaintive whispered murmur to me during Miss Jenkyns's life; but now that she was gone, I do not think that even I, who was a favourite, durst have suggested an alteration. To give an instance: we constantly adhered to the forms which were observed, at meal-times, in "my father, the rector's house." Accordingly, we had always wine and dessert; but the decanters were only filled when there was a party, and what remained was seldom touched, though we had two wine-glasses apiece every day after dinner, until the next festive occasion arrived, when the state of the remainder wine was examined into, in a family council. The dregs were often given to the poor; but occasionally, when a good deal had been left at the last party (five months ago, it might be), it was added to some of a fresh bottle, brought up from the cellar. I fancy poor Captain Brown did not much like wine, for I noticed he never finished his first glass, and most military men take several. Then, as to our dessert, Miss Jenkyns used to gather currants and gooseberries for it herself, which I sometimes thought would have tasted better fresh from the trees; but then, as Miss Jenkyns observed, there would have been nothing for dessert in summer-time. As it was, we felt very genteel with our two glasses apiece, and a dish of gooseberries at the top, of currants and biscuits at the sides, and two decanters at the bottom. When oranges came in, a curious proceeding was gone through. Miss Jenkyns did not like to cut the fruit; for, as she observed, the juice all ran out nobody knew where; sucking (only I think she used some more recondite word) was, in fact, the only way of enjoying oranges; but then there was the unpleasant association with a ceremony frequently gone through by little babies; and so, after dessert, in orange season, Miss Jenkyns and Miss Matty used to rise up, possess themselves each of an orange in silence, and withdraw to the privacy of their own rooms to indulge in sucking oranges.

I had once or twice tried, on such occasions, to prevail on Miss Matty to stay, and had succeeded in her sister's lifetime. I held up a screen, and did not look, and, as she said, she tried not to make the noise very offensive; but now that she was left alone, she seemed quite horrified when I begged her to remain with me in the warm dining-parlour, and enjoy her orange as she liked best. And so it was in everything. Miss Jenkyns's rules were made more stringent than ever, because the framer of them was gone where there could be no appeal. In all things else Miss Matilda was meek and undecided to a fault. I have heard Fanny turn her round twenty times in a morning about dinner, just as the little hussy chose; and I sometimes fancied she worked on Miss Matilda's weakness in order to bewilder her, and to make her feel more in the power of her clever servant. I determined that I would not leave her till I had seen what sort of a person Martha was; and, if I found her trustworthy, I would tell her not to trouble her mistress with every little decision.

Martha was blunt and plain-spoken to a fault; otherwise she was a brisk, well-meaning, but very ignorant girl. She had not been with us a week before Miss Matilda and I were astounded one morning by the receipt of a letter from a cousin of hers, who had been twenty or thirty years in India, and who had lately, as we had seen by *The Army List*, returned to England, bringing with him an invalid wife who had never been introduced to her English relations. Major Jenkyns wrote to propose that he and his wife should spend a night at Cranford, on his way to Scotland—at the inn, if it did not suit Miss Matilda to receive them into her house; in which case they should hope to be with her as much as possible during the day. Of course, it *must* suit her, as she said; for all Cranford knew that she had her sister's bedroom at liberty; but I am sure she wished the major had stopped in India and forgotten his cousins out and out.

"Oh! how must I manage?" asked she helplessly. "If Deborah had been alive she would have known what to do with a gentleman-visitor. Must I put razors in his dressing-room? Dear! dear! and I've got none. Deborah would have had them. And slippers, and coat-brushes?" I suggested that probably he would bring all these things with him. "And after dinner, how am I to know when to get up and leave him to his wine? Deborah would have done it so well; she would have been quite in her element. Will he want coffee, do you think?" I undertook the management of the coffee, and told her I would instruct Martha in the art of waiting—in which, it must be owned, she was terribly deficient—and that I had no doubt Major and Mrs. Jenkyns would understand the quiet mode in which a lady lived by herself in a country town. But she was sadly fluttered. I made her empty her decanters and bring up two fresh bottles of wine. I wished I could have prevented her from being present at my instructions to Martha, for she frequently cut in with some fresh direction, muddling the poor girl's mind, as she stood open-mouthed, listening to us both.

"Hand the vegetables round," said I (foolishly, I see now—for it was aiming at more than we could accomplish with quietness and simplicity); and then, seeing her look bewildered, I added, "Take the vegetables round to people, and let them help themselves."

"And mind you go first to the ladies," put in Miss Matilda. "Always go to the ladies before gentlemen when you are waiting."

"I'll do it as you tell me, ma'am," said Martha; "but I like lads best."

We felt very uncomfortable and shocked at this speech of Martha's, yet I don't think she meant any harm; and, on the whole, she attended very well to our directions, except that she "nudged" the Major when he did not help himself as soon as she expected to the potatoes, while she was handing them round.

The Major and his wife were quiet, unpretending people enough when they did come; languid, as all East Indians are, I suppose. We were rather dismayed at their bringing two servants with them—a Hindu body-servant for the major, and a steady, elderly maid for his wife: but they slept at the inn, and took off a good deal of the responsibility by attending carefully to their master's and mistress's comfort. Martha, to be sure, had never ended her staring at the East Indian's white turban and brown complexion, and I saw that Miss

Matilda shrunk away from him a little as he waited at dinner. Indeed, she asked me, when they were gone, if he did not remind me of Blue Beard? On the whole, the visit was most satisfactory, and is a subject of conversation even now with Miss Matilda; at the time it greatly excited Cranford, and even stirred up the apathetic and Honourable Mrs. Jamieson to some expression of interest, when I went to call and thank her for the kind answers she had vouchsafed to Miss Matilda's inquiries as to the arrangement of a gentleman's dressing-room—answers which, I must confess, she had given in the wearied manner of the Scandinavian prophetess—

"*Leave me, leave me to repose.*"

And *now* I come to the love affair.

It seems that Miss Pole had a cousin, once or twice removed, who had offered to Miss Matty long ago. Now, this cousin lived four or five miles from Cranford on his own estate; but his property was not large enough to entitle him to rank higher than a yeoman; or rather, with something of the "pride which apes humility," he had refused to push himself on, as so many of his class had done, into the rank of the squires. He would not allow himself to be called Thomas Holbrook, *Esq.*; he even sent back letters with this address, telling the post-mistress at Cranford that his name was *Mr.* Thomas Holbrook, yeoman. He rejected all domestic innovations; he would have the house door stand open in summer and shut in winter, without knocker or bell to summon a servant. The closed fist or the knob of the stick did this office for him if he found the door locked. He despised every refinement which had not its root deep down in humanity. If people were not ill, he saw no necessity for moderating his voice. He spoke the dialect of the country in perfection, and constantly used it in conversation; although Miss Pole (who gave me these particulars) added, that he read aloud more beautifully and with more feeling than any one she had ever heard, except the late rector.

"And how came Miss Matilda not to marry him?" asked I.

"Oh, I don't know. She was willing enough, I think; but, you know, cousin Thomas would not have been enough of a gentleman for the rector and Miss Jenkyns."

"Well! but they were not to marry him," said I impatiently.

"No; but they did not like Miss Matty to marry below her rank. You know she was the rector's daughter, and somehow they are related to Sir Peter Arley; Miss Jenkyns thought a deal of that."

"Poor Miss Matty!" said I.

"Nay, now, I don't know anything more than that he offered and was refused. Miss Matty might not like him—and Miss Jenkyns might never have said a word—it is only a guess of mine."

"Has she never seen him since?"

"No, I think not. You see Woodley, cousin Thomas's house, lies half-way between Cranford and Misselton; and I know he made Misselton his market-town very soon after he had offered to Miss Matty; and I don't think he has been into Cranford above once or twice since—once, when I was walking with Miss Matty, in High Street, and suddenly she darted from me, and went up Shire Lane. A few minutes after I was startled by meeting cousin Thomas."

"How old is he?" I asked, after a pause of castle-building.

"He must be about seventy, I think, my dear," said Miss Pole, blowing up my castle, as if by gunpowder, into small fragments.

Very soon after—at least during my long visit to Miss Matilda—I had the opportunity of seeing Mr. Holbrook; seeing, too, his first encounter with his former love, after thirty or forty years' separation. I was helping to decide whether any of the new assortment of coloured silks which they had just received at the shop would do to match a gray-and-black mousseline-de-laine that wanted a new breadth, when a tall, thin, Don Quixote-looking old man came into the shop for some woollen gloves. I had never seen the person (who was rather striking) before, and I watched him rather attentively while Miss Matty listened to the shop man. The stranger wore a blue coat with brass buttons, drab breeches, and gaiters, and drummed with his fingers on the counter until he was attended to. When he answered the shop-boy's question, "What can I have the pleasure of showing you to-day, sir?" I saw Miss Matilda start, and then suddenly sit down; and instantly I guessed who it was. She had made some inquiry which had to be carried round the other shop man.

"Miss Jenkyns wants the black sarsenet two and twopence the yard;" and Mr. Holbrook had caught the name, and was across the shop in two strides.

"Matty—Miss Matilda—Miss Jenkyns! God bless my soul! I should not have known you. How are you? how are you?" He kept shaking her hand in a way which proved the warmth of his friendship; but he repeated so often, as if to himself, "I should not have known you!" that any sentimental romance which I might be inclined to build was quite done away with by his manner.

However, he kept talking to us all the time we were in the shop; and then, waving the shop man with the unpurchased gloves on one side with "Another time, sir! another time!" he walked home with us. I am happy to say my client, Miss Matilda, also left the shop in an equally bewildered state, not having purchased either green or red silk. Mr. Holbrook was evidently full with honest, loud-spoken joy at meeting his old love again; he touched on the changes that had taken place; he even spoke of Miss Jenkyns as "Your poor sister!

Well, well! we all have our faults;" and bade us good-bye with many a hope that he should soon see Miss Matty again. She went straight to her room, and never came back till our early tea-time, when I thought she looked as if she had been crying.

CHAPTER 4

A Visit to an Old Bachelor

A few days after, a note came from Mr. Holbrook, asking us—impartially asking both of us—in a formal, old-fashioned style, to spend a day at his house—a long June day—for it was June now. He named that he had also invited his cousin, Miss Pole; so that we might join in a fly, which could be put up at his house.

I expected Miss Matty to jump at this invitation; but, no! Miss Pole and I had the greatest difficulty in persuading her to go. She thought it was improper; and was even half annoyed when we utterly ignored the idea of any impropriety in her going with two other ladies to see her old lover. Then came a more serious difficulty. She did not think Deborah would have liked her to go. This took us half a day's good hard talking to get over; but, at the first sentence of relenting, I seized the opportunity, and wrote and despatched an acceptance in her name—fixing day and hour, that all might be decided and done with.

The next morning she asked me if I would go down to the shop with her; and there, after much hesitation, we chose out three caps to be sent home and tried on, that the most becoming might be selected to take with us on Thursday.

She was in a state of silent agitation all the way to Woodley. She had evidently never been there before; and, although she little dreamed I knew anything of her early story, I could perceive she was in a tremor at the thought of seeing the place which might have been her home, and round which it is probable that many of her innocent girlish imaginations had clustered. It was a long drive there, through paved jolting lanes. Miss Matilda sat bolt upright, and looked wistfully out of the windows as we drew near the end of our journey. The aspect of the country was quiet and pastoral. Woodley stood among the fields; and there was an old-fashioned garden where roses and currant-bushes touched each other, and where the feathery asparagus formed a pretty background to the pinks and gillyflowers; there was no drive up to the door. We got out at a little gate, and walked up a straight box-edged path.

"My cousin might make a drive, I think," said Miss Pole, who was afraid of earache, and had only her cap on.

"I think it is very pretty," said Miss Matty, with a soft plaintiveness in her voice, and almost in a whisper, for just then Mr. Holbrook appeared at the door, rubbing his hands in very effervescence of hospitality. He looked more like my idea of Don Quixote than ever, and yet the likeness was only external. His respectable housekeeper stood modestly at the door to bid us welcome; and, while she led the elder ladies upstairs to a bedroom, I begged to look about the garden. My request evidently pleased the old gentleman, who took me all round the place and showed me his six-and-twenty cows, named after the different letters of the alphabet. As we went along, he surprised me occasionally by repeating apt and beautiful quotations from the poets, ranging easily from Shakespeare and George Herbert to those of our own day. He did this as naturally as if he were thinking aloud, and their true and beautiful words were the best expression he could find for what he was thinking or feeling. To be sure he called Byron "my Lord Bўrron," and pronounced the name of Goethe strictly in accordance with the English sound of the letters— "As Goethe says, 'Yeever-verdant palaces,'" etc. Altogether I never met with a man, before or since, who had spent so long a life in a secluded and not impressive country, with ever-increasing delight in the daily and yearly change of season and beauty.

When he and I went in, we found that dinner was nearly ready in the kitchen—for so, I suppose, the room ought to be called, as there were oak dressers and cupboards all round, all over by the side of the fireplace, and only a small Turkey carpet in the middle of the flag-floor. The room might have been easily made into a handsome dark oak dining-parlour by removing the oven and a few other appurtenances of a kitchen, which were evidently never used, the real cooking-place being at some distance. The room in which we were expected to sit was a stiffly-furnished, ugly apartment; but that in which we did sit was what Mr. Holbrook called the counting-house, when he paid his labourers their weekly wages at a great desk near the door. The rest of the pretty sitting-room—looking into the orchard, and all covered over with dancing tree-shadows—was filled with books. They lay on the ground, they covered the walls, they strewed the table. He was evidently half ashamed and half proud of his extravagance in this respect. They were all kinds—poetry and wild weird tales prevailing. He evidently chose his books in accordance with his own tastes, not because such and such were classical or established favourites.

"Ah!" he said, "we farmers ought not to have much time for reading; yet somehow one can't help it."

"What a pretty room!" said Miss Matty *sotto voce*.

"What a pleasant place!" said I aloud, almost simultaneously.

"Nay! if you like it," replied he; "but can you sit on these great, black leather, three-cornered chairs? I like it better than the best parlour; but I thought ladies would take that for the smarter place."

It was the smarter place, but, like most smart things, not

at all pretty, or pleasant, or homelike; so, while we were at dinner, the servant-girl dusted and scrubbed the counting-house chairs, and we sat there all the rest of the day.

We had pudding before meat; and I thought Mr. Holbrook was going to make some apology for his old-fashioned ways, for he began—

"I don't know whether you like new-fangled ways."

"Oh, not at all!" said Miss Matty.

"No more do I," said he. "My housekeeper *will* have these in her new fashion; or else I tell her that, when I was a young man, we used to keep strictly to my father's rule, 'No broth, no ball; no ball, no beef'; and always began dinner with broth. Then we had suet puddings, boiled in the broth with the beef; and then the meat itself. If we did not sup our broth, we had no ball, which we liked a deal better; and the beef came last of all, and only those had it who had done justice to the broth and the ball. Now folks begin with sweet things, and turn their dinners topsy-turvy."

When the ducks and green peas came, we looked at each other in dismay; we had only two-pronged, black-handled forks. It is true the steel was as bright as silver; but what were we to do? Miss Matty picked up her peas, one by one, on the point of the prongs, much as Amine ate her grains of rice after her previous feast with the Ghoul. Miss Pole sighed over her delicate young peas as she left them on one side of her plate untasted, for they *would* drop between the prongs. I looked at my host; the peas were going wholesale into his capacious mouth, shovelled up by his large, round-ended knife. I saw, I imitated, I survived! My friends, in spite of my precedent, could not muster up courage enough to do an ungenteel thing; and, if Mr. Holbrook had not been so heartily hungry, he would probably have seen that the good peas went away almost untouched.

After dinner, a clay pipe was brought in, and a spittoon; and, asking us to retire to another room, where he would soon join us, if we disliked tobacco-smoke, he presented his pipe to Miss Matty, and requested her to fill the bowl. This was a compliment to a lady in his youth; but it was rather inappropriate to propose it as an honour to Miss Matty, who had been trained by her sister to hold smoking of every kind in utter abhorrence. But if it was a shock to her refinement, it was also a gratification to her feelings to be thus selected; so she daintily stuffed the strong tobacco into the pipe, and then we withdrew.

"It is very pleasant dining with a bachelor," said Miss Matty softly, as we settled ourselves in the counting-house. "I only hope it is not improper; so many pleasant things are!"

"What a number of books he has!" said Miss Pole, looking round the room. "And how dusty they are!"

"I think it must be like one of the great Dr. Johnson's rooms," said Miss Matty. "What a superior man your cousin must be!"

"Yes!" said Miss Pole, "he's a great reader; but I am afraid he has got into very uncouth habits with living alone."

"Oh! uncouth is too hard a word. I should call him eccentric; very clever people always are!" replied Miss Matty.

When Mr. Holbrook returned, he proposed a walk in the fields; but the two elder ladies were afraid of damp and dirt, and had only very unbecoming calashes to put on over their caps; so they declined, and I was again his companion, in a turn which he said he was obliged to take to see after his men. He strode along, either wholly forgetting my existence, or soothed into silence by his pipe—and yet it was not silence exactly. He walked before me with a stooping gait, his hands clasped behind him; and, as some tree or cloud, or glimpse of distant upland pastures, struck him, he quoted poetry to himself, saying it out loud in a grand, sonorous voice, with just the emphasis that true feeling and appreciation give. We came upon an old cedar-tree, which stood at one end of the house.

"*The cedar spreads his dark-green layers of shade.*"

"Capital term—'layers'! Wonderful man!" I did not know whether he was speaking to me or not; but I put in an assenting "wonderful," although I knew nothing about it, just because I was tired of being forgotten, and of being consequently silent.

He turned sharp round. "Ay! you may say 'wonderful.' Why, when I saw the review of his poems in *Blackwood*, I set off within an hour, and walked seven miles to Misselton (for the horses were not in the way) and ordered them. Now, what colour are ash-buds in March?"

Is the man going mad? thought I. He is very like Don Quixote.

"What colour are they, I say?" repeated he vehemently.

"I am sure I don't know, sir," said I, with the meekness of ignorance.

"I knew you didn't. No more did I—an old fool that I am! till this young man comes and tells me. Black as ash-buds in March. And I've lived all my life in the country; more shame for me not to know. Black: they are jet-black, madam." And he went off again, swinging along to the music of some rhyme he had got hold of.

When we came back, nothing would serve him but he must read us the poems he had been speaking of; and Miss Pole encouraged him in his proposal, I thought, because she wished me to hear his beautiful reading, of which she had boasted; but she afterwards said it was because she had got to a difficult part of her crochet, and wanted to count her stitches without having to talk. Whatever he had proposed would have been right to Miss Matty; although she did fall sound asleep within five minutes after he had begun a long poem, called *Locksley Hall*, and had a comfortable nap, unobserved, till he ended; when the cessation of his voice wakened her up, and she said, feeling that something was expected, and that Miss Pole was counting—

"What a pretty book!"

"Pretty, madam! it's beautiful! Pretty, indeed!"

"Oh, yes! I meant beautiful!" said she, fluttered at his disapproval of her word. "It is so like that beautiful poem of Dr. Johnson's my sister used to read—I forget the name of it; what was it, my dear?" turning to me.

"Which do you mean, ma'am? What was it about?"

"I don't remember what it was about, and I've quite forgotten what the name of it was; but it was written by Dr. Johnson, and was very beautiful, and very like what Mr. Holbrook has just been reading."

"I don't remember it," said he reflectively. "But I don't know Dr. Johnson's poems well. I must read them."

As we were getting into the fly to return, I heard Mr. Holbrook say he should call on the ladies soon, and inquire how they got home; and this evidently pleased and fluttered Miss Matty at the time he said it; but after we had lost sight of the old house among the trees, her sentiments towards the master of it were gradually absorbed into a distressing wonder as to whether Martha had broken her word, and seized on the opportunity of her mistress's absence to have a "follower." Martha looked good, and steady, and composed enough, as she came to help us out; she was always careful of Miss Matty, and tonight she made use of this unlucky speech—

"Eh! dear, ma'am, to think of your going out in an evening in such a thin shawl! It's no better than muslin. At your age, ma'am, you should be careful."

"My age!" said Miss Matty, almost speaking crossly, for her, for she was usually gentle—"my age! Why, how old do you think I am, that you talk about my age?"

"Well, ma'am, I should say you were not far short of sixty: but folks' looks is often against them—and I'm sure I meant no harm."

"Martha, I'm not yet fifty-two!" said Matty, with grave emphasis; for probably the remembrance of her youth had come very vividly before her this day, and she was annoyed at finding that golden time so far away in the past.

But she never spoke of any former and more intimate acquaintance with Mr. Holbrook. She had probably met with so little sympathy in her early love that she had shut it up close in her heart; and it was only by a sort of watching, which I could hardly avoid since Miss Pole's confidence, that I saw how faithful her poor heart had been in its sorrow and its silence.

She gave me some good reason for wearing her best cap every day, and sat near the window, in spite of her rheumatism, in order to see, without being seen, down into the street.

He came. He put his open palms upon his knees, which were far apart, as he sat with his head bent down, whistling, after we had replied to his inquiries about our safe return. Suddenly he jumped up—

"Well, madam! have you any commands for Paris? I am going there in a week or two."

"To Paris!" we both exclaimed.

"Yes, madam! I've never been there, and always had a wish to go; and I think if I don't go soon, I mayn't go at all; so as soon as the hay is got in I shall go, before harvest-time."

We were so much astonished that we had no commissions.

Just as he was going out of the room, he turned back, with his favourite exclamation—

"God bless my soul, madam! but I nearly forgot half my errand. Here are the poems for you you admired so much the other evening at my house." He tugged away at a parcel in his coat-pocket. "Good-bye, miss," said he; "good-bye, Matty! take care of yourself." And he was gone. But he had given her a book, and he had called her Matty, just as he used to do thirty years ago.

"I wish he would not go to Paris," said Miss Matilda

anxiously. "I don't believe frogs will agree with him; he used to have to be very careful what he ate, which was curious in so strong-looking a young man."

Soon after this I took my leave, giving many an injunction to Martha to look after her mistress, and to let me know if she thought that Miss Matilda was not so well; in which case I would volunteer a visit to my old friend, without noticing Martha's intelligence to her.

Accordingly I received a line or two from Martha every now and then; and, about November, I had a note to say her mistress was "very low and sadly off her food;" and the account made me so uneasy that, although Martha did not decidedly summon me, I packed up my things and went.

I received a warm welcome, in spite of the little flurry produced by my impromptu visit, for I had only been able to give a day's notice. Miss Matilda looked miserably ill; and I prepared to comfort and cosset her.

I went down to have a private talk with Martha.

"How long has your mistress been so poorly?" I asked, as I stood by the kitchen fire.

"Well! I think it's better than a fortnight; it is, I know; it was one Tuesday, after Miss Pole had been, that she went into this moping way. I thought she was tired, and it would go off with a night's rest; but no! she has gone on and on ever since, till I thought it my duty to write to you, ma'am."

"You did quite right, Martha. It is a comfort to think she has so faithful a servant about her. And I hope you find your place comfortable."

"Well, ma'am, missus is very kind, and there's plenty to eat and drink, and no more work but what I can do easily—but—" Martha hesitated.

"But what, Martha?"

"Why, it seems so hard of missus not to let me have any followers; there's such lots of young fellows in the town; and many a one has as much as offered to keep company with me;

and I may never be in such a likely place again, and it's like wasting an opportunity. Many a girl as I know would have 'em unbeknownst to missus; but I've given my word, and I'll stick to it; or else this is just the house for missus never to be the wiser if they did come: and it's such a capable kitchen—there's such good dark corners in it—I'd be bound to hide any one. I counted up last Sunday night—for I'll not deny I was crying because I had to shut the door in Jem Hearn's face, and he's a steady young man, fit for any girl; only I had given missus my word." Martha was all but crying again; and I had little comfort to give her, for I knew, from old experience, of the horror with which both the Misses Jenkyns looked upon "followers"; and in Miss Matty's present nervous state this dread was not likely to be lessened.

I went to see Miss Pole the next day, and took her completely by surprise, for she had not been to see Miss Matilda for two days.

"And now I must go back with you, my dear, for I promised to let her know how Thomas Holbrook went on; and, I'm sorry to say, his housekeeper has sent me word today that he hasn't long to live. Poor Thomas! that journey to Paris was quite too much for him. His housekeeper says he has hardly ever been round his fields since, but just sits with his hands on his knees in the counting-house, not reading or anything, but only saying what a wonderful city Paris was! Paris has much to answer for if it's killed my cousin Thomas, for a better man never lived."

"Does Miss Matilda know of his illness?" asked I—a new light as to the cause of her indisposition dawning upon me.

"Dear! to be sure, yes! Has not she told you? I let her know a fortnight ago, or more, when first I heard of it. How odd she shouldn't have told you!"

Not at all, I thought; but I did not say anything. I felt almost guilty of having spied too curiously into that tender heart, and I was not going to speak of its secrets—hidden, Miss

Matty believed, from all the world. I ushered Miss Pole into Miss Matilda's little drawing-room, and then left them alone. But I was not surprised when Martha came to my bedroom door, to ask me to go down to dinner alone, for that missus had one of her bad headaches. She came into the drawing-room at tea-time, but it was evidently an effort to her; and, as if to make up for some reproachful feeling against her late sister, Miss Jenkyns, which had been troubling her all the afternoon, and for which she now felt penitent, she kept telling me how good and how clever Deborah was in her youth; how she used to settle what gowns they were to wear at all the parties (faint, ghostly ideas of grim parties, far away in the distance, when Miss Matty and Miss Pole were young!); and how Deborah and her mother had started the benefit society for the poor, and taught girls cooking and plain sewing; and how Deborah had once danced with a lord; and how she used to visit at Sir Peter Arley's, and try to remodel the quiet rectory establishment on the plans of Arley Hall, where they kept thirty servants; and how she had nursed Miss Matty through a long, long illness, of which I had never heard before, but which I now dated in my own mind as following the dismissal of the suit of Mr. Holbrook. So we talked softly and quietly of old times through the long November evening.

The next day Miss Pole brought us word that Mr. Holbrook was dead. Miss Matty heard the news in silence; in fact, from the account of the previous day, it was only what we had to expect. Miss Pole kept calling upon us for some expression of regret, by asking if it was not sad that he was gone, and saying—

"To think of that pleasant day last June, when he seemed so well! And he might have lived this dozen years if he had not gone to that wicked Paris, where they are always having revolutions."

She paused for some demonstration on our part. I saw Miss Matty could not speak, she was trembling so nervously;

so I said what I really felt; and after a call of some duration—all the time of which I have no doubt Miss Pole thought Miss Matty received the news very calmly—our visitor took her leave. Miss Matty made a strong effort to conceal her feelings—a concealment she practised even with me, for she has never alluded to Mr. Holbrook again, although the book he gave her lies with her Bible on the little table by her bedside. She did not think I heard her when she asked the little milliner of Cranford to make her caps something like the Honourable Mrs. Jamieson's, or that I noticed the reply—

"But she wears widows' caps, ma'am?"

"Oh? I only meant something in that style; not widows', of course, but rather like Mrs. Jamieson's."

This effort at concealment was the beginning of the tremulous motion of head and hands which I have seen ever since in Miss Matty.

The evening of the day on which we heard of Mr. Holbrook's death, Miss Matilda was very silent and thoughtful; after prayers she called Martha back, and then she stood uncertain what to say.

"Martha!" she said, at last, "you are young"—and then she made so long a pause that Martha, to remind her of her half-finished sentence, dropped a curtsy, and said—

"Yes, please, ma'am; two-and-twenty last third of October, please, ma'am."

"And, perhaps, Martha, you may some time meet with a young man you like, and who likes you. I did say you were not to have followers; but if you meet with such a young man, and tell me, and I find he is respectable, I have no objection to his coming to see you once a week. God forbid!" she said in a low voice, "that I should grieve any young hearts." She spoke as if she were providing for some distant contingency, and was rather startled when Martha made her ready, eager answer—

"Please, ma'am, there's Jem Hearn, and he's a joiner,

making three-and-sixpence a day, and six foot one in his stocking feet, please, ma'am; and if you'll ask about him tomorrow morning, every one will give him a character for steadiness; and he'll be glad enough to come tomorrow night, I'll be bound."

Though Miss Matty was startled, she submitted to Fate and Love.

CHAPTER 5

Old Letters

I have often noticed that almost every one has his own individual small economies—careful habits of saving fractions of pennies in some one peculiar direction—any disturbance of which annoys him more than spending shillings or pounds on some real extravagance. An old gentleman of my acquaintance, who took the intelligence of the failure of a Joint-stock Bank, in which some of his money was invested, with stoical mildness, worried his family all through a long summer's day because one of them had torn (instead of cutting) out the written leaves of his now useless bank-book; of course, the corresponding pages at the other end came out as well, and this little unnecessary waste of paper (his private economy) chafed him more than all the loss of his money. Envelopes fretted his soul terribly when they first came in; the only way in which he could reconcile himself to such waste of his cherished article was by patiently turning inside out all that were sent to him, and so making them serve again. Even now, though tamed by age, I see him casting wistful glances at his daughters when they send a whole instead of a half-sheet of notepaper, with the three lines of acceptance to an invitation, written on only one of the sides. I am not above owning that I have this human weakness myself. String is my foible. My pockets get full of little hanks of it, picked up and twisted together, ready for uses that never come. I am seriously annoyed if any one cuts the string of a parcel instead of patiently and faithfully undoing it fold by fold. How people can bring themselves to use india-rubber rings, which are a sort of deification of string, as lightly as they do, I cannot imagine. To me an india-rubber ring is a precious treasure. I have one which is not new—one that I picked up off the floor nearly six years ago. I have really tried to use it, but my heart failed me, and I could not commit the extravagance.

Small pieces of butter grieve others. They cannot attend to conversation because of the annoyance occasioned by the habit which some people have of invariably taking more butter than they want. Have you not seen the anxious look (almost mesmeric) which such persons fix on the article? They would feel it a relief if they might bury it out of their sight by popping it into their own mouths and swallowing it down; and they are really made happy if the person on whose plate it lies unused, suddenly breaks off a piece of toast (which he does not want at all) and eats up his butter. They think that this is not waste.

Now Miss Matty Jenkyns was chary of candles. We had many devices to use as few as possible. In the winter afternoons she would sit knitting for two or three hours—she could do this in the dark, or by firelight—and when I asked if I might not ring for candles to finish stitching my wristbands, she told me to "keep blind man's holiday." They were usually brought in with tea; but we only burned one at a time. As we lived in constant preparation for a friend who might come in any evening (but who never did), it required some contrivance to keep our two candles of the same length, ready to be lighted, and to look as if we burned two always. The candles took it in turns; and whatever we might be talking about or doing, Miss Matty's eyes were habitually fixed upon the candle, ready to jump up and extinguish it and to light the other before they had become too uneven in length to be restored to equality in the course of the evening.

One night, I remember this candle economy particularly annoyed me. I had been very much tired of my compulsory "blind man's holidays," especially as Miss Matty had fallen asleep, and I did not like to stir the fire and run the risk of awakening her, so I could not even sit on the rug, and scorch myself with sewing by firelight, according to my usual custom. I fancied Miss Matty must be dreaming of her early life; for she spoke one or two words in her uneasy sleep, bearing reference to persons who were dead long before. When Martha brought in the lighted candle and tea, Miss Matty started into wakefulness, with a strange, bewildered look around, as if we were not the people she expected to see about her. There was a little sad expression that shadowed her face as she recognised me; but immediately afterwards she tried to give me her usual smile. All through tea-time her talk ran upon the days of her childhood and youth. Perhaps this reminded her of the desirableness of looking over all the old family letters, and destroying such as ought not to be allowed to fall into the hands of strangers; for she had often spoken of the necessity of this task, but had always shrunk from it, with a timid dread of something painful. Tonight, however, she rose up after tea and went for them—in the dark; for she piqued herself on the precise neatness of all her chamber arrangements, and used to look uneasily at me when I lighted a bed-candle to go to another room for anything. When she returned there was a faint, pleasant smell of Tonquin beans in the room. I had always noticed this scent about any of the things which had belonged to her mother; and many of the letters were addressed to her—yellow bundles of love-letters, sixty or seventy years old.

Miss Matty undid the packet with a sigh; but she stifled it directly, as if it were hardly right to regret the flight of time, or of life either. We agreed to look them over separately, each taking a different letter out of the same bundle and describing its contents to the other before destroying it. I never knew what sad work the reading of old letters was before that evening, though I could hardly tell why. The letters were as happy as letters could be—at least those early letters were. There was in them a vivid and intense sense of the present time, which seemed so strong and full, as if it could never pass away, and as if the warm, living hearts that so expressed themselves could never die, and be as nothing to the sunny earth. I should have felt less melancholy, I believe, if the letters had been more so. I saw the tears stealing down the well-worn furrows of Miss Matty's cheeks, and her spectacles often wanted wiping. I trusted at last that she would light the other candle, for my own eyes were rather dim, and I wanted more light to see the pale, faded ink; but no, even through her tears, she saw and remembered her little economical ways.

The earliest set of letters were two bundles tied together, and ticketed (in Miss Jenkyns's handwriting), "Letters interchanged between my ever-honoured father and my dearly-beloved mother, prior to their marriage, in July, 1774." I should guess that the Rector of Cranford was about twenty-seven years of age when he wrote those letters; and Miss Matty told me that her mother was just eighteen at the time of her wedding. With my idea of the Rector, derived from a picture in the dining-parlour, stiff and stately, in a huge full-bottomed wig, with gown, cassock, and bands, and his hand upon a copy of the only sermon he ever published—it was strange to read these letters. They were full of eager, passionate ardour; short, homely sentences, right fresh from the heart (very different from the grand Latinised, Johnsonian style of the printed sermon, preached before some judge at assize time). His letters were a curious contrast to those of his girl-bride. She was evidently rather annoyed at his demands upon her for expressions of love, and could not quite understand what he meant by repeating the same thing over in so many different ways; but what she was quite clear about was a longing for a white "Paduasoy"—whatever that might be; and six or seven letters were principally occupied in asking her lover to use his influence with her parents (who evidently kept her in good order) to obtain this or that article of dress, more especially the white "Paduasoy." He cared nothing how she was dressed; she was always lovely enough for him, as he took pains to assure her, when she begged him to express in his answers a predilection for particular pieces of finery, in order that she might show what he said to her parents. But at length he seemed to find out that she would not be married till she had a "trousseau" to her mind; and then he sent her a letter, which had evidently accompanied a whole box full of finery, and in which he requested that she might be dressed in everything her heart desired. This was the first letter, ticketed in a frail, delicate hand, "From my dearest John." Shortly afterwards they were married—I suppose, from the intermission in their correspondence.

"We must burn them, I think," said Miss Matty, looking doubtfully at me. "No one will care for them when I am gone." And one by one she dropped them into the middle of the fire, watching each blaze up, die out, and rise away, in faint, white, ghostly semblance, up the chimney, before she gave another to the same fate. The room was light enough now; but I, like her, was fascinated into watching the destruction of those letters, into which the honest warmth of a manly heart had been poured forth.

The next letter, likewise docketed by Miss Jenkyns, was endorsed, "Letter of pious congratulation and exhortation from my venerable grandfather to my beloved mother, on occasion of my own birth. Also some practical remarks on the desirability of keeping warm the extremities of infants, from my excellent grandmother."

The first part was, indeed, a severe and forcible picture of the responsibilities of mothers, and a warning against the evils that were in the world, and lying in ghastly wait for the little baby of two days old. His wife did not write, said the old gentleman, because he had forbidden it, she being indisposed with a sprained ankle, which (he said) quite incapacitated her from holding a pen. However, at the foot of the page was a small "T.O.," and on turning it over, sure enough, there was a letter to "my dear, dearest Molly," begging her, when she left her room, whatever she did, to go *up* stairs before going *down*; and telling her to wrap her baby's feet up in flannel, and keep it warm by the fire, although it was summer, for babies were so tender.

It was pretty to see from the letters, which were evidently exchanged with some frequency between the young mother and the grandmother, how the girlish vanity was being weeded out of her heart by love for her baby. The white "Paduasoy" figured again in the letters, with almost as much vigour as before. In one, it was being made into a christening cloak for the baby. It decked it when it went with its parents to spend a day or two at Arley Hall. It added to its charms, when it was "the prettiest little baby that ever was seen. Dear mother, I wish you could see her! Without any parshality, I do think she will grow up a regular bewty!" I thought of Miss Jenkyns, gray, withered, and wrinkled, and I wondered if her mother had known her in the courts of heaven: and then I knew that she had, and that they stood there in angelic guise.

There was a great gap before any of the rector's letters appeared. And then his wife had changed her mode of endorsement. It was no longer from "My dearest John"; it was from "My honoured Husband." The letters were written on occasion of the publication of the same sermon which was represented in the picture. The preaching before "My Lord Judge," and the "publishing by request," was evidently the culminating point—the event of his life. It had been necessary for him to go up to London to superintend it through the press. Many friends had to be called upon, and consulted, before he could decide on any printer fit for so onerous a task; and at length it was arranged that J. and J. Rivingtons were to have the honourable responsibility. The worthy Rector seemed to be strung up by the occasion to a high literary pitch, for he could hardly write a letter to his wife without cropping out into Latin. I remember the end of one of his letters ran thus: "I shall ever hold the virtuous qualities of my Molly in remembrance, *dum memor ipse mei, dum spiritus regit artus;*" which, considering that the English of his correspondent was sometimes at fault in grammar, and often in spelling, might be taken as a proof of how much he "idealised his Molly"; and, as Miss Jenkyns used to say, "People talk a great deal about idealising nowadays, whatever that may mean." But this was nothing to a fit of writing classical poetry which soon seized him, in which his Molly figured away as "Maria." The letter containing the *carmen* was endorsed by her, "Hebrew verses sent me by my honoured husband, I thowt to have had a letter about killing the pig, but must wait. Mem., to send the poetry to Sir Peter Arley, as my husband desires." And in a *post-scriptum* note in his handwriting it was stated that the ode had appeared in *The Gentleman's Magazine*, December, 1782.

Her letters back to her husband (treasured as fondly by him as if they had been *M. T. Ciceronis Epistolae*) were more satisfactory to an absent husband and father than his could ever have been to her. She told him how Deborah sewed her seam very neatly every day, and read to her in the books he had set her; how she was a very "forrard," good child, but *would* ask questions her mother could not answer, but how she did not let herself down by saying she did not know, but took to stirring the fire, or sending the "forrard" child on an errand. Matty was now the mother's darling, and promised (like her sister at her age) to be a great beauty. I was reading this aloud to Miss Matty, who smiled and sighed a little at the hope, so fondly expressed, that "little Matty might not be vain, even if she were a bewty."

"I had very pretty hair, my dear," said Miss Matilda;

"and not a bad mouth." And I saw her, soon afterwards, adjust her cap and draw herself up.

But to return to Mrs. Jenkyns's letters. She told her husband about the poor in the parish; what homely, domestic medicines she had administered, what kitchen physic she had sent. She had evidently held his displeasure as a rod in pickle over the heads of all the ne'er-do-wells. She asked for his directions about the cows and pigs; and did not always obtain them, as I have shown before.

The kind old grandmother was dead when a little boy was born, soon after the publication of the sermon; but there was another letter of exhortation from the grandfather, more stringent and admonitory than ever, now that there was a boy to be guarded from the snares of the world. He described all the various sins into which men might fall, until I wondered how any man ever came to a natural death. The gallows seemed as if it must have been the termination of the lives of most of the grandfather's friends and acquaintance; and I was not surprised at the way in which he spoke of this life being "a vale of tears."

It seemed curious that I should never have heard of this brother before; but I concluded that he had died young, or else surely his name would have been alluded to by his sisters.

By and by we came to packets of Miss Jenkyns's letters. These Miss Matty did regret to burn. She said all the others had been only interesting to those who loved the writers; and that it seemed as if it would have hurt her to allow them to fall into the hands of strangers, who had not known her dear mother, and how good she was, although she did not always spell quite in the modern fashion; but Deborah's letters were so very superior! Any one might profit by reading them. It was a long time since she had read Mrs. Chapone, but she knew she used to think that Deborah could have said the same things quite as well; and as for Mrs. Carter! people thought a deal of her letters, just because she had written *Epictetus*, but she was quite sure Deborah would never have made use of such a common expression as "I canna be fashed!"

Miss Matty did grudge burning these letters, it was evident. She would not let them be carelessly passed over with any quiet reading, and skipping, to myself. She took them from me, and even lighted the second candle in order to read them aloud with a proper emphasis, and without stumbling over the big words. Oh, dear! how I wanted facts instead of reflections, before those letters were concluded! They lasted us two nights; and I won't deny that I made use of the time to think of many other things, and yet I was always at my post at the end of each sentence.

The Rector's letters, and those of his wife and mother-in-law, had all been tolerably short and pithy, written in a straight hand, with the lines very close together. Sometimes the whole letter was contained on a mere scrap of paper. The paper was very yellow, and the ink very brown; some of the sheets were (as Miss Matty made me observe) the old original post, with the stamp in the corner, representing a post boy riding for life and twanging his horn. The letters of Mrs. Jenkyns and her mother were fastened with a great round red wafer; for it was before Miss Edgeworth's *Patronage* had banished wafers from polite society. It was evident, from the tenor of what was said, that franks were in great request, and were even used as a means of paying debts by needy members of parliament. The rector sealed his epistles with an immense coat of arms, and showed by the care with which he had performed this ceremony that he expected they should be cut open, not broken by any thoughtless or impatient hand. Now, Miss Jenkyns's letters were of a later date in form and writing. She wrote on the square sheet which we have learned to call old-fashioned. Her hand was admirably calculated, together with her use of many-syllabled words, to fill up a sheet, and then came the pride and delight of crossing. Poor Miss Matty got sadly puzzled with this, for the words gathered size like snowballs, and towards the end of her letter Miss Jenkyns used to become quite sesquipedalian. In one to her father, slightly theological and controversial in its tone, she had spoken of Herod, Tetrarch of Idumae. Miss Matty read it "Herod Petrarch of Etruria," and was just as well pleased as if she had been right.

I can't quite remember the date, but I think it was in 1805 that Miss Jenkyns wrote the longest series of letters—on occasion of her absence on a visit to some friends near Newcastle-upon-Tyne. These friends were intimate with the commandant of the garrison there, and heard from him of all the preparations that were being made to repel the invasion of Buonaparte, which some people imagined might take place at the mouth of the Tyne. Miss Jenkyns was evidently very much alarmed; and the first part of her letters was often written in pretty intelligible English, conveying particulars of the preparations which were made in the family with whom she was residing against the dreaded event; the bundles of clothes that were packed up ready for a flight to Alston Moor (a wild hilly piece of ground between Northumberland and Cumberland); the signal that was to be given for this flight, and for the simultaneous turning out of the volunteers under arms—which said signal was to consist (if I remember rightly) in ringing the church bells in a particular and ominous manner. One day, when Miss Jenkyns and her hosts were at a dinner-party in Newcastle, this warning summons was actually given (not a very wise proceeding, if there be any truth in the moral attached to the fable of the Boy and the Wolf; but so it was), and Miss Jenkyns, hardly recovered from her fright, wrote the next day to describe the sound, the breathless shock, the hurry and alarm; and then, taking breath, she added: "How trivial, my dear father, do all our apprehensions of the last evening appear, at the present moment, to calm and inquiring minds!" And here Miss Matty broke in with— "But, indeed, my dear, they were not at all trivial or trifling at the time. I know I used to wake up in the night many a time and think I heard the tramp of the French entering Cranford. Many people talked of hiding themselves in the salt mines—and meat would have kept capitally down there, only perhaps we should have been thirsty. And my father preached a whole set of sermons on the occasion; one set in the mornings, all about David and Goliath, to spirit up the people to fighting with spades or bricks, if need were; and the other set in the afternoons, proving that Napoleon (that was another name for Bony, as we used to call him) was all the same as an Apollyon and Abaddon. I remember my father rather thought he should be asked to print this last set; but the parish had, perhaps, had enough of them with hearing."

Peter Marmaduke Arley Jenkyns ("poor Peter!" as Miss Matty began to call him) was at school at Shrewsbury by this time. The Rector took up his pen, and rubbed up his Latin once more, to correspond with his boy. It was very clear that the lad's were what are called show letters. They were of a highly mental description, giving an account of his studies, and his intellectual hopes of various kinds, with an occasional quotation from the classics; but, now and then, the animal nature broke out in such a little sentence as this, evidently written in a trembling hurry, after the letter had been inspected: "Mother dear, do send me a cake, and put plenty of citron in." The "mother dear" probably answered her boy in the form of cakes and "goody," for there were none of her letters among this set; but a whole collection of the rector's, to whom the Latin in his boy's letters was like a trumpet to the old war-horse. I do not know much about Latin, certainly, and it is, perhaps, an ornamental language, but not very useful, I think—at least to judge from the bits I remember out of the rector's letters. One was "You have not got that town in your map of Ireland; but *Bonus Bernardus non videt omnia*, as the *Proverbia* say." Presently it became very evident that "poor Peter" got himself into many scrapes. There were letters of stilted penitence to his father, for some wrong-doing; and among them all was a badly-written, badly-sealed, badly-directed, blotted note: "My dear, dear, dear, dearest mother, I will be a better boy; I will, indeed; but don't, please, be ill for me; I am not worth it; but I will be good, darling mother."

Miss Matty could not speak for crying, after she had read this note. She gave it to me in silence, and then got up and took it to her sacred recesses in her own room, for fear, by any chance, it might get burned. "Poor Peter!" she said; "he was always in scrapes; he was too easy. They led him wrong, and then left him in the lurch. But he was too fond of mischief. He could never resist a joke. Poor Peter!"

CHAPTER 6

Poor Peter

Poor Peter's career lay before him rather pleasantly mapped out by kind friends, but *Bonus Bernardus non videt omnia*, in his map too. He was to win honours at Shrewsbury School, and carry them thick to Cambridge, and, after that, a living a waited him, the gift of his godfather, Sir Peter Arley. Poor Peter! his lot in life was very different to what his friends had hoped and planned. Miss Matty told me all about it, and I think it was a relief to her when she had done so.

He was the darling of his mother, who seemed to dote on all her children, though she was, perhaps, a little afraid of Deborah's superior acquirements. Deborah was the favourite of her father, and when Peter disappointed him, she became his pride. The sole honour Peter brought away from Shrewsbury was the reputation of being the best good fellow that ever was, and of being the captain of the school in the art of practical joking. His father was disappointed, but set about remedying the matter in a manly way. He could not afford to send Peter to read with any tutor, but he could read with him himself; and Miss Matty told me much of the awful preparations in the way of dictionaries and lexicons that were made in her father's study the morning Peter began.

"My poor mother!" said she. "I remember how she used to stand in the hall, just near enough to the study-door to catch the tone of my father's voice. I could tell in a moment if all was going right by her face. And it did go right for a long time."

"What went wrong at last?" said I. "That tiresome Latin, I dare say."

"No! it was not the Latin. Peter was in high favour with my father, for he worked up well for him. But he seemed to think that the Cranford people might be joked about, and made fun of, and they did not like it; nobody does. He was always hoaxing them; 'hoaxing' is not a pretty word, my dear, and I hope you won't tell your father I used it, for I should not like him to think that I was not choice in my language, after living with such a woman as Deborah. And be sure you never use it yourself. I don't know how it slipped out of my mouth, except it was that I was thinking of poor Peter, and it was always his expression. But he was a very gentlemanly boy in many things. He was like dear Captain Brown in always being ready to help any old person or a child. Still, he did like joking and making fun; and he seemed to think the old ladies in Cranford would believe anything. There were many old ladies living here then; we are prin-cipally ladies now, I know, but we are not so old as the ladies used to be when I was a girl. I could laugh to think of some of Peter's jokes. No, my dear, I won't tell you of them, because they might not shock you as they ought to do, and they were very shocking. He even took in my father once, by dressing himself up as a lady that was passing through the town and wished to see the Rector of Cranford, 'who had published that admirable Assize Sermon.' Peter said he was awfully frightened himself when he saw how my father took it all in, and even offered to copy out all his Napoleon Buonaparte sermons for her—him, I mean—no, her, for Peter was a lady then. He told me he was more terrified than he ever was before, all the time my father was speaking. He did not think my father would have believed him; and yet if he had not, it would have been a sad thing for Peter. As it was, he was none so glad of it, for my father kept him hard at work copying out all those twelve Buonaparte sermons for the lady—that was for Peter himself, you know. He was the lady. And once when he wanted to go fishing, Peter said 'Confound the woman!'—very bad language, my dear, but Peter was not always so guarded as he should have been; my father was so angry with him, it nearly frightened me out of my wits; and yet I could hardly keep from laughing at the little curtsies Peter kept making, quite slyly, whenever my father spoke of the lady's excellent taste and sound discrimination."

"Did Miss Jenkyns know of these tricks?" said I.

"Oh, no! Deborah would have been too much shocked. No, no one knew but me. I wish I had always known of Peter's plans; but sometimes he did not tell me. He used to say the old ladies in the town wanted something to talk about; but I don't think they did. They had *The St. James's* Chronicle three times a week, just as we have now, and we have plenty to say; and I remember the clacking noise there always was when some of the ladies got together. But, probably, schoolboys talk more than ladies. At last there was a terrible, sad thing happened." Miss Matty got up, went to the door, and opened it; no one was there. She rang the bell for Martha, and when Martha came, her mistress told her to go for eggs to a farm at the other end of the town.

"I will lock the door after you, Martha. You are not afraid to go, are you?"

"No, ma'am, not at all; Jem Hearn will be only too proud to go with me."

Miss Matty drew herself up, and as soon as we were alone, she wished that Martha had more maidenly reserve.

"We'll put out the candle, my dear. We can talk just as

well by firelight, you know. There! Well, you see, Deborah had gone from home for a fortnight or so; it was a very still, quiet day, I remember, overhead; and the lilacs were all in flower, so I suppose it was spring. My father had gone out to see some sick people in the parish; I recollect seeing him leave the house with his wig and shovel-hat and cane. What possessed our poor Peter I don't know; he had the sweetest temper, and yet he always seemed to like to plague Deborah. She never laughed at his jokes, and thought him ungenteel, and not careful enough about improving his mind; and that vexed him.

"Well! he went to her room, it seems, and dressed himself in her old gown, and shawl, and bonnet; just the things she used to wear in Cranford, and was known by everywhere; and he made the pillow into a little—you are sure you locked the door, my dear? for I should not like any one to hear—into—into a little baby, with white long clothes. It was only, as he told me afterwards, to make something to talk about in the town; he never thought of it as affecting Deborah. And he went and walked up and down in the Filbert walk—just half-hidden by the rails, and half-seen; and he cuddled his pillow, just like a baby, and talked to it all the nonsense people do. Oh, dear! and my father came stepping stately up the street, as he always did; and what should he see but a little black crowd of people—I dare say as many as twenty—all peeping through his garden rails. So he thought, at first, they were only looking at a new rhododendron that was in full bloom, and that he was very proud of; and he walked slower, that they might have more time to admire. And he wondered if he could make out a sermon from the occasion, and thought, perhaps, there was some relation between the rhododendrons and the lilies of the field. My poor father! When he came nearer, he began to wonder that they did not see him; but their heads were all so close together peeping and peeping! My father was amongst them, meaning, he said, to ask them to walk into the garden with him, and admire the beautiful vegetable production, when—oh, my dear! I tremble to think of it—he looked through the rails himself, and saw—I don't know what he thought he saw, but old Clare told me his face went quite gray-white with anger, and his eyes blazed out under his frowning black brows: and he spoke out—oh, so terribly!—and bade them all stop where they were—not one of them to go, not one to stir a step; and, swift as light, he was in at the garden door, and down the Filbert walk, and seized hold of poor Peter, and tore his clothes off his back—bonnet, shawl, gown, and all—and threw the pillow among the people over the railings: and then he was very, very angry indeed, and before all the people he lifted up his cane and flogged Peter!

"My dear, that boy's trick, on that sunny day, when all seemed going straight and well, broke my mother's heart, and changed my father for life. It did, indeed. Old Clare said Peter looked as white as my father; and stood as still as a statue to be flogged; and my father struck hard! When my father stopped to take breath, Peter said, 'Have you done enough, sir?' quite hoarsely, and still standing quite quiet. I don't know what my father said—or if he said anything. But old Clare said Peter turned to where the people outside the railings were, and made them a low bow, as grand and as grave as any gentleman; and then walked slowly into the house. I was in the store-room helping my mother to make cowslip wine. I cannot abide the wine now, nor the scent of the flowers; they turn me sick and faint, as they did that day when Peter came in looking as haughty as any man—indeed, looking like a man, not like a boy. 'Mother!' he said, 'I am come to say, God bless you for ever.' I saw his lips quiver as he spoke; and I think he durst not say anything more loving, for the purpose that was in his heart. She looked at him rather frightened, and wondering, and asked him what was to do. He did not smile or speak, but put his arms round her and kissed her as if he did not know how to leave off; and before she could speak again, he was gone. We talked it over, and could not understand it, and she bade me go and seek my father, and ask what it was all about. I found him walking up and down, looking very highly displeased.

"'Tell your mother I have flogged Peter, and that he richly deserved it.'

"I durst not ask any more questions. When I told my mother, she sat down, quite faint, for a minute. I remember, a few days after, I saw the poor, withered cowslip flowers thrown out to the leaf heap, to decay and die there. There was no making of cowslip wine that year at the rectory, nor, indeed, ever after.

"Presently my mother went to my father. I know I thought of Queen Esther and King Ahasuerus; for my mother was very pretty and delicate-looking, and my father looked as terrible as King Ahasuerus. Some time after they came out together; and then, my mother told me what had happened, and that she was going up to Peter's room at my father's desire—though she was not to tell Peter this—to talk the matter over with him. But no Peter was there. We looked over the house; no Peter was there! Even my father, who had not liked to join in the search at first, helped us before long. The rectory was a very old house—steps up into a room, steps down into a room, all through. At first, my mother went calling low and soft, as if to reassure the poor boy, 'Peter! Peter, dear! it's only me;' but, by and by, as the servants came back from the errands my father had sent them, in different directions, to find where Peter was—as we found he was not in the garden, nor the hayloft, nor anywhere about—my mother's cry grew louder and wilder, 'Peter! Peter, my darling! where are you?' for then she felt and understood that that long kiss meant some sad kind of 'goodbye.' The afternoon went on—my mother never resting, but seeking again and again in every possible place that had been looked into twenty times before, nay, that she had looked into over and over again herself. My father sat with his head in his hands, not speaking except when his messengers came in, bringing no tidings; then he lifted up his face, so strong and sad, and told them to go again in some new direction. My mother kept passing from room to room, in and out of the house, moving noiselessly, but never ceasing. Neither she nor my father durst leave the house, which was the meeting-place for all the messengers. At last (and it was nearly dark) my father rose up. He took hold of my mother's arm as she came with wild, sad pace through one door, and quickly towards another. She started at the touch of his hand, for she had forgotten all in the world but Peter.

"'Molly!' said he, 'I did not think all this would happen.' He looked into her face for comfort—her poor face, all wild and white; for neither she nor my father had dared to acknowledge, much less act upon, the terror that was in their hearts, lest Peter should have made away with himself. My father saw no conscious look in his wife's hot, dreary eyes, and he missed the sympathy that she had always been ready to give him, strong man as he was, and, at the dumb despair in her face, his tears began to flow. But when she saw this, a gentle sorrow came over her countenance, and she said,' 'Dearest John! don't cry; come with me, and we'll find him,' almost as cheerfully as if she knew where he was. And she took my father's great hand in her little, soft one and led him along, the tears dropping as he walked on that same unceasing, weary walk, from room to room, through house and garden.

"Oh, how I wished for Deborah! I had no time for crying, for now all seemed to depend on me. I wrote for Deborah to come home. I sent a message privately to that same Mr Holbrook's house—poor Mr. Holbrook;—you know who I mean. I don't mean I sent a message to him, but I sent one that I could trust to know if Peter was at his house.

For at one time Mr. Holbrook was an occasional visitor at the rectory—you know he was Miss Pole's cousin—and he had been very kind to Peter, and taught him how to fish— he was very kind to everybody, and I thought Peter might have gone off there. But Mr. Holbrook was from home, and Peter had never been seen. It was night now; but the doors were all wide open, and my father and mother walked on and on; it was more than an hour since he had joined her, and I don't believe they had ever spoken all that time. I was getting the parlour fire lighted, and one of the servants was preparing tea, for I wanted them to have something to eat and drink and warm them, when old Clare asked to speak to me.

"'I have borrowed the nets from the weir, Miss Matty. Shall we drag the ponds tonight, or wait for the morning?'

"I remember staring in his face to gather his meaning; and when I did, I laughed out loud. The horror of that new thought—our bright, darling Peter, cold, and stark, and dead! I remember the ring of my own laugh now.

"The next day Deborah was at home before I was myself again. She would not have been so weak as to give way as I had done; but my screams (my horrible laughter had ended in crying) had roused my sweet, dear mother, whose poor wandering wits were called back and collected as soon as a child needed her care. She and Deborah sat by my bedside; I knew by the looks of each that there had been no news of Peter—no awful, ghastly news, which was what I most had dreaded in my dull state between sleeping and waking.

"The same result of all the searching had brought something of the same relief to my mother, to whom, I am sure, the thought that Peter might even then be hanging dead on some of the familiar home places had caused that never-ending walk of yesterday. Her soft eyes never were the same again after that; they had always a restless, craving look, as if seeking for what they could not find. Oh! it was an awful time; coming down like a thunderbolt on the still sunny day when the lilacs were all in bloom."

"Where was Mr. Peter?" said I.

"He had made his way to Liverpool; and there was war then; and some of the king's ships lay off the mouth of the Mersey; and they were only too glad to have a fine likely boy such as him (five foot nine he was) come to offer himself. The captain wrote to my father, and Peter wrote to my mother. Stay! those letters will be somewhere here."

We lighted the candle, and found the captain's letter and Peter's too. And we also found a little simple begging letter from Mrs. Jenkyns to Peter, addressed to him at the house of an old school-fellow, whither she fancied he might have gone. They had returned it unopened; and unopened it had remained ever since, having been inadvertently put among by the other letters of that time. This is it:

> *My dearest Peter,*
> *You did not think we should be so sorry as we are,*
> *I know, or you would never have gone away. You*
> *are too good. Your father sits and sighs till my*
> *heart aches to hear him. He cannot hold up his*
> *head for grief; and yet he only did what he thought*
> *was right. Perhaps he has been too severe, and*
> *perhaps I have not been kind enough; but God*
> *knows how we love you, my dear only boy. Don*
> *looks so sorry you are gone. Come back, and make*
> *us happy, who love you so much. I know you will*
> *come back.*

But Peter did not come back. That spring day was the last time he ever saw his mother's face. The writer of the letter—the last—the only person who had ever seen what was written in it, was dead long ago; and I, a stranger, not born at the time when this occurrence took place, was the one to open it.

The captain's letter summoned the father and mother to Liverpool instantly, if they wished to see their boy; and, by some of the wild chances of life, the captain's letter had been detained somewhere, somehow.

Miss Matty went on: "And it was race-time, and all the post-horses at Cranford were gone to the races; but my father and mother set off in our own gig—and oh! my dear, they were too late—the ship was gone! And now read Peter's letter to my mother!"

It was full of love, and sorrow, and pride in his new profession, and a sore sense of his disgrace in the eyes of the people at Cranford; but ending with a passionate entreaty that she would come and see him before he left the Mersey: "Mother, we may go into the battle. I hope we shall, and lick those French; but I must see you again before that time."

"And she was too late," said Miss Matty; "too late!"

We sat in silence, pondering on the full meaning of those sad, sad words. At length I asked Miss Matty to tell me how her mother bore it.

"Oh!" she said, "she was patience itself. She had never been strong, and this weakened her terribly. My father used to sit looking at her: far more sad than she was. He seemed as if he could look at nothing else when she was by; and he was so humble—so very gentle now. He would, perhaps, speak in his old way—laying down the law, as it were—and then, in a minute or two, he would come round and put his hand on our shoulders, and ask us in a low voice, if he had said anything to hurt us. I did not wonder at his speaking so to Deborah, for she was so clever; but I could not bear to hear him talking so to me.

"But, you see, he saw what we did not—that it was killing my mother. Yes! killing her (put out the candle, my dear; I can talk better in the dark), for she was but a frail woman, and ill-fitted to stand the fright and shock she had gone through; and she would smile at him and comfort him, not in words, but in her looks and tones, which were always cheerful when he was there. And she would speak of how she thought Peter stood a good chance of being admiral very soon—he was so brave and clever; and how she thought of seeing him in his navy uniform, and what sort of hats admirals wore; and how much more fit he was to be a sailor than a clergyman; and all in that way, just to make my father think she was quite glad of what came of that unlucky morning's work, and the flogging which was always in his mind, as we all knew. But oh, my dear! the bitter, bitter crying she had when she was alone; and at last, as she grew weaker, she could not keep her tears in when Deborah or me was by, and would give us message after message for Peter (his ship had gone to the Mediterranean, or somewhere down there, and then he was ordered off to India, and there was no overland route then); but she still said that no one knew where their death lay in wait, and that we were not to think hers was near. We did not think it, but we knew it, as we saw her fading away.

"Well, my dear, it's very foolish of me, I know, when in all likelihood I am so near seeing her again.

"And only think, love! the very day after her death—for she did not live quite a twelvemonth after Peter went away, the very day after—came a parcel for her from India—from her poor boy. It was a large, soft, white India shawl, with just a little narrow border all round; just what my mother would have liked.

"We thought it might rouse my father, for he had sat with her hand in his all night long; so Deborah took it in to him, and Peter's letter to her, and all. At first he took no notice; and we tried to make a kind of light careless talk about the shawl, opening it out and admiring it. Then, suddenly, he got up, and spoke: 'She shall be buried in it,' he said. 'Peter shall have that comfort; and she would have liked it.'

"Well, perhaps it was not reasonable, but what could we do or say? One gives people in grief their own way. He took it up and felt it: 'It is just such a shawl as she wished for when she was married, and her mother did not give it her. I did not know of it till after, or she should have had it—she should; but she shall have it now.'

"My mother looked so lovely in her death! She was always pretty, and now she looked fair, and waxen, and young—younger than Deborah, as she stood trembling and shivering by her. We decked her in the long soft folds; she lay smiling, as if pleased; and people came—all Cranford came—to beg to see her, for they had loved her dearly, as well they might; and the countrywomen brought posies; old Clare's wife brought some white violets, and begged they might lie on her breast.

"Deborah said to me the day of my mother's funeral that if she had a hundred offers she never would marry and leave my father. It was not very likely she would have so many—I don't know that she had one; but it was not less to her credit to say so. She was such a daughter to my father as I think there never was before or since. His eyes failed him, and she read book after book, and wrote, and copied, and was always at his service in any parish business. She could do many more things than my poor mother could; she even once wrote a letter to the bishop for my father. But he missed my mother sorely; the whole parish noticed it. Not that he was less active; I think he was more so, and more patient in helping every one. I did all I could to set Deborah at liberty to be with him; for I knew I was good for little, and that my best work in the world was to do odd jobs quietly, and set others at liberty. But my father was a changed man."

"Did Mr. Peter ever come home?"

"Yes, once. He came home a lieutenant; he did not get to be admiral. And he and my father were such friends! My father took him into every house in the parish, he was so proud of him. He never walked out without Peter's arm to lean upon. Deborah used to smile (I don't think we ever laughed again after my mother's death), and say she was quite put in a corner. Not but what my father always wanted her when there was letter-writing or reading to be done, or anything to be settled."

"And then?" said I, after a pause

"Then Peter went to sea again; and, by and by, my father died, blessing us both, and thanking Deborah for all she had been to him; and, of course, our circumstances were changed; and, instead of living at the rectory, and keeping three maids and a man, we had to come to this small house, and be content with a servant-of-all-work; but, as Deborah used to say, we have always lived genteelly, even if circumstances have compelled us to simplicity. Poor Deborah!"

"And Mr. Peter?" asked I.

"Oh, there was some great war in India—I forget what they call it—and we have never heard of Peter since then. I believe he is dead myself; and it sometimes fidgets me that we have never put on mourning for him. And then, again, when I sit by myself, and all the house is still, I think I hear his step coming up the street, and my heart begins to flutter and beat; but the sound always goes past—and Peter never comes.

"That's Martha back? No! I'll go, my dear; I can always find my way in the dark, you know. And a blow of fresh air at the door will do my head good, and it's rather got a trick of aching."

So she pattered off. I had lighted the candle, to give the room a cheerful appearance against her return.

"Was it Martha?" asked I.

"Yes. And I am rather uncomfortable, for I heard such a strange noise, just as I was opening the door."

"Where?" I asked, for her eyes were round with affright.

"In the street—just outside—it sounded like—"

"Talking?" I put in, as she hesitated a little.

"No! kissing—"

CHAPTER 7

Visiting

One morning, as Miss Matty and I sat at our work—it was before twelve o'clock, and Miss Matty had not changed the cap with yellow ribbons that had been Miss Jenkyns's best, and which Miss Matty was now wearing out in private, putting on the one made in imitation of Mrs. Jamieson's at all times when she expected to be seen—Martha came up, and asked if Miss Betty Barker might speak to her mistress. Miss Matty assented, and quickly disappeared to change the yellow ribbons, while Miss Barker came upstairs; but, as she had forgotten her spectacles, and was rather flurried by the unusual time of the visit, I was not surprised to see her return with one cap on the top of the other. She was quite unconscious of it herself, and looked at us with bland satisfaction. Nor do I think Miss Barker perceived it; for, putting aside the little circumstance that she was not so young as she had been, she was very much absorbed in her errand, which she delivered herself of with an oppressive modesty that found vent in endless apologies.

Miss Betty Barker was the daughter of the old clerk at Cranford who had officiated in Mr. Jenkyns's time. She and her sister had pretty good situations as ladies'-maids, and had saved money enough to set up a milliner's shop, which had been patronised by the ladies in the neighbourhood. Lady Arley, for instance, would occasionally give Miss Barkers the pattern of an old cap of hers, which they immediately copied and circulated among the *élite* of Cranford. I say the *élite*, for Miss Barkers had caught the trick of the place, and piqued themselves upon their "aristocratic connection." They would not sell their caps and ribbons to any one without a pedigree. Many a farmer's wife or daughter turned away huffed from Miss Barkers' select millinery, and went rather to the universal shop, where the profits of brown soap and moist sugar enabled the proprietor to go straight to (Paris, he said, until he found his customers too patriotic and John Bullish to wear what the Mounseers wore) London; where, as he often told his customers, Queen Adelaide had appeared, only the very week before, in a cap exactly like the one he showed them, trimmed with yellow and blue ribbons, and had been complimented by King William on the becoming nature of her headdress.

Miss Barkers, who confined themselves to truth, and did not approve of miscellaneous customers, throve notwithstanding. They were self-denying, good people. Many a time have I seen the eldest of them (she that had been maid to Mrs. Jamieson) carrying out some delicate mess to a poor person. They only aped their betters in having "nothing to do" with the class immediately below theirs. And when Miss Barker died, their profits and income were found to be such that Miss Betty was justified in shutting up shop and retiring from business. She also (as I think I have before said) set up her cow; a mark of respectability in Cranford almost as decided as setting up a gig is among some people. She dressed finer than any lady in Cranford; and we did not wonder at it; for it was understood that she was wearing out all the bonnets and caps and outrageous ribbons which had once formed her stock-in-trade. It was five or six years since she had given up shop, so in any other place than Cranford her dress might have been considered *passee*.

And now Miss Betty Barker had called to invite Miss

Matty to tea at her house on the following Tuesday. She gave me also an impromptu invitation, as I happened to be a visitor—though I could see she had a little fear lest, since my father had gone to live in Drumble, he might have engaged in that "horrid cotton trade," and so dragged his family down out of "aristocratic society." She prefaced this invitation with so many apologies that she quite excited my curiosity.

"Her presumption" was to be excused. What had she been doing? She seemed so overpowered by it, I could only think that she had been writing to Queen Adelaide to ask for a receipt for washing lace; but the act which she so characterised was only an invitation she had carried to her sister's former mistress, Mrs. Jamieson. "Her former occupation considered, could Miss Matty excuse the liberty?" Ah! thought I, she has found out that double cap, and is going to rectify Miss Matty's head-dress. No! it was simply to extend her invitation to Miss Matty and to me. Miss Matty bowed acceptance; and I wondered that, in the graceful action, she did not feel the unusual weight and extraordinary height of her headdress. But I do not think she did, for she recovered her balance, and went on talking to Miss Betty in a kind, condescending manner, very different from the fidgety way she would have had if she had suspected how singular her appearance was.

"Mrs. Jamieson is coming, I think you said?" asked Miss Matty.

"Yes. Mrs. Jamieson most kindly and condescendingly said she would be happy to come. One little stipulation she made, that she should bring Carlo. I told her that if I had a weakness, it was for dogs."

"And Miss Pole?" questioned Miss Matty, who was thinking of her pool at preference, in which Carlo would not be available as a partner.

"I am going to ask Miss Pole. Of course, I could not think of asking her until I had asked you, madam—the rector's daughter, madam. Believe me, I do not forget the situation my father held under yours."

"And Mrs. Forrester, of course?"

"And Mrs. Forrester. I thought, in fact, of going to her before I went to Miss Pole. Although her circumstances are changed, madam, she was born at Tyrrell, and we can never forget her alliance to the Bigges, of Bigelow Hall."

Miss Matty cared much more for the little circumstance of her being a very good card-player.

"Mrs. Fitz-Adam—I suppose—"

"No, madam. I must draw a line somewhere. Mrs. Jamieson would not, I think, like to meet Mrs. Fitz-Adam. I have the greatest respect for Mrs. Fitz-Adam—but I cannot think her fit society for such ladies as Mrs. Jamieson and Miss Matilda Jenkyns."

Miss Betty Barker bowed low to Miss Matty, and pursed up her mouth. She looked at me with sidelong dignity, as much as to say, although a retired milliner, she was no democrat, and understood the difference of ranks.

"May I beg you to come as near half-past six to my little dwelling, as possible, Miss Matilda? Mrs. Jamieson dines at five, but has kindly promised not to delay her visit beyond that time—half-past six." And with a swimming curtsy Miss Betty Barker took her leave.

My prophetic soul foretold a visit that afternoon from Miss Pole, who usually came to call on Miss Matilda after any event—or, indeed, in sight of any event—to talk it over with her.

"Miss Betty told me it was to be a choice and select few," said Miss Pole, as she and Miss Matty compared notes.

"Yes, so she said. Not even Mrs. Fritz-Adam."

Now, Mrs. Fitz-Adam was the widowed sister of the Cranford surgeon, whom I have named before. Their parents were respectable farmers, content with their station. The name of these good people was Hoggins. Mr. Hoggins was the Cranford doctor now; we disliked the name, and considered it coarse; but, as Miss Jenkyns said, if he changed it to Piggins, it would not be much better. We had hoped to discover a relationship between him and that Marchioness of Exeter, whose name was Molly Hoggins; but the man, careless of his own interests, utterly ignored and denied any such relationship, although, as dear Miss Jenkyns had said, he had a sister called Mary, and the same Christian names were very apt to run in families.

Soon after Miss Mary Hoggins married Mr. Fitz-Adam she disappeared from the neighbourhood for many years. She did not move in a sphere in Cranford society sufficiently high to make any of us care to know what Mr. Fitz-Adam was. He died and was gathered to his fathers without our ever having thought about him at all. And then Mrs. Fitz-Adam reappeared in Cranford ("as bold as a lion," Miss Pole said), a well-to-do widow, dressed in rustling black silk, so soon after her husband's death that poor Miss Jenkyns was justified in the remark she made, that "bombazine would have shown a deeper sense of her loss."

I remember the convocation of ladies who assembled to decide whether or not Mrs. Fitz-Adam should be called upon by the old blue-blooded inhabitants of Cranford. She had taken a large rambling house, which had been usually considered to confer a patent of gentility upon its tenant, because, once upon a time, seventy or eighty years before, the spinster daughter of an earl had resided in it. I am not sure if the inhabiting this house was not also believed to convey some unusual power of intellect; for the earl's daughter, Lady Jane, had a sister, Lady Anne, who had married a general officer in the time of the American war, and this general officer had written one or two comedies, which were still acted on the London boards, and which, when we saw them advertised, made us all draw up, and feel that Drury Lane was paying a very pretty compliment to Cranford. Still, it was not at all a settled thing that Mrs. Fitz-Adam was to be visited, when dear Miss Jenkyns died; and, with her, something of the clear knowledge of the strict code of gentility went out too. As Miss Pole observed, "As most of the ladies of good family in Cranford were elderly spinsters, or widows without children, if we did not relax a little, and become less exclusive, by and by we should have no society at all."

Mrs. Forrester continued on the same side.

"She had always understood that Fitz meant something aristocratic; there was Fitz-Roy—she thought that some of the king's children had been called Fitz-Roy; and there was Fitz-Clarence now—they were the children of dear good King William the Fourth. Fitz-Adam!—it was a pretty name, and she thought it very probably meant 'Child of Adam.' No one who had not some good blood in their veins would dare to be called Fitz; there was a deal in a name; she had had a cousin who spelt his name with two little ffs—ffoulkes—and he always looked down upon capital letters, and said they belonged to late-invented families. She had been afraid he would die a bachelor, he was so very choice. When he met with a Mrs. ffarringdon, at a watering-place, he took to her immediately; and a very pretty, genteel woman she was—a widow, with a very good fortune; and 'my cousin,' Mr. ffoulkes, married her; and it was all owing to her two little ffs."

Mrs. Fitz-Adam did not stand a chance of meeting with Mr. Fitz-anything in Cranford, so that could not have been her motive for settling there. Miss Matty thought it might have been the hope of being admitted into the society of the place, which would certainly be a very agreeable rise for *ci-devant* Miss Hoggins; and if this had been her hope it would be cruel to disappoint her.

So everybody called upon Mrs. Fitz-Adam—everybody but Mrs. Jamieson, who used to show how honourable she was by never seeing Mrs. Fitz-Adam when they met at the Cranford parties. There would be only eight or ten ladies in the room, and Mrs. Fitz-Adam was the largest of all, and she invariably used to stand up when Mrs. Jamieson came in, and curtsy very low to her whenever she turned in her direction—so low, in fact, that I think Mrs. Jamieson must have looked at the wall above her, for she never moved a muscle of her face, no more than she had not seen her. Still Mrs. Fitz-Adam persevered.

The spring evenings were getting bright and long when three or four ladies in calashes met at Miss Barker's door. Do you know what a calash is? It is a covering worn over caps, not unlike the heads fastened on old-fashioned gigs; but sometimes it is not quite so large. This kind of head-gear always made an awful impression on the children in Cranford; and now two or three left off their play in the quiet, sunny little street, and gathered in wondering silence round Miss Pole, Miss Matty, and myself. We were silent too, so that we could hear loud, suppressed whispers inside Miss Barker's house: "Wait, Peggy! wait till I've run upstairs and washed my hands. When I cough, open the door; I'll not be a minute."

And, true enough, it was not a minute before we heard a noise, between a sneeze and a crow; on which the door flew open. Behind it stood a round-eyed maiden, all aghast at the honourable company of calashes, who marched in without a word. She recovered presence of mind enough to usher us into a small room, which had been the shop, but was now converted into a temporary dressing-room. There we unpinned and shook ourselves, and arranged our features before the glass into a sweet and gracious company-face; and then, bowing backwards with "After you, ma'am," we allowed Mrs. Forrester to take precedence up the narrow staircase that led to Miss Barker's drawing-room. There she sat, as stately and composed as though we had never heard that odd-sounding cough, from which her throat must have been even then sore and rough. Kind, gentle, shabbily-dressed Mrs. Forrester was immediately conducted to the second place of honour—a seat arranged something like Prince Albert's near the queen's—good, but not so good. The place of pre-eminence was, of course, reserved for the Honourable Mrs. Jamieson, who presently came panting up the stairs—Carlo rushing round her on her progress, as if he meant to trip her up.

And now Miss Betty Barker was a proud and happy woman! She stirred the fire, and shut the door, and sat as near to it as she could, quite on the edge of her chair. When Peggy came in, tottering under the weight of the tea-tray, I noticed that Miss Barker was sadly afraid lest Peggy should not keep her distance sufficiently. She and her mistress were on very familiar terms in their everyday intercourse, and Peggy wanted now to make several little confidences to her, which Miss Barker was on thorns to hear, but which she thought it her duty, as a lady, to repress. So she turned away from all Peggy's asides and signs; but she made one or two very mala-propos answers to what was said; and at last, seized with a bright idea, she exclaimed, "Poor sweet Carlo! I'm forgetting him. Come downstairs with me, poor ittie doggie, and it shall have its tea, it shall!"

In a few minutes she returned, bland and benignant as before; but I thought she had forgotten to give the "poor ittie doggie" anything to eat, judging by the avidity with which he swallowed down chance pieces of cake. The tea-tray was abundantly loaded—I was pleased to see it, I was so hungry; but I was afraid the ladies present might think it vulgarly heaped up. I know what they would have done at their own houses; but somehow the heaps disappeared here. I saw Mrs. Jamieson eating seed-cake, slowly and considerately, as she did everything; and I was rather surprised, for I knew she had told us, on the occasion of her last party, that she never had it in her house, it reminded her so much of scented soap. She always gave us Savoy biscuits. However, Mrs. Jamieson was kindly indulgent to Miss Barker's want of knowledge of the customs of high life; and, to spare her feelings, ate three large pieces of seed-cake, with a placid, ruminating expression of countenance, not unlike a cow's.

After tea there was some little demur and difficulty. We were six in number; four could play at preference, and for the other two there was cribbage. But all, except myself (I was rather afraid of the Cranford ladies at cards, for it was the most earnest and serious business they ever engaged in), were anxious to be of the "pool." Even Miss Barker, while declaring she did not know spadille from manille, was evidently hankering to take a hand. The dilemma was soon put an end to by a singular kind of noise. If a baron's daughter-in-law could ever be supposed to snore, I should have said Mrs. Jamieson did so then; for, overcome by the heat of the room, and inclined to doze by nature, the temptation of that very comfortable armchair had been too much for her, and Mrs. Jamieson was nodding. Once or twice she opened her eyes with an effort, and calmly but unconsciously smiled upon us; but by and by, even her benevolence was not equal to this exertion, and she was sound asleep.

"It is very gratifying to me," whispered Miss Barker at the card-table to three opponents, whom, notwithstanding her ignorance of the game, she was "basting" most unmercifully—"very gratifying indeed, to see how completely Mrs. Jamieson feels at home in my poor little dwelling; she could not have paid me a greater compliment."

Miss Barker provided me with some literature in the shape of three or four handsomely bound fashion-books, ten or twelve years old, observing, as she put a little table and a candle for my special benefit, that she knew young people liked to look at pictures. Carlo lay and snorted, and started at his mistress's feet. He, too, was quite at home.

The card-table was an animated scene to watch; four ladies' heads, with niddle-noddling caps, all nearly meeting over the middle of the table in their eagerness to whisper quick enough and loud enough: and every now and then came

Miss Barker's "Hush, ladies! if you please, hush, Mrs. Jamieson is asleep."

It was very difficult to steer clear between Mrs. Forrester's deafness and Mrs. Jamieson's sleepiness. But Miss Barker managed her arduous task well. She repeated the whisper to Mrs. Forrester, distorting her face considerably, in order to show, by the motions of her lips, what was said; and then she smiled kindly all round at us, and murmured to herself, "Very gratifying, indeed; I wish my poor sister had been alive to see this day."

Presently the door was thrown wide open; Carlo started to his feet, with a loud, snapping bark, and Mrs. Jamieson awoke: or, perhaps, she had not been asleep—as she said almost directly, the room had been so light she had been glad to keep her eyes shut, but had been listening with great interest to all our amusing and agreeable conversation. Peggy came in once more, red with importance. Another tray! "Oh, gentility!" thought I, "can you endure this last shock?" For Miss Barker had ordered (nay, I doubt not, prepared, although she did say, "Why, Peggy, what have you brought us?" and looked pleasantly surprised at the unexpected pleasure) all sorts of good things for supper—scalloped oysters, potted lobsters, jelly, a dish called "little Cupids" (which was in great favour with the Cranford ladies, although too expensive to be given, except on solemn and state occasions—macaroons sopped in brandy, I should have called it, if I had not known its more refined and classical name). In short, we were evidently to be feasted with all that was sweetest and best; and we thought it better to submit graciously, even at the cost of our gentility—which never ate suppers in general, but which, like most non-supper-eaters, was particularly hungry on all special occasions.

Miss Barker, in her former sphere, had, I dare say, been made acquainted with the beverage they call cherry-brandy. We none of us had ever seen such a thing, and rather shrank back when she proffered it us: "Just a little, leetle glass, ladies;

after the oysters and lobsters, you know. Shell-fish are some-times thought not very wholesome." We all shook our heads like female mandarins; but, at last, Mrs. Jamieson suffered herself to be persuaded, and we followed her lead. It was not exactly unpalatable, though so hot and so strong that we thought ourselves bound to give evidence that we were not accustomed to such things by coughing terribly—almost as strangely as Miss Barker had done before we were admitted by Peggy.

"It's very strong," said Miss Pole, as she put down her empty glass; "I do believe there is spirit in it."

"Only a little drop—just necessary to make it keep," said Miss Barker. "You know we put brandy-paper over preserves to make them keep. I often feel tipsy myself from eating damson tart."

I question whether damson tart would have opened Mrs. Jamieson's heart as the cherry-brandy did; but she told us of a coming event, respecting which she had been quite silent till that moment.

"My sister-in-law, Lady Glenmire, is coming to stay with me."

There was a chorus of "Indeed!" and then a pause. Each one rapidly viewed her wardrobe, as to its fitness to appear in the presence of a baron's widow; for, of course, a series of small festivals were always held in Cranford on the arrival of a visitor at any of our friends' houses. We felt very pleasantly excited on the present occasion.

Not long after this the maids and the lanterns were announced. Mrs. Jamieson had the sedan-chair, which had squeezed itself into Miss Barker's narrow lobby with some difficulty, and most literally "stopped the way." It required some skilful manoeuvring on the part of the old chairmen (shoemakers by day, but when summoned to carry the sedan, dressed up in a strange old livery—long greatcoats, with small capes, coeval with the sedan, and similar to the dress of the class in Hogarth's pictures) to edge, and back, and try at it again, and finally to succeed in carrying their burden out of Miss Barker's front door. Then we heard their quick pit-a-pat along the quiet little street as we put on our calashes and pinned up our gowns; Miss Barker hovering about us with offers of help, which, if she had not remembered her former occupation, and wished us to forget it, would have been much more pressing.

CHAPTER 8

"Your Ladyship"

Early the next morning—directly after twelve—Miss Pole made her appearance at Miss Matty's. Some very trifling piece of business was alleged as a reason for the call; but there was evidently something behind. At last out it came.

"By the way, you'll think I'm strangely ignorant, but, do you really know, I am puzzled how we ought to address Lady Glenmire. Do you say 'Your ladyship,' where you would say 'you' to a common person? I have been puzzling all morning; and are we to say 'My lady,' instead of 'Ma'am'? Now you knew Lady Arley—will you kindly tell me the most correct way of speaking to the peerage?"

Poor Miss Matty! she took off her spectacles and she put them on again—but how Lady Arley was addressed she could not remember.

"It is so long ago," she said. "Dear! dear! how stupid I am! I don't think I ever saw her more than twice. I know we used to call Sir Peter 'Sir Peter'—but he came much oftener to see us than Lady Arley did. Deborah would have known in a minute. 'My lady'—'Your ladyship.' It sounds very strange, and as if it was not natural. I never thought of it before; but, now you have named it, I am all in a puzzle."

It was very certain Miss Pole would obtain no wise

decision from Miss Matty, who got more bewildered every moment, and more perplexed as to etiquettes of address.

"Well, I really think," said Miss Pole, "I had better just go and tell Mrs. Forrester about our little difficulty. One sometimes grows nervous; and yet one would not have Lady Glenmire think we were quite ignorant of the etiquettes of high life in Cranford."

"And will you just step in here, dear Miss Pole, as you come back, please, and tell me what you decide upon? Whatever you and Mrs. Forrester fix upon will be quite right, I'm sure. 'Lady Arley,' 'Sir Peter,'" said Miss Matty to herself, trying to recall the old form of words.

"Who is Lady Glenmire?" asked I.

"Oh, she's the widow of Mr. Jamieson—that's Mrs. Jamieson's late husband, you know—widow of his eldest brother. Mrs. Jamieson was a Miss Walker, daughter of Governor Walker. 'Your ladyship.' My dear, if they fix on that way of speaking, you must just let me practise a little on you first, for I shall feel so foolish and hot saying it the first time to Lady Glenmire."

It was really a relief to Miss Matty when Mrs. Jamieson came on a very unpolite errand. I notice that apathetic people have more quiet impertinence than others; and Mrs. Jamieson came now to insinuate pretty plainly that she did not particularly wish that the Cranford ladies should call upon her sister-in-law. I can hardly say how she made this clear; for I grew very indignant and warm, while with slow deliberation she was explaining her wishes to Miss Matty, who, a true lady herself, could hardly understand the feeling which made Mrs. Jamieson wish to appear to her noble sister-in-law as if she only visited "county" families. Miss Matty remained puzzled and perplexed long after I had found out the object of Mrs. Jamieson's visit.

When she did understand the drift of the honourable lady's call, it was pretty to see with what quiet dignity she received the intimation thus uncourteously given. She was not in the least hurt—she was of too gentle a spirit for that; nor was she exactly conscious of disapproving of Mrs. Jamieson's conduct; but there was something of this feeling in her mind, I am sure, which made her pass from the subject to others in a less flurried and more composed manner than usual. Mrs. Jamieson was, indeed, the more flurried of the two, and I could see she was glad to take her leave.

A little while afterwards Miss Pole returned, red and indignant. "Well! to be sure! You've had Mrs. Jamieson here, I find from Martha; and we are not to call on Lady Glenmire. Yes! I met Mrs. Jamieson, half-way between here and Mrs. Forrester's, and she told me; she took me so by surprise, I had nothing to say. I wish I had thought of something very sharp and sarcastic; I dare say I shall tonight. And Lady Glenmire is but the widow of a Scotch baron after all! I went on to look at Mrs. Forrester's *Peerage,* to see who this lady was that is to be kept under a glass case: widow of a Scotch peer—never sat in the House of Lords—and as poor as Job, I dare say; and she—fifth daughter of some Mr. Campbell or other. You are the daughter of a rector, at any rate, and related to the Arleys; and Sir Peter might have been Viscount Arley, every one says."

Miss Matty tried to soothe Miss Pole, but in vain. That lady, usually so kind and good-humoured, was now in a full flow of anger.

"And I went and ordered a cap this morning, to be quite ready," said she at last, letting out the secret which gave sting to Mrs. Jamieson's intimation. "Mrs. Jamieson shall see if it is so easy to get me to make fourth at a pool when she has none of her fine Scotch relations with her!"

In coming out of church, the first Sunday on which Lady Glenmire appeared in Cranford, we sedulously talked together, and turned our backs on Mrs. Jamieson and her guest. If we might not call on her, we would not even look at her, though we were dying with curiosity to know what she was like. We had the comfort of questioning Martha in the afternoon. Martha did not belong to a sphere of society whose observation could be an implied compliment to Lady Glenmire, and Martha had made good use of her eyes.

"Well, ma'am! is it the little lady with Mrs. Jamieson, you mean? I thought you would like more to know how young Mrs. Smith was dressed, her being a bride." (Mrs. Smith was the butcher's wife.)

Miss Pole said, "Good gracious me! as if we cared about a Mrs. Smith;" but was silent as Martha resumed her speech.

"The little lady in Mrs. Jamieson's pew had on, ma'am, rather an old black silk, and a shepherd's plaid cloak, ma'am, and very bright, black eyes she had, ma'am, and a pleasant, sharp face; not over young, ma'am, but yet, I should guess, younger than Mrs. Jamieson herself. She looked up and down the church, like a bird, and nipped up her petticoats, when she came out, as quick and sharp as ever I see. I'll tell you what, ma'am, she's more like Mrs. Deacon, at the Coach and Horses, nor any one."

"Hush, Martha!" said Miss Matty, "that's not respectful."

"Isn't it, ma'am? I beg pardon, I'm sure; but Jem Hearn said so as well. He said, she was just such a sharp, stirring sort of a body—"

"Lady," said Miss Pole.

"Lady—as Mrs. Deacon."

Another Sunday passed away, and we still averted our eyes from Mrs. Jamieson and her guest, and made remarks to ourselves that we thought were very severe—almost too much so. Miss Matty was evidently uneasy at our sarcastic manner of speaking.

Perhaps by this time Lady Glenmire had found out that Mrs. Jamieson's was not the gayest, liveliest house in the world; perhaps Mrs. Jamieson had found out that most of the county families were in London, and that those who remained in the country were not so alive as they might have been to the circumstance of Lady Glenmire being in their neighbour-hood. Great events spring out of small causes; so I will not pretend to say what induced Mrs. Jamieson to alter her deter-mination of excluding the Cranford ladies, and send notes of invitation all round for a small party on the following Tuesday. Mr. Mulliner himself brought them round. He *would* always ignore the fact of there being a back door to any house, and gave a louder rat-tat than his mistress, Mrs. Jamieson. He had three little notes, which he carried in a large basket, in order to impress his mistress with an idea of their great weight, though they might easily have gone into his waistcoat pocket.

Miss Matty and I quietly decided we would have a previous engagement at home: it was the evening on which Miss Matty usually made candle-lighters of all the notes and letters of the week; for on Mondays her accounts were always made straight—not a penny owing from the week before; so, by a natural arrangement, making candle-lighters fell upon a Tuesday evening, and gave us a legitimate excuse for declining Mrs. Jamieson's invitation. But before our answer was written, in came Miss Pole, with an open note in her hand.

"So!" she said. "Ah! I see you have got your note too. Better late than never. I could have told my Lady Glenmire she would be glad enough of our society before a fortnight was over."

"Yes," said Miss Matty, "we're asked for Tuesday evening. And perhaps you would just kindly bring your work across and drink tea with us that night. It is my usual regular time for looking over the last week's bills, and notes, and letters, and making candle-lighters of them; but that does not seem quite reason enough for saying I have a previous engagement at home, though I meant to make it do. Now, if you would come, my conscience would be quite as ease, and luckily the note is not written yet."

I saw Miss Pole's countenance change while Miss Matty was speaking.

"Don't you mean to go, then?" asked she.

"Oh, no!" said Miss Matty quietly. "You don't either, I suppose?"

"I don't know," replied Miss Pole. "Yes, I think I do," said she rather briskly; and, on seeing Miss Matty looked surprised, she added, "You see, one would not like Mrs. Jamieson to think that anything she could do, or say, was of consequence enough to give offence; it would be a kind of letting down of ourselves, that I, for one, should not like. It would be too flattering to Mrs. Jamieson if we allowed her to suppose that what she had said affected us a week, nay, ten days, afterwards."

"Well! I suppose it is wrong to be hurt and annoyed so long about anything; and, perhaps, after all, she did not mean to vex us. But I must say, I could not have brought myself to say the things Mrs. Jamieson did about our not calling. I really don't think I shall go."

"Oh, come! Miss Matty, you must go; you know our friend Mrs. Jamieson is much more phlegmatic than most people, and does not enter into the little delicacies of feeling which you possess in so remarkable a degree."

"I thought you possessed them too, that day Mrs. Jamieson called to tell us not to go," said Miss Matty innocently.

But Miss Pole, in addition to her delicacies of feeling, possessed a very smart cap, which she was anxious to show to an admiring world; and so she seemed to forget all her angry words uttered not a fortnight before, and to be ready to act on what she called the great Christian principle of "Forgive and forget"; and she lectured dear Miss Matty so long on this head that she absolutely ended by assuring her it was her duty, as a deceased rector's daughter, to buy a new cap and go to the party at Mrs. Jamieson's. So "we were most happy to accept," instead of "regretting that we were obliged to decline."

The expenditure on dress in Cranford was principally in that one article referred to. If the heads were buried in smart new caps, the ladies were like ostriches, and cared not what became of their bodies. Old gowns, white and venerable collars, any number of brooches, up and down and everywhere (some with dog's eyes painted in them; some that were like small picture-frames with mausoleums and weeping-willows neatly executed in hair inside; some, again, with miniatures of ladies and gentlemen sweetly smiling out of a nest of stiff muslin), old brooches for a permanent ornament, and new caps to suit the fashion of the day—the ladies of Cranford always dressed with chaste elegance and propriety, as Miss Barker once prettily expressed it.

And with three new caps, and a greater array of brooches than had ever been seen together at one time since Cranford was a town, did Mrs. Forrester, and Miss Matty, and Miss Pole appear on that memorable Tuesday evening. I counted seven brooches myself on Miss Pole's dress. Two were fixed negligently in her cap (one was a butterfly made of Scotch pebbles, which a vivid imagination might believe to be the real insect); one fastened her net neckerchief; one her collar; one ornamented the front of her gown, midway between her throat and waist; and another adorned the point of her stomacher. Where the seventh was I have forgotten, but it was somewhere about her, I am sure.

But I am getting on too fast, in describing the dresses of the company. I should first relate the gathering on the way to Mrs. Jamieson's. That lady lived in a large house just outside the town. A road which had known what it was to be a street ran right before the house, which opened out upon it without any intervening garden or court. Whatever the sun was about, he never shone on the front of that house. To be sure, the living-rooms were at the back, looking on to a pleasant garden; the front windows only belonged to kitchens and house-keepers' rooms, and pantries, and in one of them Mr. Mulliner was reported to sit. Indeed, looking askance, we often saw the back of a head covered with hair-powder, which also extended itself over his coat collar down to his very waist; and this imposing back was always engaged in reading *The St. James's Chronicle*, opened wide, which, in some degree, accounted for the length of time the said newspaper was in reaching us—equal subscribers with Mrs. Jamieson, though, in right of her honourableness, she always had the reading of it first. This very Tuesday, the delay in forwarding the last number had been particularly aggravating; just when both Miss Pole and Miss Matty, the former more especially, had been wanting to see it, in order to coach up the court news, ready for the evening's interview with aristocracy. Miss Pole told us she had absolutely taken time by the forelock, and been dressed by five o'clock, in order to be ready if *The St. James's Chronicle* should come in at the last moment—the very *St. James's Chronicle* which the powdered head was tranquilly and composedly reading as we passed the accustomed window this evening.

"The impudence of the man!" said Miss Pole in a low, indignant whisper. "I should like to ask him whether his mistress pays her quarter share for his exclusive use."

We looked at her in admiration of the courage of her thought; for Mr. Mulliner was an object of great awe to all of us. He seemed never to have forgotten his condescension in coming to live at Cranford. Miss Jenkyns, at times, had stood forth as the undaunted champion of her sex, and spoken to him on terms of equality; but even Miss Jenkyns could get no higher. In his pleasantest and most gracious moods he looked like a sulky cockatoo. He did not speak except in gruff monosyllables. He would wait in the hall when we begged him not to wait, and then look deeply offended because we had kept him there, while, with trembling, hasty hands, we prepared ourselves for appearing in company.

Miss Pole ventured on a small joke as we went upstairs,

intended, though addressed to us, to afford Mr. Mulliner some slight amusement. We all smiled, in order to seem as if we felt at our ease, and timidly looked for Mr. Mulliner's sympathy. Not a muscle of that wooden face had relaxed; and we were grave in an instant.

Mrs. Jamieson's drawing-room was cheerful; the evening sun came streaming into it, and the large square window was clustered round with flowers. The furniture was white and gold; not the later style, Louise Quatorze, I think they call it, all shells and twirls; no, Mrs. Jamieson's chairs and tables had not a curve or bend about them. The chair and table legs diminished as they neared the ground, and were straight and square in all their corners. The chairs were all a-row against the walls, with the exception of four or five which stood in a circle round the fire. They were railed with white bars across the back, and knobbed with gold; neither the railings nor the knobs invited to ease. There was a japanned table devoted to literature, on which lay a Bible, a *Peerage*, and a Prayer-book. There was another square Pembroke table dedicated to the fine arts, on which were a kaleidoscope, conversation-cards, puzzle cards (tied together to an interminable length with faded pink satin ribbon), and a box painted in fond imitation of the drawings which decorate tea-chests. Carlo lay on the worsted-worked rug, and ungraciously barked at us as we entered. Mrs. Jamieson stood up, giving us each a torpid smile of welcome, and looking helplessly beyond us at Mr. Mulliner, as if she hoped he would place us in chairs, for, if he did not, she never could. I suppose he thought we could find our way to the circle round the fire, which reminded me of Stonehenge, I don't know why. Lady Glenmire came to the rescue of our hostess, and, somehow or other, we found ourselves for the first time placed agreeably, and not formally, in Mrs. Jamieson's house. Lady Glenmire, now we had time to look at her, proved to be a bright little woman of middle age, who had been very pretty in the days of her youth, and who was even yet very pleasant-looking. I saw Miss Pole appraising her dress in the first five minutes, and I take her word when she said the next day—

"My dear! ten pounds would have purchased every stitch she had on—lace and all."

It was pleasant to suspect that a peeress could be poor, and partly reconciled us to the fact that her husband had never sat in the House of Lords; which, when we first heard of it, seemed a kind of swindling us out of our respect on false pretences; a sort of "A Lord and No Lord" business.

We were all very silent at first. We were thinking what we could talk about, that should be high enough to interest My Lady. There had been a rise in the price of sugar, which, as preserving-time was near, was a piece of intelligence to all our housekeeping hearts, and would have been the natural topic if Lady Glenmire had not been by. But we were not sure if the peerage ate preserves—much less knew how they were made. At last Miss Pole who had always a great deal of courage and *savoir faire*, spoke to Lady Glenmire, who on her part had seemed just as much puzzled to know how to break the silence as we were.

"Has your ladyship been to Court lately?" asked she; and then gave a little glance round at us, half timid and half triumphant, as much as to say, "See how judiciously I have chosen a subject befitting the rank of the stranger."

"I never was there in my life," said Lady Glenmire, with a broad Scotch accent, but in a very sweet voice. And then, as if she had been too abrupt, she added: "We very seldom went to London—only twice, in fact, during all my married life; and before I was married my father had far too large a family" (fifth daughter of Mr. Campbell was in all our minds, I am sure) "to take us often from our home, even to Edinburgh. Ye'll have been in Edinburgh, maybe?" said she, suddenly brightening up with the hope of a common interest. We had none of us been there; but Miss Pole had an uncle who once had passed a night there, which was very pleasant.

Mrs. Jamieson, meanwhile, was absorbed in wonder why Mr. Mulliner did not bring the tea; and at length the wonder oozed out of her mouth.

"I had better ring the bell, my dear, had not I?" said Lady Glenmire briskly.

"No—I think not—Mulliner does not like to be hurried."

We should have liked our tea, for we dined at an earlier hour than Mrs. Jamieson. I suspect Mr. Mulliner had to finish *The St. James's Chronicle* before he chose to trouble himself about tea. His mistress fidgeted and fidgeted, and kept saying, "I can't think why Mulliner does not bring tea. I can't think what he can be about." And Lady Glenmire at last grew quite impatient, but it was a pretty kind of impatience after all; and she rang the bell rather sharply, on receiving a half-permission from her sister-in-law to do so. Mr. Mulliner appeared in dignified surprise. "Oh!" said Mrs. Jamieson, "Lady Glenmire rang the bell; I believe it was for tea."

In a few minutes tea was brought. Very delicate was the china, very old the plate, very thin the bread-and-butter, and very small the lumps of sugar. Sugar was evidently Mrs. Jamieson's favourite economy. I question if the little filigree sugar-tongs, made something like scissors, could have opened themselves wide enough to take up an honest, vulgar, good-sized piece; and when I tried to seize two little minnikin pieces at once, so as not to be detected in too many returns to the sugar-basin, they absolutely dropped one, with a little sharp clatter, quite in a malicious and unnatural manner. But before this happened we had had a slight disappointment. In the little silver jug was cream, in the larger one was milk. As soon as Mr. Mulliner came in, Carlo began to beg, which was a thing our manners forbade us to do, though I am sure we were just as hungry; and Mrs. Jamieson said she was certain we would excuse her if she gave her poor dumb Carlo his tea first. She accordingly mixed a saucerful for him, and put it down for him to lap; and then she told us how intelligent and sensible the dear little fellow was; he knew cream quite well, and constantly refused tea with only milk in it: so the milk was left for us; but we silently thought we were quite as intelligent and sensible as Carlo, and felt as if insult were added to injury when we were called upon to admire the gratitude evinced by his wagging his tail for the cream which should have been ours.

After tea we thawed down into common-life subjects. We were thankful to Lady Glenmire for having proposed some more bread-and-butter, and this mutual want made us better acquainted with her, than we should ever have been with talking about the Court, though Miss Pole did say she had hoped to know how the dear queen was from some one who had seen her.

The friendship began over bread-and-butter extended on to cards. Lady Glenmire played preference to admiration, and was a complete authority as to ombre and quadrille. Even Miss Pole forgot to say "my lady," and "your ladyship," and said "Basto! ma'am;" "you have spadille, I believe," just as quietly as if we had never held the great Cranford parliament on the subject of the proper mode of addressing a peeress.

As a proof of how thoroughly we had forgotten that we were in the presence of one who might have sat down to tea with a coronet, instead of a cap, on her head, Mrs. Forrester related a curious little fact to Lady Glenmire—an anecdote known to the circle of her intimate friends, but of which even Mrs. Jamieson was not aware. It related to some fine old lace, the sole relic of better days, which Lady Glenmire was admiring on Mrs. Forrester's collar.

"Yes," said that lady, "such lace cannot be got now for either love or money; made by the nuns abroad, they tell me. They say that they can't make it now, even there. But perhaps they can now they've passed the Catholic Emancipation Bill. I should not wonder. But, in the meantime, I treasure up my lace very much. I daren't even trust the washing of it to my maid" (the little charity schoolgirl I have named before, but who sounded well as "my maid"). "I always wash it myself. And once it had a narrow escape. Of course, your ladyship knows that such lace must never be starched or ironed. Some people wash it in sugar and water, and some in coffee, to make it the right yellow colour; but I myself have a very good receipt for washing it in milk, which stiffens it enough, and gives it a very good creamy colour. Well, ma'am, I had tacked it together (and the beauty of this fine lace is that, when it is wet, it goes into a very little space), and put it to soak in milk, when, unfortunately, I left the room; on my return, I found pussy on the table, looking very like a thief, but gulping very uncomfortably, as if she was half-choked with something she wanted to swallow and could not. And, would you believe it?—at first I pitied her, and said, 'Poor pussy! poor pussy!' till, all at once, I looked and saw the cup of milk empty—cleaned out! 'You naughty cat!' said I; and I believe I was provoked enough to give her a slap, which did no good, but only helped the lace down—just as one slaps a choking child on the back. I could have cried, I was so vexed; but I determined I would not give the lace up without a struggle for it. I hoped the lace might disagree with her, at any rate; but it would have been too much for Job, if he had seen, as I did, that cat come in, quite placid and purring, not a quarter of an hour after, and almost expecting to be stroked. 'No, pussy!' said I, 'if you have any conscience you ought not to expect that!' And then a thought struck me; and I rang the bell for my maid, and sent her to Mr. Hoggins, with my compliments, and would he be kind enough to lend me one of his top-boots for an hour? I did not think there was anything odd in the message; but Jenny said the young men in the surgery laughed as if they would be ill at my wanting a top-boot. When it came, Jenny and I put pussy in, with her fore-feet straight down, so that they were fastened, and could not scratch, and we gave her a teaspoonful of currant-jelly in which (your ladyship must excuse me) I had mixed some tartar emetic. I shall never forget how anxious I was for the next half-hour. I took pussy to my own room, and spread a clean towel on the floor. I could have kissed her when she returned the lace to sight, very much as it had gone down. Jenny had boiling water ready, and we soaked it and soaked it, and spread it on a lavender-bush in the sun before I could touch it again, even to put it in milk. But now your ladyship would never guess that it had been in pussy's inside."

We found out in the course of the evening that Lady Glenmire was going to pay Mrs. Jamieson a long visit, as she had given up her apartments in Edinburgh, and had no ties to take her back there in a hurry. On the whole, we were rather glad to hear this, for she had made a pleasant impression upon us; and it was also very comfortable to find, from things which dropped out in the course of conversation, that, in addition to many other genteel qualities, she was far removed from the "vulgarity of wealth."

"Don't you find it very unpleasant walking?" asked Mrs. Jamieson, as our respective servants were announced. It was a pretty regular question from Mrs. Jamieson, who had her own carriage in the coach-house, and always went out in a sedan-chair to the very shortest distances. The answers were nearly as much a matter of course.

"Oh, dear, no! it is so pleasant and still at night!" "Such a refreshment after the excitement of a party!" "The stars are so beautiful!" This last was from Miss Matty.

"Are you fond of astronomy?" Lady Glenmire asked.

"Not very," replied Miss Matty, rather confused at the moment to remember which was astronomy and which was astrology—but the answer was true under either circumstance, for she read, and was slightly alarmed at, Francis Moore's astrological predictions; and, as to astronomy, in a private and confidential conversation, she had told me she never could believe that the earth was moving constantly, and that she would not believe it if she could, it made her feel so tired and dizzy whenever she thought about it.

In our pattens we picked our way home with extra care that night, so refined and delicate were our perceptions after drinking tea with "my lady."

CHAPTER 9

Signor Brunoni

Soon after the events of which I gave an account in my last paper, I was summoned home by my father's illness; and for a time I forgot, in anxiety about him, to wonder how my dear friends at Cranford were getting on, or how Lady Glenmire could reconcile herself to the dullness of the long visit which she was still paying to her sister-in-law, Mrs. Jamieson. When my father grew a little stronger I accompanied him to the seaside, so that altogether I seemed banished from Cranford, and was deprived of the opportunity of hearing any chance intelligence of the dear little town for the greater part of that year.

Late in November, when we had returned home again, and my father was once more in good health, I received a letter from Miss Matty; and a very mysterious letter it was. She began many sentences without ending them, running then one into another, in much the same confused sort of way in which written words run together on blotting-paper. All I could make out was that, if my father was better (which she hoped he was), and would take warning and wear a greatcoat from Michaelmas to Lady-day, if turbans were in fashion, could I tell her? Such a piece of gaiety was going to happen as had not been seen or known of since Wombwell's lions came, when one of them ate a little child's arm; and she was, perhaps, too old to care about dress, but a new cap she must have; and, having heard that turbans were worn, and some of the county families likely to come, she would like to look tidy, if I would bring her a cap from the milliner I employed; and, oh, dear! how careless of her to forget that she wrote to beg I would come and pay her a visit next Tuesday; when she hoped to have something to offer me in the way of amusement, which she would not now more particularly describe, only sea-green was her favourite colour. So she ended her letter; but, in a *P.S.* she added, she thought she might as well tell me what was the peculiar attraction to Cranford just now; Signor Brunoni was going to exhibit his wonderful magic in the Cranford Assembly Rooms on Wednesday and Friday evening in the following week.

I was very glad to accept the invitation from my dear Miss Matty, independently of the conjurer, and most particularly anxious to prevent her from disfiguring her small, gentle, mousey face with a great Saracen's head turban; and accordingly I bought her a pretty, neat, middle-aged cap, which, however, was rather a disappointment to her when, on my arrival, she followed me into my bedroom, ostensibly to poke the fire, but in reality, I do believe, to see if the sea-green turban was not inside the cap-box with which I had travelled. It was in vain that I twirled the cap round on my hand to exhibit back and side fronts; her heart had been set upon a turban, and all she could do was to say, with resignation in her look and voice—

"I am sure you did your best, my dear. It is just like the caps all the ladies in Cranford are wearing, and they have had theirs for a year, I dare say. I should have liked something newer, I confess—something more like the turbans Miss Betty Barker tells me Queen Adelaide wears; but it is very pretty, my dear. And I dare say lavender will wear better than sea-green. Well, after all, what is dress, that we should care about it? You'll tell me if you want anything, my dear. Here is the bell. I suppose turbans have not got down to Drumble yet?"

So saying, the dear old lady gently bemoaned herself out of the room, leaving me to dress for the evening, when, as she informed me, she expected Miss Pole and Mrs. Forrester, and she hoped I should not feel myself too much tired to join the party. Of course I should not; and I made some haste to unpack and arrange my dress; but, with all my speed, I heard the arrivals and the buzz of conversation in the next room before I was ready. Just as I opened the door, I caught the words, "I was foolish to expect anything very genteel out of the Drumble shops; poor girl! she did her best, I've no doubt." But, for all that, I had rather that she blamed Drumble and me than disfigured herself with a turban.

Miss Pole was always the person, in the trio of Cranford ladies now assembled, to have had adventures. She was in the habit of spending the morning in rambling from shop to shop, not to purchase anything (except an occasional reel of cotton, or a pieces of tape), but to see the new articles and report upon them, and to collect all the stray pieces of intelligence in the town. She had a way, too, of demurely popping hither and thither into all sorts of places to gratify her curiosity on any point—a way which, if she had not looked so very genteel and prim, might have been considered impertinent. And now, by the expressive way in which she cleared her throat, and waited for all minor subjects (such as caps and turbans) to be cleared off the course, we knew she had something very particular to relate, when the due pause came—and I defy any people possessed of common modesty to keep up a conversation long, where one among them sits up aloft in silence, looking down upon all the things they chance to say as trivial and contemptible compared to what they could disclose, if properly entreated. Miss Pole began—

"As I was stepping out of Gordon's shop to-day, I chanced to go into 'The George' (my Betty has a second cousin who is chambermaid there, and I thought Betty would like to hear how she was), and, not seeing any one about, I strolled up the staircase, and found myself in the passage leading to the assembly room (you and I remember the assembly room, I am sure, Miss Matty! and the *menuets de la cour*!); so I went on, not thinking of what I was about, when, all at once, I perceived that I was in the middle of the preparations for tomorrow night—the room being divided with great clothes-maids, over which Crosby's men were tacking red flannel; very dark and odd it seemed; it quite bewildered me, and I was going on behind the screens, in my absence of mind, when a gentleman (quite the gentleman, I can assure you) stepped forwards and asked if I had any business he could arrange for me. He spoke such pretty broken English, I could not help thinking of Thaddeus of Warsaw, and the Hungarian Brothers, and Santo Sebastiani; and while I was busy picturing his past life to myself, he had bowed me out of the room. But wait a minute! You have not heard half my story yet! I was going downstairs, when who should I meet but Betty's second cousin. So, of course, I stopped to speak to her for Betty's sake; and she told me that I had really seen the conjurer—the gentleman who spoke broken English was Signor Brunoni himself. Just at this moment he passed us on the stairs, making such a graceful bow! in reply to which I dropped a curtsey—all foreigners have such polite manners, one catches something of it. But, when he had gone downstairs, I bethought me that I had dropped my glove in the assembly room (it was safe in my muff all the time, but I never found it till afterwards); so I went back, and, just as I was creeping up the passage left on one side of the great screen that goes nearly across the room, who should I see but the very same gentleman that had met me before, and passed me on the stairs, coming now forward from the inner part of the room, to which there is no entrance—you remember, Miss Matty—and just repeating, in his pretty broken English, the inquiry if I had any business there?—I don't mean that he put it quite so bluntly, but he seemed very determined that I should not pass the screen—so, of course, I explained about my glove, which, curiously enough, I found at that very moment."

Miss Pole, then, had seen the conjurer—the real, live conjurer! and numerous were the questions we all asked her. "Had he a beard?"

"Was he young or old?" "Fair or dark?" "Did he look—" (unable to shape my question prudently, I put it in another form)—"How did he look?" In short, Miss Pole was the heroine of the evening, owing to her morning's encounter. If she was not the rose (that is to say, the conjurer), she had been near it.

Conjuration, sleight of hand, magic, witchcraft, were the subjects of the evening. Miss Pole was slightly sceptical, and inclined to think there might be a scientific solution found for even the proceedings of the Witch of Endor. Mrs. Forrester believed everything, from ghosts to death-watches. Miss Matty ranged between the two—always convinced by the last speaker. I think she was naturally more inclined to Mrs. Forrester's side, but a desire of proving herself a worthy sister to Miss Jenkyns kept her equally balanced—Miss Jenkyns, who would never allow a servant to call the little rolls of tallow that formed themselves round candles "winding sheets," but insisted on their being spoken of as "roley-poleys!" A sister of hers to be superstitious! It would never do.

After tea, I was despatched downstairs into the dining-parlour for that volume of the old *Encyclopaedia* which contained the nouns beginning with C, in order that Miss Pole might prime herself with scientific explanations for the tricks of the following evening. It spoiled the pool at preference which Miss Matty and Mrs. Forrester had been looking forward to, for Miss Pole became so much absorbed in her subject, and the plates by which it was illustrated, that we felt it would be cruel to disturb her otherwise than by one or two well-timed yawns, which I threw in now and then, for I was really touched by the meek way in which the two ladies were bearing their disappointment. But Miss Pole only read the more zealously, imparting to us no more interesting information than this:

"Ah! I see; I comprehend perfectly. A represents the ball. Put A between B and D—no! between C and F, and turn the second joint of the third finger of your left hand over the wrist of your right H. Very clear indeed! My dear Mrs. Forrester, conjuring and witchcraft is a mere affair of the alphabet. Do let me read you this one passage!"

Mrs. Forrester implored Miss Pole to spare her, saying, from a child upwards she never could understand being read aloud to; and I dropped the pack of cards, which I had been shuffling very audibly, and by this discreet movement I obliged Miss Pole to perceive that preference was to have been the order of the evening, and to propose, rather unwillingly, that the pool should commence. The pleasant brightness that stole over the other two ladies' faces on this! Miss Matty had one or two twinges of self-reproach for having interrupted Miss Pole in her studies; and did not remember her cards well, or give her full attention to the game, until she had soothed her conscience by offering to lend the volume of the *Encyclopaedia* to Miss Pole, who accepted it thankfully, and said Betty should take it home when she came with the lantern.

The next evening we were all in a little gentle flutter at the idea of the gaiety before us. Miss Matty went up to dress betimes, and hurried me until I was ready, when we found we had an hour and a half to wait before the "doors opened at seven precisely." And we had only twenty yards to go! However, as Miss Matty said, it would not do to get too much absorbed in anything, and forget the time; so she thought we had better sit quietly, without lighting the candles, till five minutes to seven. So Miss Matty dozed and I knitted.

At length we set off; and at the door, under the carriage-way at the George, we met Mrs. Forrester and Miss Pole: the latter was discussing the subject of the evening with more vehemence than ever, and throwing A's and B's at our heads like hailstones. She had even copied one or two of the "receipts," as she called them, for the different tricks, on backs of letters, ready to explain and to detect Signor Brunoni's arts.

We went into the cloak-room adjoining the assembly room; Miss Matty gave a sigh or two to her departed youth, and the remembrance of the last time she had been there, as she adjusted her pretty new cap before the strange, quaint old mirror in the cloak-room. The assembly room had been added to the inn, about a hundred years before, by the different county families, who met together there once a month during the winter to dance and play at cards. Many a county beauty had first swam through the minuet that she afterwards danced before Queen Charlotte in this very room. It was said that one of the Gunnings had graced the apartment with her beauty; it was certain that a rich and beautiful widow, Lady Williams, had here been smitten with the noble figure of a young artist, who was staying with some family in the neighbourhood for professional purposes, and accompanied his patrons to the Cranford Assembly. And a pretty bargain poor Lady Williams had of her handsome husband, if all tales were true. Now, no beauty blushed and dimpled along the sides of the Cranford assembly room; no handsome artist won hearts by his bow, *chapeau bras* in hand; the old room was dingy; the salmon-coloured paint had faded into a drab; great pieces of plaster had chipped off from the white wreaths and festoons on its walls; but still a mouldy odour of aristocracy lingered about the place, and a dusty recollection of the days that were gone made Miss Matty and Mrs. Forrester bridle up as they entered, and walk mincingly up the room, as if there were a number of genteel observers, instead of two little boys with a stick of toffee between them with which to beguile the time.

We stopped short at the second front row; I could hardly understand why, until I heard Miss Pole ask a stray waiter if any of the county families were expected; and when he shook his head, and believed not, Mrs. Forrester and Miss Matty moved forward, and our party represented a conversational square. The front row was soon augmented and enriched by Lady Glenmire and Mrs. Jamieson. We six occupied the two front rows, and our aristocratic seclusion was respected by the groups of shopkeepers who strayed in from time to time and huddled together on the back benches. At least I conjectured so, from the noise they made, and the sonorous bumps they gave in sitting down; but when, in weariness of the obstinate green curtain that would not draw up, but would stare at me with two odd eyes, seen through holes, as in the old tapestry story, I would fain have looked round at the merry, chattering people behind me, Miss Pole clutched my arm, and begged me not to turn, for "it was not the thing." What "the thing" was I never could find out, but it must have been something eminently dull and tiresome. However, we all sat eyes right, square front, gazing at the tantalising curtain, and hardly speaking intelligibly, we were so afraid of being caught in the vulgarity of making any noise in a place of public amusement. Mrs. Jamieson was the most fortunate, for she fell asleep.

At length the eyes disappeared, the curtain quivered, one side went up before the other, which stuck fast; it was dropped again, and with a fresh effort and a vigorous pull from some unseen hand, it flew up, revealing to our sight a magnificent gentleman in the Turkish costume, seated before a little table, gazing at us (I should have said with the same eyes that I had last seen through the hole in the curtain) with calm and condescending dignity "like a being of another sphere," as I heard a sentimental voice ejaculate behind me.

"That's not Signor Brunoni!" said Miss Pole decidedly, and so audibly that I am sure he heard, for he glanced down over his flowing beard at our party with an air of mute reproach. "Signor Brunoni had no beard—but perhaps he'll come soon." So she lulled herself into patience Meanwhile, Miss Matty had reconnoitred through her eyeglass, wiped it, and looked again. Then she turned round and said to me in a kind, mild, sorrowful tone:

"You see, my dear, turbans *are* worn."

But we had no time for more conversation. The Grand Turk, as Miss Pole chose to call him, arose and announced himself as Signor Brunoni.

"I don't believe him!" exclaimed Miss Pole, in a defiant manner. He looked at her again, with the same dignified upbraiding in his countenance. "I don't!" she repeated more positively than ever. "Signor Brunoni had not got that muffy sort of thing about his chin, but looked like a close-shaved Christian gentleman."

Miss Pole's energetic speeches had the good effect of wakening up Mrs. Jamieson, who opened her eyes wide, in sign of the deepest attention, a proceeding which silenced Miss Pole and encouraged the Grand Turk to proceed, which he did in very broken English—so broken that there was no cohesion between the parts of his sentences; a fact which he himself perceived at last, and so left off speaking and proceeded to action.

Now we *were* astonished. How he did his tricks I could not imagine; no, not even when Miss Pole pulled out her pieces of paper and began reading aloud, or at least in a very audible whisper, the separate "receipts" for the most common of his tricks. If ever I saw a man frown and look enraged, I saw the Grand Turk frown at Miss Pole; but, as she said, what could be expected but unchristian looks from a Mussulman? If Miss Pole were sceptical, and more engrossed with her receipts and diagrams than with his tricks, Miss Matty and

Mrs. Forrester were mystified and perplexed to the highest degree. Mrs. Jamieson kept taking her spectacles off and wiping them, as if she thought it was something defective in them which made the legerdemain; and Lady Glenmire, who had seen many curious sights in Edinburgh, was very much struck with the tricks, and would not at all agree with Miss Pole, who declared that anybody could do them with a little practice, and that she would herself undertake to do all he did, with two hours given to study the *Encyclopaedia* and make her third finger flexible.

At last Miss Matty and Mrs. Forrester became perfectly awe-stricken. They whispered together. I sat just behind them, so I could not help hearing what they were saying. Miss Matty asked Mrs. Forrester "if she thought it was quite right to have come to see such things? She could not help fearing they were lending encouragement to something that was not quite—" A little shake of the head filled up the blank. Mrs. Forrester replied that the same thought had crossed her mind; she, too, was feeling very uncomfortable, it was so very strange. She was quite certain that it was her pocket-handkerchief which was in that loaf just now; and it had been in her own hand not five minutes before. She wondered who had furnished the bread? She was sure it could not be Dakin, because he was the churchwarden. Suddenly Miss Matty half turned towards me.

"Will you look, my dear—you are a stranger in the town, and it won't give rise to unpleasant reports—will you just look round and see if the rector is here? If he is, I think we may conclude that this wonderful man is sanctioned by the Church, and that will be a great relief to my mind."

I looked, and I saw the tall, thin, dry, dusty rector, sitting surrounded by national school boys, guarded by troops of his own sex from any approach of the many Cranford spinsters. His kind face was all agape with broad smiles, and the boys around him were in chinks of laughing. I told Miss

Matty that the Church was smiling approval, which set her mind at case.

I have never named Mr. Hayter, the rector, because I, as a well-to-do and happy young woman, never came in contact with him. He was an old bachelor, but as afraid of matrimonial reports getting abroad about him as any girl of eighteen; and he would rush into a shop, or dive down an entry, sooner than encounter any of the Cranford ladies in the street; and, as for the preference parties, I did not wonder at his not accepting invitations to them. To tell the truth, I always suspected Miss Pole of having given very vigorous chase to Mr. Hayter when he first came to Cranford; and not the less because now she appeared to share so vividly in his dread lest her name should ever be coupled with his. He found all his interests among the poor and helpless; he had treated the national school boys this very night to the performance; and virtue was for once its own reward, for they guarded him right and left, and clung round him as if he had been the queen-bee and they the swarm. He felt so safe in their environment that he could even afford to give our party a bow as we filed out. Miss Pole ignored his presence, and pretended to be absorbed in convincing us that we had been cheated, and had not seen Signor Brunoni after all.

CHAPTER 10

The Panic

I think a series of circumstances dated from Signor Brunoni's visit to Cranford, which seemed at the time connected in our minds with him, though I don't know that he had anything really to do with them. All at once all sorts of uncomfortable rumours got afloat in the town. There were one or two robberies—real *bona fide* robberies; men had up before the magistrates and committed for trial—and that seemed to make us all afraid of being robbed; and for a long time at Miss Matty's, I know, we used to make a regular expedition all round the kitchens and cellars every night, Miss Matty leading the way, armed with the poker, I following with the hearth brush, and Martha carrying the shovel and fire-irons with which to sound the alarm; and by the accidental hitting together of them she often frightened us so much that we bolted ourselves up, all three together, in the back kitchen, or storeroom, or wherever we happened to be, till, when our affright was over, we recollected ourselves, and set out afresh with double valiance. By day we heard strange stories from the shopkeepers and cottagers, of carts that went about in the dead of night, drawn by horses shod with felt, and guarded by men in dark clothes, going round the town, no doubt in search of some unwatched house or some unfastened door.

Miss Pole, who affected great bravery herself, was the

principal person to collect and arrange these reports so as to make them assume their most fearful aspect. But we discovered that she had begged one of Mr. Hoggins's worn-out hats to hang up in her lobby, and we (at least I) had doubts as to whether she really would enjoy the little adventure of having her house broken into, as she protested she should. Miss Matty made no secret of being an arrant coward, but she went regularly through her housekeeper's duty of inspection—only the hour for this became earlier and earlier, till at last we went the rounds at half-past six, and Miss Matty adjourned to bed soon after seven, "in order to get the night over the sooner."

Cranford had so long piqued itself on being an honest and moral town that it had grown to fancy itself too genteel and well-bred to be otherwise, and felt the stain upon its character at this time doubly. But we comforted ourselves with the assurance which we gave to each other that the robberies could never have been committed by any Cranford person; it must have been a stranger, or strangers, who brought this disgrace upon the town, and occasioned as many precautions as if we were living among the Red Indians or the French.

This last comparison of our nightly state of defence and fortification was made by Mrs. Forrester, whose father had served under General Burgoyne in the American war, and whose husband had fought the French in Spain. She, indeed, inclined to the idea that, in some way, the French were connected with the small thefts, which were ascertained facts, and the burglaries and highway robberies, which were rumours. She had been deeply impressed with the idea of French spies at some time in her life; and the notion could never be fairly eradicated, but sprang up again from time to time. And now her theory was this: the Cranford people respected themselves too much, and were too grateful to the aristocracy who were so kind as to live near the town, ever to disgrace their bringing up by being dishonest or immoral;

therefore, we must believe that the robbers were strangers—if strangers, why not foreigners?—if foreigners, who so likely as the French? Signor Brunoni spoke broken English like a Frenchman; and, though he wore a turban like a Turk, Mrs. Forrester had seen a print of Madame de Staül with a turban on, and another of Mr. Denon in just such a dress as that in which the conjurer had made his appearance, showing clearly that the French, as well as the Turks, wore turbans. There could be no doubt Signor Brunoni was a Frenchman—a French spy come to discover the weak and undefended places of England, and doubtless he had his accomplices. For her part, she, Mrs. Forrester, had always had her own opinion of Miss Pole's adventure at the George Inn, seeing two men where only one was believed to be. French people had ways and means which, she was thankful to say, the English knew nothing about; and she had never felt quite easy in her mind about going to see that conjurer; it was rather too much like a forbidden thing, though the Rector was there. In short, Mrs. Forrester grew more excited than we had ever known her before, and, being an officer's daughter and widow, we looked up to her opinion, of course.

Really I do not know how much was true or false in the reports which flew about like wildfire just at this time; but it seemed to me then that there was every reason to believe that at Mardon (a small town about eight miles from Cranford) houses and shops were entered by holes made in the walls, the bricks being silently carried away in the dead of the night, and all done so quietly that no sound was heard either in or out of the house. Miss Matty gave it up in despair when she heard of this. "What was the use," said she, "of locks and bolts, and bells to the windows, and going round the house every night? That last trick was fit for a conjurer. Now she did believe that Signor Brunoni was at the bottom of it."

One afternoon, about five o'clock, we were startled by

a hasty knock at the door. Miss Matty bade me run and tell Martha on no account to open the door till she (Miss Matty) had reconnoitred through the window; and she armed herself with a footstool to drop down on the head of the visitor in case he should show a face covered with black crape, as he looked up in answer to her inquiry of who was there. But it was nobody but Miss Pole and Betty. The former came upstairs, carrying a little hand-basket, and she was evidently in a state of great agitation.

"Take care of that!" said she to me, as I offered to relieve her of her basket. "It's my plate. I am sure there is a plan to rob my house tonight. I am come to throw myself on your hospitality, Miss Matty. Betty is going to sleep with her cousin at the 'George.' I can sit up here all night if you will allow me; but my house is so far from any neighbours, and I don't believe we could be heard if we screamed ever so!"

"But," said Miss Matty, "what has alarmed you so much? Have you seen any men lurking about the house?"

"Oh, yes!" answered Miss Pole. "Two very bad-looking men have gone three times past the house very slowly; and an Irish beggar-woman came not half an hour ago, and all but forced herself in past Betty, saying her children were starving, and she must speak to the mistress. You see, she said 'mistress,' though there was a hat hanging up in the hall, and it would have been more natural to have said 'master.' But Betty shut the door in her face, and came up to me, and we got the spoons together, and sat in the parlour window watching till we saw Thomas Jones going from his work, when we called to him and asked him to take care of us into the town."

We might have triumphed over Miss Pole, who had professed such bravery until she was frightened; but we were too glad to perceive that she shared in the weaknesses of humanity to exult over her; and I gave up my room to her very willingly, and shared Miss Matty's bed for the night. But before we retired, the two ladies rummaged up, out of the recesses of their memory, such horrid stories of robbery and murder that I quite quaked in my shoes. Miss Pole was evidently anxious to prove that such terrible events had occurred within her experience that she was justified in her sudden panic; and Miss Matty did not like to be outdone, and capped every story with one yet more horrible, till it reminded me, oddly enough, of an old story I had read somewhere of a nightingale and a musician who strove one against the other which could produce the most admirable music, till poor Philomel dropped down dead.

One of the stories that haunted me for a long time afterwards was of a girl who was left in charge of a great house in Cumberland on some particular fair-day, when the other servants all went off to the gaieties. The family were away in London, and a pedlar came by, and asked to leave his large and heavy pack in the kitchen, saying he would call for it again at night; and the girl (a gamekeeper's daughter) roaming about in search of amusement, chanced to hit upon a gun hanging up in the hall, and took it down to look at the chasing; and it went off through the open kitchen door, hit the pack, and a slow, dark thread of blood came oozing out. (How Miss Pole enjoyed this part of the story, dwelling on each word as if she loved it!) She rather hurried over the further account of the girl's bravery, and I have but a confused idea that somehow she baffled the robbers with Italian irons, heated red-hot, and then restored to blackness by being dipped in grease.

We parted for the night with an awe-stricken wonder as to what we should hear of in the morning; and, on my part, with a vehement desire for the night to be over and gone—I was so afraid lest the robbers should have seen, from some dark lurking-place, that Miss Pole had carried off her plate, and thus have a double motive for attacking our house.

But until Lady Glenmire came to call next day we heard

of nothing unusual. The kitchen fire-irons were in exactly the same position against the back-door as when Martha and I had skilfully piled them up, like spillikins, ready to fall with an awful clatter if only a cat had touched the outside panels. I had wondered what we should all do if thus awakened and alarmed, and had proposed to Miss Matty that we should cover up our faces under the bedclothes, so that there should be no danger of the robbers thinking that we could identify them; but Miss Matty, who was trembling very much, scouted this idea, and said we owed it to society to apprehend them, and that she should certainly do her best to lay hold of them and lock them up in the garret till morning.

When Lady Glenmire came we almost felt jealous of her. Mrs. Jamieson's house had really been attacked; at least there were men's footsteps to be seen on the flower borders underneath the kitchen windows, "where nae men should be;" and Carlo had barked all through the night as if strangers were abroad. Mrs. Jamieson had been awakened by Lady Glenmire, and they had rung the bell which communicated with Mr. Mulliner's room in the third storey, and when his night capped head had appeared over the banisters, in answer to the summons, they had told him of their alarm, and the reasons for it; whereupon he retreated into his bedroom and locked the door (for fear of draughts, as he informed them in the morning), and opened the window, and called out valiantly to say, if the supposed robbers would come to him he would fight them; but, as Lady Glenmire observed, that was but poor comfort, since they would have to pass by Mrs. Jamieson's room and her own before they could reach him, and must be of a very pugnacious disposition indeed if they neglected the opportunities of robbery presented by the unguarded lower storeys, to go up to a garret, and there force a door in order to get at the champion of the house. Lady Glenmire, after waiting and listening for some time in the drawing-room, had proposed to Mrs. Jamieson that they should go to bed; but that lady said she should not feel comfortable unless she sat up and watched; and, accordingly, she packed herself warmly up on the sofa, where she was found by the housemaid when she came into the room at six o'clock, fast asleep; but Lady Glenmire went to bed, and kept awake all night.

When Miss Pole heard of this, she nodded her head in great satisfaction. She had been sure we should hear of something happening in Cranford that night; and we had heard. It was clear enough they had first proposed to attack her house; but when they saw that she and Betty were on their guard, and had carried off the plate, they had changed their tactics and gone to Mrs. Jamieson's, and no one knew what might have happened if Carlo had not barked, like a good dog that he was!

Poor Carlo! his barking days were nearly over. Whether the gang who infested the neighbourhood were afraid of him; or whether they were revengeful enough—for the way in which he had baffled them on the night in question—to poison him; or whether, as some among the more uneducated people thought, he died of apoplexy, brought on by too much feeding and too little exercise; at any rate, it is certain that, two days after this eventful night, Carlo was found dead, with his poor little legs stretched out stiff in the attitude of running, as if by such unusual exertion he could escape the sure pursuer, Death.

We were all sorry for Carlo, the old familiar friend who had snapped at us for so many years; and the mysterious mode of his death made us very uncomfortable. Could Signor Brunoni be at the bottom of this? He had apparently killed a canary with only a word of command; his will seemed of deadly force; who knew but what he might yet be lingering in the neighbourhood willing all sorts of awful things!

We whispered these fancies among ourselves in the evenings; but in the mornings our courage came back with the daylight, and in a week's time we had got over the shock of Carlo's death; all but Mrs. Jamieson. She, poor thing, felt it as she had felt no event since her husband's death; indeed, Miss Pole said, that as the Honourable Mr. Jamieson drank a good deal, and occasioned her much uneasiness, it was possible that Carlo's death might be the greater affliction. But there was always a tinge of cynicism in Miss Pole's remarks. However, one thing was clear and certain—it was necessary for Mrs. Jamieson to have some change of scene; and Mr. Mulliner was very impressive on this point, shaking his head whenever we inquired after his mistress, and speaking of her loss of appetite and bad nights very ominously; and with justice, too, for if she had two characteristics in her natural state of health they were a facility of eating and sleeping. If she could neither eat nor sleep, she must be indeed out of spirits and out of health.

Lady Glenmire (who had evidently taken very kindly to Cranford) did not like the idea of Mrs. Jamieson's going to Cheltenham, and more than once insinuated pretty plainly that it was Mr. Mulliner's doing, who had been much alarmed on the occasion of the house being attacked, and since had said, more than once, that he felt it a very responsible charge to have to defend so many women. Be that as it might, Mrs. Jamieson went to Cheltenham, escorted by Mr. Mulliner; and Lady Glenmire remained in possession of the house, her ostensible office being to take care that the maid-servants did not pick up followers. She made a very pleasant-looking dragon; and as soon as it was arranged for her to stay in Cranford, she found out that Mrs. Jamieson's visit to Cheltenham was just the best thing in the world. She had let her house in Edinburgh, and was for the time houseless, so the charge of her sister-in-law's comfortable abode was very convenient and acceptable.

Miss Pole was very much inclined to install herself as a heroine, because of the decided steps she had taken in flying from the two men and one woman, whom she entitled "that murderous gang." She described their appearance in glowing colours, and I noticed that every time she went over the story some fresh trait of villainy was added to their appearance. One was tall—he grew to be gigantic in height before we had done with him; he, of course, had black hair—and by and by it hung in elf-locks over his forehead and down his back. The other was short and broad—and a hump sprouted out on his shoulder before we heard the last of him; he had red hair—which deepened into carroty; and she was almost sure he had a cast in the eye—a decided squint. As for the woman, her eyes glared, and she was masculine-looking—a perfect virago; most probably a man dressed in woman's clothes: afterwards we heard of a beard on her chin, and a manly voice and a stride.

If Miss Pole was delighted to recount the events of that afternoon to all inquirers, others were not so proud of their adventures in the robbery line. Mr. Hoggins, the surgeon, had been attacked at his own door by two ruffians, who were concealed in the shadow of the porch, and so effectually silenced him that he was robbed in the interval between ringing his bell and the servant's answering it. Miss Pole was sure it would turn out that this robbery had been committed by "her men," and went the very day she heard the report to have her teeth examined, and to question Mr. Hoggins. She came to us afterwards; so we heard what she had heard, straight and direct from the source, while we were yet in the excitement and flutter of the agitation caused by the first intelligence; for the event had only occurred the night before.

"Well!" said Miss Pole, sitting down with the decision of a person who has made up her mind as to the nature of life and the world (and such people never tread lightly, or seat themselves without a bump), "well, Miss Matty! men will be men. Every mother's son of them wishes to be considered Samson and Solomon rolled into one—too strong ever to be beaten or discomfited—too wise ever to be outwitted. If you will notice, they have always foreseen events, though they never tell one for one's warning before the events happen. My father was a man, and I know the sex pretty well."

She had talked herself out of breath, and we should have been very glad to fill up the necessary pause as chorus, but we did not exactly know what to say, or which man had suggested this diatribe against the sex; so we only joined in generally, with a grave shake of the head, and a soft murmur of, "They are very incomprehensible, certainly!"

"Now, only think," said she. "There I have undergone the risk of having one of my remaining teeth drawn (for one is terribly at the mercy of any surgeon-dentist; and I, for one, always speak them fair till I have got my mouth out of their clutches), and, after all, Mr. Hoggins is too much of a man to own that he was robbed last night."

"Not robbed!" exclaimed the chorus.

"Don't tell me!" Miss Pole exclaimed, angry that we could be for a moment imposed upon. "I believe he was robbed, just as Betty told me, and he is ashamed to own it; and, to be sure, it was very silly of him to be robbed just at his own door; I dare say he feels that such a thing won't raise him in the eyes of Cranford society, and is anxious to conceal it—but he need not have tried to impose upon me, by saying I must have heard an exaggerated account of some petty theft of a neck of mutton, which, it seems, was stolen out of the safe in his yard last week; he had the impertinence to add, he believed that that was taken by the cat. I have no doubt, if I could get at the bottom of it, it was that Irishman dressed up in woman's clothes, who came spying about my house, with the story about the starving children."

After we had duly condemned the want of candour which Mr. Hoggins had evinced, and abused men in general, taking him for the representative and type, we got round to the subject about which we had been talking when Miss Pole came in; namely, how far, in the present disturbed state of the country, we could venture to accept an invitation which Miss Matty had just received from Mrs. Forrester, to come as usual and keep the anniversary of her wedding-day by drinking tea with her at five o'clock, and playing a quiet pool afterwards. Mr. Forrester had said that she asked us with some diffidence, because the roads were, she feared, very unsafe. But she suggested that perhaps one of us would not object to take the sedan, and that the others, by walking briskly, might keep up with the long trot of the chairmen, and so we might all arrive safely at Over Place, a suburb of the town. (No; that is too large an expression: a small cluster of houses separated from Cranford by about two hundred yards of a dark and lonely lane.) There was no doubt but that a similar note was awaiting Miss Pole at home; so her call was a very fortunate affair, as it enabled us to consult together . . . We would all much rather have declined this invitation; but we felt that it would not be quite kind to Mrs. Forrester, who would otherwise be left to a solitary retrospect of her not very happy or fortunate life. Miss Matty and Miss Pole had been visitors on this occasion for many years, and now they gallantly determined to nail their colours to the mast, and to go through Darkness Lane rather than fail in loyalty to their friend.

But when the evening came, Miss Matty (for it was she who was voted into the chair, as she had a cold), before being shut down in the sedan, like Jack-in-a-box, implored the chairmen, whatever might befall, not to run away and leave her fastened up there, to be murdered; and even after they had promised, I saw her tighten her features into the stern determination of a martyr, and she gave me a melancholy and ominous shake of the head through the glass. However, we got there safely, only rather out of breath, for it was who could trot hardest through Darkness Lane, and I am afraid poor Miss Matty was sadly jolted.

Mrs. Forrester had made extra preparations, in

acknowledgment of our exertion in coming to see her through such dangers. The usual forms of genteel ignorance as to what her servants might send up were all gone through; and harmony and preference seemed likely to be the order of the evening, but for an interesting conversation that began I don't know how, but which had relation, of course, to the robbers who infested the neighbourhood of Cranford.

Having braved the dangers of Darkness Lane, and thus having a little stock of reputation for courage to fall back upon; and also, I dare say, desirous of proving ourselves superior to men (*videlicet* Mr. Hoggins) in the article of candour, we began to relate our individual fears, and the private precautions we each of us took. I owned that my pet apprehension was eyes—eyes looking at me, and watching me, glittering out from some dull, flat, wooden surface; and that if I dared to go up to my looking-glass when I was panic-stricken, I should certainly turn it round, with its back towards me, for fear of seeing eyes behind me looking out of the darkness. I saw Miss Matty nerving herself up for a confession; and at last out it came. She owned that, ever since she had been a girl, she had dreaded being caught by her last leg, just as she was getting into bed, by some one concealed under it. She said, when she was younger and more active, she used to take a flying leap from a distance, and so bring both her legs up safely into bed at once; but that this had always annoyed Deborah, who piqued herself upon getting into bed gracefully, and she had given it up in consequence. But now the old terror would often come over her, especially since Miss Pole's house had been attacked (we had got quite to believe in the fact of the attack having taken place), and yet it was very unpleasant to think of looking under a bed, and seeing a man concealed, with a great, fierce face staring out at you; so she had bethought herself of something—perhaps I had noticed that she had told Martha to buy her a penny ball, such as children play with—and now she rolled this ball under the bed every night: if it came out on the other side, well and good; if not, she always took care to have her hand on the bell rope, and meant to call out John and Harry, just as if she expected men-servants to answer her ring.

We all applauded this ingenious contrivance, and Miss Matty sank back into satisfied silence, with a look at Mrs. Forrester as if to ask for *her* private weakness.

Mrs. Forrester looked askance at Miss Pole, and tried to change the subject a little by telling us that she had borrowed a boy from one of the neighbouring cottages and promised his parents a hundredweight of coals at Christmas, and his supper every evening, for the loan of him at nights. She had instructed him in his possible duties when he first came; and, finding him sensible, she had given him the Major's sword (the Major was her late husband), and desired him to put it very carefully behind his pillow at night, turning the edge towards the head of the pillow. He was a sharp lad, she was sure; for, spying out the major's cocked hat, he had said, if he might have that to wear, he was sure he could frighten two Englishmen, or four Frenchmen, any day. But she had impressed upon him anew that he was to lose no time in putting on hats or anything else; but, if he heard any noise, he was to run at it with his drawn sword. On my suggesting that some accident might occur from such slaughterous and indiscriminate directions, and that he might rush on Jenny getting up to wash, and have spitted her before he had discovered that she was not a Frenchman, Mrs. Forrester said she did not think that that was likely, for he was a very sound sleeper, and generally had to be well shaken or cold-pigged in a morning before they could rouse him. She sometimes thought such dead sleep must be owing to the hearty suppers the poor lad ate, for he was half-starved at home, and she told Jenny to see that he got a good meal at night.

Still this was no confession of Mrs. Forrester's peculiar timidity, and we urged her to tell us what she thought would frighten her more than anything. She paused, and stirred the fire, and snuffed the candles, and then she said, in a sounding whisper:

"Ghosts!"

She looked at Miss Pole, as much as to say, she had declared it, and would stand by it. Such a look was a challenge in itself. Miss Pole came down upon her with indigestion, spectral illusions, optical delusions, and a great deal out of Dr. Ferrier and Dr. Hibbert besides. Miss Matty had rather a leaning to ghosts, as I have mentioned before, and what little she did say was all on Mrs. Forrester's side, who, emboldened by sympathy, protested that ghosts were a part of her religion; that sure she, the widow of a major in the army, knew what to be frightened at, and what not; in short, I never saw Mrs. Forrester so warm either before or since, for she was a gentle, meek, enduring old lady in most things. Not all the elder-wine that ever was mulled could this night wash out the remembrances of this difference between Miss Pole and her hostess. Indeed, when the elder-wine was brought in, it gave rise to a new burst of discussion; for Jenny, the little maiden who staggered under the tray, had to give evidence of having seen a ghost with her own eyes, not so many nights ago, in Darkness Lane, the very lane we were to go through on our way home.

In spite of the uncomfortable feeling which this last consideration gave me, I could not help being amused at Jenny's position, which was exceedingly like that of a witness being examined and cross-examined by two counsel who are not at all scrupulous about asking leading questions. The conclusion I arrived at was, that Jenny had certainly seen something beyond what a fit of indigestion would have caused. A lady all in white, and without her head, was what she deposed and adhered to, supported by a consciousness of the secret sympathy of her mistress under the withering scorn with which Miss Pole regarded her. And not only she, but many others, had seen this headless lady, who sat by the roadside wringing her hands as in deep grief. Mrs. Forrester looked at us from time to time with an air of conscious triumph; but then she had not to pass through Darkness Lane before she could bury herself beneath her own familiar bedclothes.

We preserved a discreet silence as to the headless lady while we were putting on our things to go home, for there was no knowing how near the ghostly head and ears might be, or what spiritual connection they might be keeping up with the unhappy body in Darkness Lane; and, therefore, even Miss Pole felt that it was as well not to speak lightly on such subjects, for fear of vexing or insulting that woebegone trunk. At least, so I conjecture; for, instead of the busy clatter usual in the operation, we tied on our cloaks as sadly as mutes at a funeral. Miss Matty drew the curtains round the windows of the chair to shut out disagreeable sights, and the men (either because they were in spirits that their labours were so nearly ended, or because they were going down hill) set off at such a round and merry pace that it was all Miss Pole and I could do to keep up with them. She had breath for nothing beyond an imploring "Don't leave me!" uttered as she clutched my arm so tightly that I could not have quitted her, ghost or no ghost. What a relief it was when the men, weary of their burden, and their quick trot, stopped just where Headingley Causeway branches off from Darkness Lane! Miss Pole unloosed me and caught at one of the men.

"Could not you—could not you take Miss Matty round by Headingley Causeway?—the pavement in Darkness Lane jolts so, and she is not very strong?"

A smothered voice was heard from the inside of the chair—

"Oh! pray go on! What is the matter? What is the matter? I will give you sixpence more to go on very fast; pray don't stop here."

"And I'll give you a shilling," said Miss Pole, with tremulous dignity, "if you'll go by Headingley Causeway."

The two men grunted acquiescence and took up the chair, and went along the causeway, which certainly answered Miss Pole's kind purpose of saving Miss Matty's bones; for it was covered with soft, thick mud, and even a fall there would have been easy till the getting-up came, when there might have been some difficulty in extrication.

CHAPTER 11

Samuel Brown

The next morning I met Lady Glenmire and Miss Pole setting out on a long walk to find some old woman who was famous in the neighbourhood for her skill in knitting woollen stockings. Miss Pole said to me, with a smile half kindly and half contemptuous upon her countenance, "I have been just telling Lady Glenmire of our poor friend Mrs. Forrester and her terror of ghosts. It comes from living so much alone, and listening to the bug-a-boo stories of that Jenny of hers." She was so calm and so much above superstitious fears herself that I was almost ashamed to say how glad I had been of her Headingley Causeway proposition the night before, and turned off the conversation to something else.

In the afternoon Miss Pole called on Miss Matty to tell her of the adventure—the real adventure they had met with on their morning's walk. They had been perplexed about the exact path which they were to take across the fields in order to find the knitting old woman, and had stopped to inquire at a little wayside public-house, standing on the high road to London, about three miles from Cranford. The good woman had asked them to sit down and rest themselves while she fetched her husband, who could direct them better than she could; and, while they were sitting in the sanded parlour, a little girl came in. They thought that she belonged to the landlady, and began some trifling conversation with her; but, on Mrs. Roberts's return, she told them that the little thing was the only child of a couple who were staying in the house. And then she began a long story, out of which Lady Glenmire and Miss Pole could only gather one or two decided facts, which were that, about six weeks ago, a light spring-cart had broken down just before their door, in which there were two men, one woman, and this child. One of the men was seriously hurt—no bones broken, only "shaken," the landlady called it; but he had probably sustained some severe internal injury, for he had languished in their house ever since, attended by his wife, the mother of this little girl. Miss Pole had asked what he was, what he looked like. And Mrs. Roberts had made answer that he was not like a gentleman, nor yet like a common person; if it had not been that he and his wife were such decent, quiet people, she could almost have thought he was a mountebank, or something of that kind, for they had a great box in the cart, full of she did not know what. She had helped to unpack it, and take out their linen and clothes, when the other man—his twin-brother, she believed he was— had gone off with the horse and cart.

Miss Pole had begun to have her suspicions at this point, and expressed her idea that it was rather strange that the box and cart and horse and all should have disappeared; but good Mrs. Roberts seemed to have become quite indignant at Miss Pole's implied suggestion; in fact, Miss Pole said, she was as angry as if Miss Pole had told her that she herself was a swindler. As the best way of convincing the ladies, she bethought her of begging them to see the wife; and, as Miss Pole said, there was no doubting the honest, worn, bronzed face of the woman, who, at the first tender word from Lady Glenmire, burst into tears, which she was too weak to check until some word from the landlady made her swallow down her sobs, in order that she might testify to the Christian kindness shown by Mr. and Mrs. Roberts. Miss Pole came round with a swing to as vehement a belief in the sorrowful tale as she had been sceptical before; and, as a proof of this, her energy in the poor sufferer's behalf was nothing daunted when she found out that he, and no other, was our Signor Brunoni, to whom all Cranford had been attributing all manner of evil this six weeks past! Yes! his wife said his proper name was Samuel Brown— "Sam," she called him—but to the last we preferred calling him "the Signor"; it sounded so much better.

The end of their conversation with the Signora Brunoni was that it was agreed that he should be placed under medical advice, and for any expense incurred in procuring this Lady Glenmire promised to hold herself responsible, and had accordingly gone to Mr. Hoggins to beg him to ride over to the Rising Sun that very afternoon, and examine into the signor's real state; and, as Miss Pole said, if it was desirable to remove him to Cranford to be more immediately under Mr. Hoggin's eye, she would undertake to see for lodgings and arrange about the rent. Mrs. Roberts had been as kind as could be all throughout, but it was evident that their long residence there had been a slight inconvenience.

Before Miss Pole left us, Miss Matty and I were as full of the morning's adventure as she was. We talked about it all the evening, turning it in every possible light, and we went to bed anxious for the morning, when we should surely hear from some one what Mr. Hoggins thought and recommended; for, as Miss Matty observed, though Mr. Hoggins did say "Jack's up," "a fig for his heels," and called preference "pref.," she believed he was a very worthy man and a very clever surgeon. Indeed, we were rather proud of our doctor at Cranford, as a doctor. We often wished, when we heard of Queen Adelaide or the Duke of Wellington being ill, that they would send for Mr. Hoggins; but, on consideration, we were rather glad they did not, for, if we were ailing, what should we do if Mr. Hoggins had been appointed physician-in-ordinary to the Royal Family? As a surgeon we were proud of him; but as a man, or rather, I should say, as a gentleman, we could only shake our heads over his name and himself, and wished that he had read Lord Chesterfield's *Letters* in the days when his manners were susceptible of improvement. Nevertheless, we all regarded his dictum in the signor's case as infallible, and when he said that with care and attention he might rally, we had no more fear for him.

But, although we had no more fear, everybody did as much as if there was great cause for anxiety—as indeed there was until Mr. Hoggins took charge of him. Miss Pole looked out clean and comfortable, if homely, lodgings; Miss Matty sent the sedan-chair for him, and Martha and I aired it well before it left Cranford by holding a warming-pan full of red-hot coals in it, and then shutting it up close, smoke and all, until the time when he should get into it at the Rising Sun. Lady Glenmire undertook the medical department under Mr. Hoggins's directions, and rummaged up all Mrs. Jamieson's medicine glasses, and spoons, and bed-tables, in a free-and-easy way, that made Miss Matty feel a little anxious as to what that lady and Mr. Mulliner might say, if they knew. Mrs. Forrester made some of the bread-jelly, for which she was so famous, to have ready as a refreshment in the lodgings when he should arrive. A present of this bread-jelly was the highest mark of favour dear Mrs. Forrester could confer. Miss Pole had once asked her for the receipt, but she had met with a very decided rebuff; that lady told her that she could not part with it to any one during her life, and that after her death it was bequeathed, as her executors would find, to Miss Matty. What Miss Matty—or, as Mrs. Forrester called her (remembering the clause in her will and the dignity of the occasion), Miss Matilda Jenkyns—might choose to do with the receipt when it came into her possession—whether to make it public, or to hand it down as an heirloom—she did not know, nor would she dictate. And a mould of this admirable, digestible, unique bread-jelly was sent by Mrs. Forrester to our poor sick conjurer. Who says that the aristocracy are proud? Here was a lady by birth a Tyrrell, and descended from the great Sir Walter that shot King Rufus, and in whose veins ran the blood of him who murdered the little princes in the Tower, going every day to see what dainty dishes she could prepare for Samuel Brown, a mountebank! But, indeed, it was wonderful to see what kind feelings were called out by this poor man's coming amongst us. And also wonderful to see how the great Cranford panic, which had been occasioned by his first coming in his Turkish dress, melted away into thin air on his second coming—pale and feeble, and with his heavy, filmy eyes, that only brightened a very little when they fell upon the countenance of his faithful wife, or their pale and sorrowful little girl.

Somehow we all forgot to be afraid. I dare say it was that finding out that he, who had first excited our love of the marvellous by his unprecedented arts, had not sufficient everyday gifts to manage a shying horse, made us feel as if we were ourselves again. Miss Pole came with her little basket at all hours of the evening, as if her lonely house and the unfrequented roads to it had never been infested by that "murderous gang"; Mrs. Forrester said she thought that neither Jenny nor she need mind the headless lady who wept and wailed in Darkness Lane, for surely the power was never given to such beings to harm those who went about to try to do what little good was in their power, to which Jenny tremblingly assented; but the mistress's theory had little effect on the maid's practice until she had sewn two pieces of red flannel in the shape of a cross on her inner garment.

I found Miss Matty covering her penny ball—the ball that she used to roll under the bed—with gay-coloured worsted in rainbow stripes.

"My dear," said she, "my heart is sad for that little careworn child. Although her father is a conjurer, she looks as if she had never had a good game of play in her life. I used to make very pretty balls in this way when I was a girl, and I thought I would try if I could not make this one smart and take it to Phoebe this afternoon. I think 'the gang' must have left the neighbourhood, for one does not hear any more of their violence and robbery now."

We were all of us far too full of the Signor's precarious state to talk either about robbers or ghosts. Indeed, Lady Glenmire said she never had heard of any actual robberies, except that two little boys had stolen some apples from Farmer Benson's orchard, and that some eggs had been missed on a market-day off Widow Hayward's stall. But that was expecting too much of us; we could not acknowledge that we had only had this small foundation for all our panic. Miss Pole drew herself up at this remark of Lady Glenmire's, and said, "that she wished she could agree with her as to the very small reason we had had for alarm, but with the recollection of a man disguised as a woman who had endeavoured to force himself into her house while his confederates waited outside; with the knowledge gained from Lady Glenmire herself, of the footprints seen on Mrs. Jamieson's flower borders; with the fact before her of the audacious robbery committed on Mr. Hoggins at his own door—" But here Lady Glenmire broke in with a very strong expression of doubt as to whether this last story was not an entire fabrication founded upon the theft of a cat. She grew so red while she was saying all this that I was not surprised at Miss Pole's manner of bridling up, and I am certain, if Lady Glenmire had not been "her ladyship," we should have had a more emphatic contradiction than the "Well, to be sure!" and similar fragmentary éjaculations, which were all that she ventured upon in my lady's presence. But when she was gone Miss Pole began a long congratulation to Miss Matty that so far they had escaped marriage, which she noticed always made people credulous to the last degree; indeed, she thought it argued great natural credulity in a woman if she could not keep herself from being married; and in what Lady

Glenmire had said about Mr. Hoggin's robbery we had a specimen of what people came to if they gave way to such a weakness; evidently Lady Glenmire would swallow anything if she could believe the poor vamped-up story about a neck of mutton and a pussy with which he had tried to impose on Miss Pole, only she had always been on her guard against believing too much of what men said.

We were thankful, as Miss Pole desired us to be, that we had never been married; but I think, of the two, we were even more thankful that the robbers had left Cranford; at least I judge so from a speech of Miss Matty's that evening, as we sat over the fire, in which she evidently looked upon a husband as a great protector against thieves, burglars, and ghosts; and said that she did not think that she should dare to be always warning young people against matrimony, as Miss Pole did continually; to be sure, marriage was a risk, as she saw, now she had had some experience; but she remembered the time when she had looked forward to being married as much as any one.

"Not to any particular person, my dear," said she, hastily checking herself up, as if she were afraid of having admitted too much; "only the old story, you know, of ladies always saying '*When* I marry,' and gentlemen '*If* I marry.'" It was a joke spoken in rather a sad tone, and I doubt if either of us smiled; but I could not see Miss Matty's face by the flickering firelight. In a little while she continued:

"But, after all, I have not told you the truth. It is so long ago, and no one ever knew how much I thought of it at the time, unless, indeed, my dear mother guessed; but I may say that there was a time when I did not think I should have been only Miss Matty Jenkyns all my life; for even if I did meet with any one who wished to marry me now (and, as Miss Pole says, one is never too safe), I could not take him—I hope he would not take it too much to heart, but I could *not* take him or any one but the person I once thought I should be married to; and he is dead and gone, and he never knew how it all came about that I said 'No,' when I had thought many and many a time—Well, it's no matter what I thought. God ordains it all, and I am very happy, my dear. No one has such kind friends as I," continued she, taking my hand and holding it in hers.

If I had never known of Mr. Holbrook, I could have said something in this pause, but as I had, I could not think of anything that would come in naturally, and so we both kept silence for a little time.

"My father once made us," she began, "keep a diary, in two columns; on one side we were to put down in the morning what we thought would be the course and events of the coming day, and at night we were to put down on the other side what really had happened. It would be to some people rather a sad way of telling their lives" (a tear dropped upon my hand at these words)—"I don't mean that mine has been sad, only so very different to what I expected. I remember, one winter's evening, sitting over our bedroom fire with Deborah—I remember it as if it were yesterday—and we were planning our future lives, both of us were planning, though only she talked about it. She said she should like to marry an archdeacon, and write his charges; and you know, my dear, she never was married, and, for aught I know, she never spoke to an unmarried archdeacon in her life. I never was ambitious, nor could I have written charges, but I thought I could manage a house (my mother used to call me her right hand), and I was always so fond of little children—the shyest babies would stretch out their little arms to come to me; when I was a girl, I was half my leisure time nursing in the neighbouring cottages; but I don't know how it was, when I grew sad and grave—which I did a year or two after this time—the little things drew back from me, and I am afraid I lost the knack, though I am just as fond of children as ever, and have a strange yearning at my heart whenever I see a mother with her baby in her arms. Nay, my dear" (and, by a sudden blaze which sprang up from a fall of the unstirred coals, I saw that her eyes were full of tears—gazing intently on some vision of what might have been), "do you know I dream sometimes that I have a little child—always the same—a little girl of about two years old; she never grows older, though I have dreamed about her for many years. I don't think I ever dream of any words or sound she makes; she is very noiseless and still, but she comes to me when she is very sorry or very glad, and I have wakened with the clasp of her dear little arms round my neck. Only last night—perhaps because I had gone to sleep thinking of this ball for Phoebe—my little darling came in my dream, and put up her mouth to be kissed, just as I have seen real babies do to real mothers before going to bed. But all this is nonsense, dear! only don't be frightened by Miss Pole from being married. I can fancy it may be a very happy state, and a little credulity helps one on through life very smoothly—better than always doubting and doubting and seeing difficulties and disagreeables in everything."

If I had been inclined to be daunted from matrimony, it would not have been Miss Pole to do it; it would have been the lot of poor Signor Brunoni and his wife. And yet again, it was an encouragement to see how, through all their cares and sorrows, they thought of each other and not of themselves; and how keen were their joys, if they only passed through each other, or through the little Phoebe.

The Signora told me one day a good deal about their lives up to this period. It began by my asking her whether Miss Pole's story of the twin-brothers was true; it sounded so wonderful a likeness, that I should have had my doubts, if Miss Pole had not been unmarried. But the Signora, or (as we found out she preferred to be called) Mrs. Brown, said it was quite true; that her brother-in-law was by many taken for her husband, which was of great assistance to them in their profession; "though," she continued, "how people can mistake

Thomas for the real Signor Brunoni, I can't conceive; but he says they do; so I suppose I must believe him. Not but what he is a very good man; I am sure I don't know how we should have paid our bill at the Rising Sun but for the money he sends; but people must know very little about art if they can take him for my husband. Why, miss, in the ball trick, where my husband spreads his fingers wide, and throws out his little finger with quite an air and a grace, Thomas just clumps up his hand like a fist, and might have ever so many balls hidden in it. Besides, he has never been in India, and knows nothing of the proper sit of a turban."

"Have you been in India?" said I, rather astonished.

"Oh, yes! many a year, ma'am. Sam was a sergeant in the 31st; and when the regiment was ordered to India, I drew a lot to go, and I was more thankful than I can tell; for it seemed as if it would only be a slow death to me to part from my husband. But, indeed, ma'am, if I had known all, I don't know whether I would not rather have died there and then than gone through what I have done since. To be sure, I've been able to comfort Sam, and to be with him; but, ma'am, I've lost six children," said she, looking up at me with those strange eyes that I've never noticed but in mothers of dead children—with a kind of wild look in them, as if seeking for what they never more might find. "Yes! Six children died off, like little buds nipped untimely, in that cruel India. I thought, as each died, I never could—I never would—love a child again; and when the next came, it had not only its own love, but the deeper love that came from the thoughts of its little dead brothers and sisters. And when Phoebe was coming, I said to my husband, 'Sam, when the child is born, and I am strong, I shall leave you; it will cut my heart cruel; but if this baby dies too I shall go mad; the madness is in me now; but if you let me go down to Calcutta, carrying my baby step by step, it will, maybe, work itself off; and I will save, and I will hoard, and I will beg—and I will die, to get a passage home to England, where our baby may live. God bless him! he said I might go; and he saved up his pay, and I saved every piece I could get for washing or any way; and when Phoebe came, and I grew strong again, I set off. It was very lonely; through the thick forests, dark again with their heavy trees—along by the riverside (but I had been brought up near the Avon in Warwickshire, so that flowing noise sounded like home)—from station to station, from Indian village to village, I went along, carrying my child. I had seen one of the officer's ladies with a little picture, ma'am—done by a Catholic foreigner, ma'am—of the Virgin and the little Saviour, ma'am. She had Him on her arm, and her form was softly curled round Him, and their cheeks touched. Well, when I went to bid good-bye to this lady, for whom I had washed, she cried sadly; for she, too, had lost her children, but she had not another to save like me; and I was bold enough to ask her would she give me that print. And she cried the more, and said *her* children were with that little blessed Jesus; and gave it me, and told me she had heard it had been painted on the bottom of a cask, which made it have that round shape. And when my body was very weary, and my heart was sick (for there were times when I misdoubted if I could ever reach my home, and there were times when I thought of my husband, and one time when I thought my baby was dying), I took out that picture and looked at it, till I could have thought the mother spoke to me, and comforted me. And the natives were very kind. We could not understand one another; but they saw my baby on my breast, and they came out to me and brought me rice and milk, and sometimes flowers—I have got some of the flowers dried. Then, the next morning, I was so tired; and they wanted me to stay with them—I could tell that—and tried to frighten me from going into the deep woods, which, indeed, looked very strange and dark; but it seemed to me as if Death was following me to take my baby away from me; and as if I must go on and on—and I thought how God had cared for mothers ever since the world was made, and would care for me; so I bade them goodbye, and set off afresh. And once when my baby was ill, and both she and I needed rest, He led me to a place where I found a kind Englishman lived, right in the midst of the natives."

"And you reached Calcutta safely at last?"

"Yes, safely! Oh! when I knew I had only two days' journey more before me, I could not help it, ma'am—it might be idolatry, I cannot tell—but I was near one of the native temples, and I went into it with my baby to thank God for His great mercy; for it seemed to me that where others had prayed before to their God, in their joy or in their agony, was of itself a sacred place. And I got as servant to an invalid lady, who grew quite fond of my baby aboard-ship; and, in two years' time, Sam earned his discharge, and came home to me, and to our child. Then he had to fix on a trade; but he knew of none; and once, once upon a time, he had learned some tricks from an Indian juggler; so he set up conjuring, and it answered so well that he took Thomas to help him—as his man, you know, not as another conjurer, though Thomas has set it up now on his own hook. But it has been a great help to us that likeness between the twins, and made a good many tricks go off well that they made up together. And Thomas is a good brother, only he has not the fine carriage of my husband, so that I can't think how he can be taken for Signor Brunoni himself, as he says he is."

"Poor little Phoebe!" said I, my thoughts going back to the baby she carried all those hundred miles.

"Ah! you may say so! I never thought I should have reared her, though, when she fell ill at Chunderabaddad; but that good, kind Aga Jenkyns took us in, which I believe was the very saving of her."

"Jenkyns!" said I.

"Yes, Jenkyns. I shall think all people of that name are kind; for here is that nice old lady who comes every day to take Phoebe a walk!"

But an idea had flashed through my head: could the Aga Jenkyns be the lost Peter? True, he was reported by many to be dead. But, equally true, some had said that he had arrived at the dignity of Great Lama of Thibet. Miss Matty thought he was alive. I would make further inquiry.

CHAPTER 12

Engaged to be Married

Was the "poor Peter" of Cranford the Aga Jenkyns of Chunderabaddad, or was he not? As somebody says, that was the question.

In my own home, whenever people had nothing else to do, they blamed me for want of discretion. Indiscretion was my bugbear fault. Everybody has a bugbear fault; a sort of standing characteristic—a *pièce de résistance* for their friends to cut at; and in general they cut and come again. I was tired of being called indiscreet and incautious; and I determined for once to prove myself a model of prudence and wisdom. I would not even hint my suspicions respecting the Aga. I would collect evidence and carry it home to lay before my father, as the family friend of the two Misses Jenkyns.

In my search after facts I was often reminded of a description my father had once given of a ladies' committee that he had had to preside over. He said he could not help thinking of a passage in Dickens, which spoke of a chorus in which every man took the tune he knew best, and sang it to his own satisfaction. So, at this charitable committee, every lady took the subject uppermost in her mind, and talked about it to her own great contentment, but not much to the advancement of the subject they had met to discuss. But even that committee could have been nothing to the Cranford ladies when I attempted to gain some clear and definite information as to poor Peter's height, appearance, and when and where he was seen and heard of last. For instance, I remember asking Miss Pole (and I thought the question was very opportune, for I put it when I met her at a call at Mrs. Forrester's, and both the ladies had known Peter, and I imagined that they might refresh each other's memories)—I asked Miss Pole what was the very last thing they had ever heard about him; and then she named the absurd report to which I have alluded, about his having been elected Great Lama of Thibet; and this was a signal for each lady to go off on her separate idea. Mrs. Forrester's start was made on the veiled prophet in *Lalla Rookh*—whether I thought he was meant for the Great Lama, though Peter was not so ugly, indeed, rather handsome, if he had not been freckled. I was thankful to see her double upon Peter; but, in a moment, the delusive lady was off upon Rowland's Kalydor, and the merits of cosmetics and hair oils in general, and holding forth so fluently that I turned to listen to Miss Pole who (through the llamas, the beasts of burden) had got to Peruvian bonds, and the share market, and her poor opinion of joint-stock banks in general, and of that one in particular in which Miss Matty's money was invested. In vain I put in "When was it—in what year was it that you heard that Mr. Peter was the Great Lama?" They only joined issue to dispute whether llamas were carnivorous animals or not; in which dispute they were not quite on fair grounds, as Mrs. Forrester (after they had grown warm and cool again) acknowledged that she always confused carnivorous and graminivorous together, just as she did horizontal and perpendicular; but then she apologised for it very prettily, by saying that in her day the only use people made of four-syllabled words was to teach how they should be spelled.

The only fact I gained from this conversation was that certainly Peter had last been heard of in India, "or that neighbourhood"; and that this scanty intelligence of his whereabouts had reached Cranford in the year when Miss Pole had bought her Indian muslin gown, long since worn out (we washed it and mended it, and traced its decline and fall into a window-blind before we could go on); and in a year when Wombwell came to Cranford, because Miss Matty had wanted to see an elephant, in order that she might the better imagine Peter riding on one; and had seen a boa-constrictor too, which was more than she wished to imagine in her fancy pictures of Peter's locality; and in a year when Miss Jenkyns had learned some piece of poetry off by heart, and used to say, at all the Cranford parties, how Peter was "surveying mankind from China to Peru," which everybody had thought very grand, and rather appropriate, because India was between China and Peru, if you took care to turn the globe to the left instead of the right.

I suppose all these inquiries of mine, and the consequent curiosity excited in the minds of my friends, made us blind and deaf to what was going on around us. It seemed to me as if the sun rose and shone, and as if the rain rained on Cranford just as usual, and I did not notice any sign of the times that could be considered as a prognostic of any uncommon event; and, to the best of my belief, not only Miss Matty and Mrs. Forrester, but even Miss Pole herself, whom we looked upon as a kind of prophetess, from the knack she had of foreseeing things before they came to pass—although she did not like to disturb her friends by telling them her foreknowledge—even Miss Pole herself was breathless with astonishment when she came to tell us of the astounding piece of news. But I must recover myself; the contemplation of it, even at this distance of time, has taken away my breath and my grammar, and unless I subdue my emotion my spelling will go too.

We were sitting—Miss Matty and I—much as usual, she in the blue chintz easy-chair, with her back to the light and her knitting in her hand, I reading aloud *The St. James's Chronicle*. A few minutes more, and we should have gone to make the little alterations in dress usual before calling-time (twelve o'clock) in Cranford. I remember the scene and the date well. We had been talking of the signor's rapid recovery since the warmer weather had set in, and praising Mr. Hoggins's skill, and lamenting his want of refinement and manner (it seems a curious coincidence that this should have been our subject, but so it was), when a knock was heard—a caller's knock—three distinct taps—and we were flying (that is to say, Miss Matty could not walk very fast, having had a touch of rheumatism) to our rooms, to change cap and collars, when Miss Pole arrested us by calling out, as she came up the stairs, "Don't go—I can't wait—it is not twelve, I know—but never mind your dress—I must speak to you." We did our best to look as if it was not we who had made the hurried movement, the sound of which she had heard; for, of course, we did not like to have it supposed that we had any old clothes that it was convenient to wear out in the "sanctuary of home," as Miss Jenkyns once prettily called the back parlour, where she was tying up preserves. So we threw our gentility with double force into our manners, and very genteel we were for two minutes while Miss Pole recovered breath, and excited our curiosity strongly by lifting up her hands in amazement, and bringing them down in silence, as if what she had to say was too big for words, and could only be expressed by pantomime.

"What do you think, Miss Matty? What *do* you think? Lady Glenmire is to marry—is to be married, I mean—Lady Glenmire—Mr Hoggins—Mr. Hoggins—Mr. Hoggins is going to marry Lady Glenmire!"

"Marry!" said we. "Marry! Madness!"

"Marry!" said Miss Pole, with the decision that belonged to her character. "*I* said marry! as you do; and I also said, 'What a fool my lady is going to make of herself!' I could have said 'Madness!' but I controlled myself, for it was in a public shop that I heard of it. Where feminine delicacy is gone to,

I don't know. You and I, Miss Matty, would have been ashamed to have known that our marriage was spoken of in a grocer's shop, in the hearing of shop men!"

"But," said Miss Matty, sighing as one recovering from a blow, "perhaps it is not true. Perhaps we are doing her injustice."

"No," said Miss Pole. "I have taken care to ascertain that. I went straight to Mrs. Fitz-Adam, to borrow a cookery-book which I knew she had; and I introduced my congratulations *a propos* of the difficulty gentlemen must have in housekeeping; and Mrs. Fitz-Adam bridled up, and said that she believed it was true, though how and where I could have heard it she did not know. She said her brother and Lady Glenmire had come to an understanding at last. 'Understanding!' such a coarse word! But my lady will have to come down to many a want of refinement. I have reason to believe Mr. Hoggins sups on bread-and-cheese and beer every night."

"Marry!" said Miss Matty once again. "Well! I never thought of it. Two people that we know going to be married. It's coming very near!"

"So near that my heart stopped beating when I heard of it, while you might have counted twelve," said Miss Pole.

"One does not know whose turn may come next. Here, in Cranford, poor Lady Glenmire might have thought herself safe," said Miss Matty, with a gentle pity in her tones.

"Bah!" said Miss Pole, with a toss of her head. "Don't you remember poor dear Captain Brown's song, *Tibbie Fowler* and the line—

Set her on the Tintock Tap,
The wind will blaw a man till her.

That was because Tibbie Fowler was rich, I think."

"Well, there is a kind of attraction about Lady Glenmire that I, for one, should be ashamed to have."

I put in my wonder. "But how can she have fancied Mr. Hoggins? I am not surprised that Mr. Hoggins has liked her."

"Oh! I don't know. Mr. Hoggins is rich, and very pleasant-looking," said Miss Matty, "and very good-tempered and kind-hearted."

"She has married for an establishment, that's it. I suppose she takes the surgery with it," said Miss Pole, with a little dry laugh at her own joke. But, like many people who think they have made a severe and sarcastic speech, which yet is clever of its kind, she began to relax in her grimness from the moment when she made this allusion to the surgery; and we turned to speculate on the way in which Mrs. Jamieson would receive the news. The person whom she had left in charge of her house to keep off followers from her maids to set up a follower of her own! and that follower a man whom Mrs. Jamieson had tabooed as vulgar, and inadmissible to Cranford society, not merely on account of his name, but because of his voice, his complexion, his boots, smelling of the stable, and himself, smelling of drugs. Had he ever been to see Lady Glenmire at Mrs. Jamieson's? Chloride of lime would not purify the house in its owner's estimation if he had. Or had their interviews been confined to the occasional meetings in the chamber of the poor sick conjurer, to whom, with all our sense of the *mésalliance*, we could not help allowing that they had both been exceedingly kind? And now it turned out that a servant of Mrs. Jamieson's had been ill, and Mr. Hoggins had been attending her for some weeks. So the wolf had got into the fold, and now he was carrying off the shepherdess. What would Mrs. Jamieson say? We looked into the darkness of futurity as a child gazes after a rocket up in the cloudy sky, full of wondering expectation of the rattle, the discharge, and the brilliant shower of sparks and light. Then we brought ourselves down to earth and the present time by questioning each other (being all equally ignorant, and all equally without the slightest data to build any conclusions upon) as to when IT would take place? Where? How much a year Mr. Hoggins had? Whether she would drop her title? And how Martha and the other correct servants in Cranford would ever be brought to announce a married couple as Lady Glenmire and Mr. Hoggins? But would they be visited? Would Mrs. Jamieson let us? Or must we choose between the Honourable Mrs. Jamieson and the degraded Lady Glenmire? We all liked Lady Glenmire the best. She was bright, and kind, and sociable, and agreeable; and Mrs. Jamieson was dull, and inert, and pompous, and tiresome. But we had acknowledged the sway of the latter so long, that it seemed like a kind of disloyalty now even to meditate disobedience to the prohibition we anticipated.

Mrs. Forrester surprised us in our darned caps and patched collars; and we forgot all about them in our eagerness to see how she would bear the information, which we honourably left to Miss Pole to impart, although, if we had been inclined to take unfair advantage, we might have rushed in ourselves, for she had a most out-of-place fit of coughing for five minutes after Miss Forrester entered the room. I shall never forget the imploring expression of her eyes, as she looked at us over her pocket-handkerchief. They said as plain as words could speak, "Don't let Nature deprive me of the treasure which is mine, although for a time I can make no use of it." And we did not.

Mrs. Forrester's surprise was equal to ours; and her sense of injury rather greater, because she had to feel for her Order, and saw more fully than we could do how such conduct brought stains on the aristocracy.

When she and Miss Pole left us we endeavoured to subside into calmness; but Miss Matty was really upset by the intelligence she had heard. She reckoned it up, and it was more than fifteen years since she had heard of any of her acquaintance going to be married, with the one exception of Miss Jessie Brown; and, as she said, it gave her quite a shock, and made her feel as if she could not think what would happen, next.

I don't know whether it is a fancy of mine, or a real fact, but I have noticed that, just after the announcement of an engagement in any set, the unmarried ladies in that set flutter out in an unusual gaiety and newness of dress, as much as to say, in a tacit and unconscious manner, "We also are spinsters." Miss Matty and Miss Pole talked and thought more about bonnets, gowns, caps, and shawls, during the fortnight that succeeded this call, than I had known them do for years before. But it might be the spring weather, for it was a warm and pleasant March; and merinos and beavers, and woollen materials of all sorts, were but ungracious receptacles of the bright sun's glancing rays. It had not been Lady Glenmire's dress that had won Mr. Hoggins's heart, for she went about on her errands of kindness more shabby than ever. Although, in the hurried glimpses I caught of her at church or elsewhere, she appeared rather to shun meeting any of her friends, her face seemed to have almost something of the flush of youth in it; her lips looked redder and more trembling full than in their old compressed state, and her eyes dwelt on all things with a lingering light, as if she was leaning to love Cranford and its belongings. Mr. Hoggins looked broad and radiant, and creaked up the middle aisle at church in a brand-new pair of top-boots—an audible, as well as visible, sign of his purposed change of state; for the tradition went, that the boots he had worn till now were the identical pair in which he first set out on his rounds in Cranford twenty-five years ago; only they had been new-pieced, high and low, top and bottom, heel and sole, black leather and brown leather, more times than any one could tell.

None of the ladies in Cranford chose to sanction the marriage by congratulating either of the parties. We wished to ignore the whole affair until our liege lady, Mrs. Jamieson, returned. Till she came back to give us our cue, we felt that it would be better to consider the engagement in the same light as the Queen of Spain's legs—facts which certainly existed, but the less said about the better. This restraint upon our tongues—for, you see, if we did not speak about it to any of the parties concerned, how could we get answers to the questions that we longed to ask?—was beginning to be irksome, and our idea of the dignity of silence was paling before our curiosity, when another direction was given to our thoughts, by an announcement on the part of the principal shopkeeper of Cranford, who ranged the trades from grocer and cheesemonger to man-milliner, as occasion required, that the spring fashions were arrived, and would be exhibited on the following Tuesday at his rooms in High Street. Now, Miss Matty had been only waiting for this before buying herself a new silk gown. I had offered, it is true, to send to Drumble for patterns, but she had rejected my proposal, gently implying that she had not forgotten her disappointment about the sea green turban. I was thankful that I was on the spot now, to counteract the dazzling fascination of any yellow or scarlet silk.

I must say a word or two here about myself. I have spoken of my father's old friendship for the Jenkyns family; indeed, I am not sure if there was not some distant relationship. He had willingly allowed me to remain all the winter at Cranford, in consideration of a letter which Miss Matty had written to him about the time of the panic, in which I suspect she had exaggerated my powers and my bravery as a defender of the house. But now that the days were longer and more cheerful, he was beginning to urge the necessity of my return; and I only delayed in a sort of odd forlorn hope that if I could obtain any clear information, I might make the account given by the Signora of the Aga Jenkyns tally with that of "Poor Peter," his appearance and disappearance, which I had winnowed out of the conversation of Miss Pole and Mrs. Forrester.

CHAPTER 13

Stopped Payment

The very Tuesday morning on which Mr. Johnson was going to show the fashions, the post-woman brought two letters to the house. I say the post-woman, but I should say the post-man's wife. He was a lame shoemaker, a very clean, honest man, much respected in the town; but he never brought the letters round except on unusual occasions, such as Christmas Day or Good Friday; and on those days the letters, which should have been delivered at eight in the morning, did not make their appearance until two or three in the afternoon, for every one liked poor Thomas, and gave him a welcome on these festive occasions. He used to say, "He was welly stawed wi' eating, for there were three or four houses where nowt would serve 'em but he must share in their breakfast;" and by the time he had done his last breakfast, he came to some other friend who was beginning dinner; but come what might in the way of temptation, Tom was always sober, civil, and smiling; and, as Miss Jenkyns used to say, it was a lesson in patience, that she doubted not would call out that precious quality in some minds, where, but for Thomas, it might have lain dormant and undiscovered. Patience was certainly very dormant in Miss Jenkyns's mind. She was always expecting letters, and always drumming on the table till the post-woman had called or gone past. On Christmas Day and Good Friday she drummed from breakfast till church, from church-time till two o'clock—unless when the fire wanted stirring, when she invariably knocked down the fire-irons, and scolded Miss Matty for it. But equally certain was the hearty welcome and the good dinner for Thomas; Miss Jenkyns standing over him like a bold dragoon, questioning him as to his children, what they were doing, what school they went to; upbraiding him if another was likely to make its appearance, but sending even the little babies the shilling and the mince-pie which was her gift to all the children, with half a crown in addition for both father and mother. The post was not half of so much conse-quence to dear Miss Matty; but not for the world would she have diminished Thomas's welcome and his dole, though I could see that she felt rather shy over the ceremony, which had been regarded by Miss Jenkyns as a glorious opportunity for giving advice and benefiting her fellow-creatures. Miss Matty would steal the money all in a lump into his hand, as if she were ashamed of herself. Miss Jenkyns gave him each individual coin separate, with a "There! that's for yourself; that's for Jenny," etc. Miss Matty would even beckon Martha out of the kitchen while he ate his food: and once, to my knowledge, winked at its rapid disappearance into a blue cotton pocket-handkerchief. Miss Jenkyns almost scolded him if he did not leave a clean plate, however heaped it might have been, and gave an injunction with every mouthful.

I have wandered a long way from the two letters that awaited us on the breakfast-table that Tuesday morning. Mine was from my father. Miss Matty's was printed. My father's was just a man's letter; I mean it was very dull, and gave no information beyond that he was well, that they had had a good deal of rain, that trade was very stagnant, and there were many disagreeable rumours afloat. He then asked me if I knew whether Miss Matty still retained her shares in the Town and County Bank, as there were very unpleasant reports about it, though nothing more than he had always foreseen, and had prophesied to Miss Jenkyns years ago, when she would invest their little property in it—the only unwise step that clever woman had ever taken, to his knowledge (the only time she ever acted against his advice, I knew). However, if anything had gone wrong, of course I was not to think of leaving Miss Matty while I could be of any use, etc.

"Who is your letter from, my dear? Mine is a very civil invitation, signed 'Edwin Wilson,' asking me to attend an important meeting of the shareholders of the Town and County Bank, to be held in Drumble, on Thursday the twenty-first. I am sure it is very attentive of them to remember me."

I did not like to hear of this "important meeting," for, though I did not know much about business, I feared it confirmed what my father said: however, I thought, ill news came fast enough, so I resolved to say nothing about my alarm, and merely told her that my father was well, and sent his kind regards to her. She kept turning over and admiring her letter. At last she spoke—"I remember their sending one to Deborah just like this; but that I did not wonder at, for everybody knew she was so clear-headed. I am afraid I could not help them much; indeed, if they came to accounts, I should be quite in the way, for I never could do sums in my head. Deborah, I know, rather wished to go, and went so far as to order a new bonnet for the occasion; but, when the time came, she had a bad cold; so they sent her a very polite account of what they had done. Chosen a director, I think it was. Do you think they want me to help to choose a director? I am sure I should choose your father at once."

"My father has no shares in the bank," said I.

"Oh, no! I remember. He objected very much to Deborah's buying any, I believe. But she was quite the woman of business, and always judged for herself; and here, you see, they have paid eight per cent all these years."

It was a very uncomfortable subject to me, with my

half-knowledge; so I thought I would change the conversation, and I asked what time she thought we had better go and see the fashions. "Well, my dear," she said, "the thing is this, it is not etiquette to go till after twelve; but then, you see, all Cranford will be there, and one does not like to be too curious about dress and trimmings and caps with all the world looking on. It is never genteel to be over-curious on these occasions. Deborah had the knack of always looking as if the latest fashion was nothing new to her; a manner she had caught from Lady Arley, who did see all the new modes in London, you know. So I thought we would just slip down this morning, soon after breakfast—for I do want half a pound of tea—and then we could go up and examine the things at our leisure, and see exactly how my new silk gown must be made; and then, after twelve, we could go with our minds disengaged, and free from thoughts of dress."

We began to talk of Miss Matty's new silk gown. I discovered that it would be really the first time in her life that she had had to choose anything of consequence for herself: for Miss Jenkyns had always been the more decided character, whatever her taste might have been; and it is astonishing how such people carry the world before them by the mere force of will. Miss Matty anticipated the sight of the glossy folds with as much delight as if the five sovereigns, set apart for the purchase, could buy all the silks in the shop; and (remembering my own loss of two hours in a toy-shop before I could tell on what wonder to spend a silver threepence) I was very glad that we were going early, that dear Miss Matty might have leisure for the delights of perplexity.

If a happy sea-green could be met with, the gown was to be sea-green; if not, she inclined to maize, and I to silver gray; and we discussed the requisite number of breadths until we arrived at the shop-door. We were to buy the tea, select the silk, and then clamber up the iron corkscrew stairs that led into what was once a loft, though now a fashion showroom.

The young men at Mr. Johnson's had on their best looks, and their best cravats, and pivoted themselves over the counter with surprising activity. They wanted to show us upstairs at once; but on the principle of business first and pleasure afterwards, we stayed to purchase the tea. Here Miss Matty's absence of mind betrayed itself. If she was made aware that she had been drinking green tea at any time, she always thought it her duty to lie awake half through the night afterward (I have known her take it in ignorance many a time without such effects), and consequently green tea was prohibited the house; yet today she herself asked for the obnoxious article, under the impression that she was talking about the silk. However, the mistake was soon rectified; and then the silks were unrolled in good truth. By this time the shop was pretty well filled, for it was Cranford market day, and many of the farmers and country people from the neighbourhood round came in, sleeking down their hair, and glancing shyly about, from under their eyelids, as anxious to take back some notion of the unusual gaiety to the mistress or the lasses at home, and yet feeling that they were out of place among the smart shop men and gay shawls and summer prints. One honest-looking man, however, made his way up to the counter at which we stood, and boldly asked to look at a shawl or two. The other country folk confined themselves to the grocery side; but our neighbour was evidently too full of some kind intention towards mistress, wife, or daughter, to be shy; and it soon became a question with me, whether he or Miss Matty would keep their shop man the longest time. He thought each shawl more beautiful than the last; and, as for Miss Matty, she smiled and sighed over each fresh bale that was brought out; one colour set off another, and the heap together would, as she said, make even the rainbow look poor.

"I am afraid," said she, hesitating, "whichever I choose

I shall wish I had taken another. Look at this lovely crimson! it would be so warm in winter. But spring is coming on, you know. I wish I could have a gown for every season," said she, dropping her voice—as we all did in Cranford whenever we talked of anything we wished for but could not afford. "However," she continued, in a louder and more cheerful tone, "it would give me a great deal of trouble to take care of them if I had them; so, I think, I'll only take one. But which must it be, my dear?"

And now she hovered over a lilac with yellow spots, while I pulled out a quiet sage-green that had faded into insignificance under the more brilliant colours, but which was nevertheless a good silk in its humble way. Our attention was called off to our neighbour. He had chosen a shawl of about thirty shillings' value; and his face looked broadly happy, under the anticipation, no doubt, of the pleasant surprise he should give to some Molly or Jenny at home; he had tugged a leathern purse out of his breeches-pocket, and had offered a five-pound note in payment for the shawl, and for some parcels which had been brought round to him from the grocery counter; and it was just at this point that he attracted our notice. The shop man was examining the note with a puzzled doubtful air.

"Town and County Bank! I am not sure, sir, but I believe we have received a warning against notes issued by this bank only this morning. I will just step and ask Mr. Johnson, sir; but I'm afraid I must trouble you for payment in cash, or in a note of a different bank."

I never saw a man's countenance fall so suddenly into dismay and bewilderment. It was almost piteous to see the rapid change.

"Dang it!" said he, striking his fist down on the table, as if to try which was the harder, "the chap talks as if notes and gold were to be had for the picking up."

Miss Matty had forgotten her silk gown in her interest

for the man. I don't think she had caught the name of the bank, and in my nervous cowardice I was anxious that she should not; and so I began admiring the yellow-spotted lilac gown that I had been utterly condemning only a minute before. But it was of no use.

"What bank was it? I mean, what bank did your note belong to?"

"Town and County Bank."

"Let me see it," said she quietly to the shop man, gently taking it out of his hand, as he brought it back to return it to the farmer.

Mr. Johnson was very sorry, but, from information he had received, the notes issued by that bank were little better than waste paper.

"I don't understand it," said Miss Matty to me in a low voice. "That is our bank, is it not?—the Town and County Bank?"

"Yes," said I. "This lilac silk will just match the ribbons in your new cap, I believe," I continued, holding up the folds so as to catch the light, and wishing that the man would make haste and be gone, and yet having a new wonder, that had only just sprung up, how far it was wise or right in me to allow Miss Matty to make this expensive purchase, if the affairs of the bank were really so bad as the refusal of the note implied.

But Miss Matty put on the soft, dignified manner peculiar to her, rarely used, and yet which became her so well, and, laying her hand gently on mine, she said:

"Never mind the silks for a few minutes, dear. I don't understand you, sir," turning now to the shop man, who had been attending to the farmer. "Is this a forged note?"

"Oh, no, ma'am. It is a true note of its kind; but, you see, ma'am, it is a joint-stock bank, and there are reports out that it is likely to break. Mr. Johnson is only doing his duty, ma'am, as I am sure Mr. Dobson knows."

But Mr. Dobson could not respond to the appealing bow

by any answering smile. He was turning the note absently over in his fingers, looking gloomily enough at the parcel containing the lately-chosen shawl.

"It's hard upon a poor man," said he, "as earns every farthing with the sweat of his brow. However, there's no help for it. You must take back your shawl, my man; Lizzie must do on with her cloak for awhile. And yon figs for the little ones—I promised them to 'em—I'll take them; but the 'bacco and the other things—"

"I will give you five sovereigns for your note, my good man," said Miss Matty. "I think there is some great mistake about it, for I am one of the shareholders, and I'm sure they would have told me if things had not been going on right."

The shop man whispered a word or two across the table to Miss Matty. She looked at him with a dubious air.

"Perhaps so," said she. "But I don't pretend to understand business; I only know that if it is going to fail, and if honest people are to lose their money because they have taken our notes—I can't explain myself," said she, suddenly becoming aware that she had got into a long sentence with four people for audience—"only I would rather exchange my gold for the note, if you please," turning to the farmer, "and then you can take your wife the shawl. It is only going without my gown a few days longer," she continued, speaking to me. "Then, I have no doubt, everything will be cleared up."

"But if it is cleared up the wrong way?" said I.

"Why, then, it will only have been common honesty in me, as a shareholder, to have given this good man the money. I am quite clear about it in my own mind; but, you know, I can never speak quite as comprehensibly as others can; only you must give me your note, Mr. Dobson, if you please, and go on with your purchases with these sovereigns."

The man looked at her with silent gratitude—too awkward to put his thanks into words; but he hung back for a minute or two, fumbling with his note.

"I'm loth to make another one lose instead of me, if it is a loss; but, you see, five pounds is a deal of money to a man with a family; and, as you say, ten to one in a day or two the note will be as good as gold again."

"No hope of that, my friend," said the shop man.

"The more reason why I should take it," said Miss Matty, quietly. She pushed her sovereigns towards the man, who slowly laid his note down in exchange. "Thank you. I will wait a day or two before I purchase any of these silks; perhaps you will then have a greater choice. My dear, will you come upstairs?"

We inspected the fashions with as minute and curious an interest as if the gown to be made after them had been bought. I could not see that the little event in the shop below had in the least damped Miss Matty's curiosity as to the make of sleeves or the sit of skirts. She once or twice exchanged congratulations with me on our private and leisurely view of the bonnets and shawls; but I was, all the time, not so sure that our examination was so utterly private, for I caught glimpses of a figure dodging behind the cloaks and mantles; and, by a dexterous move, I came face to face with Miss Pole, also in morning costume (the principal feature of which was her being with out teeth, and wearing a veil to conceal the deficiency), come on the same errand as ourselves. But she quickly took her departure, because as she said, she had a bad headache, and did not feel herself up to conversation.

As we came down through the shop, the civil Mr. Johnson was awaiting us; he had been informed of the exchange of the note for gold, and with much good feeling and real kindness, but with a little want of tact, he wished to condole with Miss Matty, and impress upon her the true state of the case. I could only hope that he had heard an exaggerated rumour, for he said that her shares were worse than nothing, and that the bank could not pay a shilling in the pound. I was glad that Miss Matty seemed still a little incredulous; but I could not tell how much of this was real or assumed, with that self-control which seemed habitual to ladies of Miss Matty's standing in Cranford, who would have thought their dignity compromised by the slightest expression of surprise, dismay, or any similar feeling to an inferior in station, or in a public shop. However, we walked home very silently. I am ashamed to say I believe I was rather vexed and annoyed at Miss Matty's conduct in taking the note to herself so decidedly. I had so set my heart upon her having a new silk gown, which she wanted sadly; in general, she was so undecided anybody might turn her round; in this case I had felt that it was no use attempting it, but I was not the less put out at the result.

Somehow, after twelve o'clock, we both acknowledged to a sated curiosity about the fashions, and to a certain fatigue of body (which was, in fact, depression of mind) that indisposed us to go out again. But still we never spoke of the note; till, all at once, something possessed me to ask Miss Matty if she would think it her duty to offer sovereigns for all the notes of the Town and County Bank she met with? I could have bitten my tongue out the minute I had said it. She looked up rather sadly, and as if I had thrown a new perplexity into her already distressed mind; and for a minute or two she did not speak. Then she said—my own dear Miss Matty—without a shade of reproach in her voice—

"My dear, I never feel as if my mind was what people call very strong; and it's often hard enough work for me to settle what I ought to do with the case right before me. I was very thankful to—I was very thankful that I saw my duty this morning, with the poor man standing by me; but it's rather a strain upon me to keep thinking and thinking what I should do if such and such a thing happened; and, I believe, I had rather wait and see what really does come; and I don't doubt I shall be helped then, if I don't fidget myself, and get too anxious beforehand. You know, love, I'm not like Deborah. If Deborah had lived, I've no doubt she would have seen after them, before they had got themselves into this state."

We had neither of us much appetite for dinner, though we tried to talk cheerfully about indifferent things. When we returned into the drawing-room, Miss Matty unlocked her desk and began to look over her account-books. I was so penitent for what I had said in the morning, that I did not choose to take upon myself the presumption to suppose that I could assist her; I rather left her alone, as, with puzzled brow, her eye followed her pen up and down the ruled page. By and by she shut the book, locked her desk, and came and drew a chair to mine, where I sat in moody sorrow over the fire. I stole my hand into hers; she clasped it, but did not speak a word. At last she said, with forced composure in her voice, "If that bank goes wrong, I shall lose one hundred and forty-nine pounds thirteen shillings and fourpence a year; I shall only have thirteen pounds a year left." I squeezed her hand hard and tight. I did not know what to say. Presently (it was too dark to see her face) I felt her fingers work convulsively in my grasp; and I knew she was going to speak again. I heard the sobs in her voice as she said, "I hope it's not wrong—not wicked—but, oh! I am so glad poor Deborah is spared this. She could not have borne to come down in the world—she had such a noble, lofty spirit."

This was all she said about the sister who had insisted upon investing their little property in that unlucky bank. We were later in lighting the candle than usual that night, and until that light shamed us into speaking, we sat together very silently and sadly.

However, we took to our work after tea with a kind of forced cheerfulness (which soon became real as far as it went), talking of that never-ending wonder—Lady Glenmire's engagement. Miss Matty was almost coming round to think it a good thing.

"I don't mean to deny that men are troublesome in a

house. I don't judge from my own experience, for my father was neatness itself, and wiped his shoes on coming in as carefully as any woman; but still a man has a sort of knowledge of what should be done in difficulties that it is very pleasant to have one at hand ready to lean upon. Now, Lady Glenmire, instead of being tossed about, and wondering where she is to settle, will be certain of a home among pleasant and kind people, such as our good Miss Pole and Mrs. Forrester. And Mr. Hoggins is really a very personable man; and as for his manners, why, if they are not very polished, I have known people with very good hearts, and very clever minds too, who were not what some people reckoned refined, but who were both true and tender."

She fell off into a soft reverie about Mr. Holbrook, and I did not interrupt her, I was so busy maturing a plan I had had in my mind for some days, but which this threatened failure of the bank had brought to a crisis. That night, after Miss Matty went to bed, I treacherously lighted the candle again, and sat down in the drawing-room to compose a letter to the Aga Jenkyns, a letter which should affect him if he were Peter, and yet seem a mere statement of dry facts if he were a stranger. The church clock pealed out two before I had done.

The next morning news came, both official and otherwise, that the Town and County Bank had stopped payment. Miss Matty was ruined.

She tried to speak quietly to me; but when she came to the actual fact that she would have but about five shillings a week to live upon, she could not restrain a few tears.

"I am not crying for myself, dear," said she, wiping them away; "I believe I am crying for the very silly thought of how my mother would grieve if she could know; she always cared for us so much more than for herself. But many a poor person has less, and I am not very extravagant, and, thank God, when the neck of mutton, and Martha's wages, and the rent are paid, I have not a farthing owing. Poor Martha! I think she'll be sorry to leave me."

Miss Matty smiled at me through her tears, and she would fain have had me see only the smile, not the tears.

CHAPTER 14

Friends in Need

It was an example to me, and I fancy it might be to many others, to see how immediately Miss Matty set about the retrenchment which she knew to be right under her altered circumstances. While she went down to speak to Martha, and break the intelligence to her, I stole out with my letter to the Aga Jenkyns, and went to the Signor's lodgings to obtain the exact address. I bound the Signora to secrecy; and, indeed, her military manners had a degree of shortness and reserve in them which made her always say as little as possible, except when under the pressure of strong excitement. Moreover (which made my secret doubly sure), the Signor was now so far recovered as to be looking forward to travelling and conjuring again in the space of a few days, when he, his wife, and little Phoebe would leave Cranford. Indeed, I found him looking over a great black-and-red placard, in which the Signor Brunoni's accomplishments were set forth, and to which only the name of the town where he would next display them was wanting. He and his wife were so much absorbed in deciding where the red letters would come in with most effect (it might have been the Rubric for that matter), that it was some time before I could get my question asked privately, and not before I had given several decisions, the wisdom of which I questioned afterwards with equal sincerity as soon as the Signor threw in his doubts and reasons on the important subject. At last I got the address, spelt by sound, and very queer it looked. I dropped it in the post on my way home, and then for a minute I stood looking at the wooden pane with a gaping slit which divided me from the letter but a moment ago in my hand. It was gone from me like life, never to be recalled. It would get tossed about on the sea, and stained with sea-waves perhaps, and be carried among palm trees, and scented with all tropical fragrance; the little piece of paper, but an hour ago so familiar and commonplace, had set out on its race to the strange wild countries beyond the Ganges! But I could not afford to lose much time on this speculation. I hastened home, that Miss Matty might not miss me. Martha opened the door to me, her face swollen with crying. As soon as she saw me she burst out afresh, and taking hold of my arm she pulled me in, and banged the door to, in order to ask me if indeed it was all true that Miss Matty had been saying.

"I'll never leave her! No; I won't. I telled her so, and said I could not think how she could find in her heart to give me warning. I could not have had the face to do it, if I'd been her. I might ha' been just as good for nothing as Mrs. Fitz-Adam's Rosy, who struck for wages after living seven years and a half in one place. I said I was not one to go and serve Mammon at that rate; that I knew when I'd got a good missus, if she didn't know when she'd got a good servant—"

"But, Martha—" said I, cutting in while she wiped her eyes.

"Don't 'but Martha' me," she replied to my deprecatory tone.

"Listen to reason—"

"I'll not listen to reason," she said, now in full possession of her voice, which had been rather choked with sobbing. "Reason always means what someone else has got to say. Now

I think what I've got to say is good enough reason; but, reason or not, I'll say it, and I'll stick to it. I've money in the Savings Bank, and I've a good stock of clothes, and I'm not going to leave Miss Matty. No, not if she gives me warning every hour in the day!"

She put her arms akimbo, as much as to say she defied me; and, indeed, I could hardly tell how to begin to remonstrate with her, so much did I feel that Miss Matty, in her increasing infirmity, needed the attendance of this kind and faithful woman.

"Well—" said I at last.

"I'm thankful you begin with 'well!' If you'd ha' begun with 'but,' as you did afore, I'd not ha' listened to you. Now you may go on."

"I know you would be a great loss to Miss Matty, Martha—"

"I told her so. A loss she'd never cease to be sorry for," broke in Martha triumphantly.

"Still, she will have so little—so very little—to live upon, that I don't see just now how she could find you food—she will even be pressed for her own. I tell you this, Martha, because I feel you are like a friend to dear Miss Matty, but you know she might not like to have it spoken about."

Apparently this was even a blacker view of the subject than Miss Matty had presented to her, for Martha just sat down on the first chair that came to hand, and cried out loud (we had been standing in the kitchen).

At last she put her apron down, and looking me earnestly in the face, asked, "Was that the reason Miss Matty wouldn't order a pudding today? She said she had no great fancy for sweet things, and you and she would just have a mutton-chop. But I'll be up to her. Never you tell, but I'll make her a pudding, and a pudding she'll like, too, and I'll pay for it myself; so mind you see she eats it. Many a one has been comforted in their sorrow by seeing a good dish come upon the table."

I was rather glad that Martha's energy had taken the immediate and practical direction of pudding-making, for it staved off the quarrelsome discussion as to whether she should or should not leave Miss Matty's service. She began to tie on a clean apron, and otherwise prepare herself for going to the shop for the butter, eggs, and what else she might require. She would not use a scrap of the articles already in the house for her cookery, but went to an old teapot in which her private store of money was deposited, and took out what she wanted.

I found Miss Matty very quiet, and not a little sad; but by and by she tried to smile for my sake. It was settled that I was to write to my father, and ask him to come over and hold a consultation, and as soon as this letter was despatched we began to talk over future plans. Miss Matty's idea was to take a single room, and retain as much of her furniture as would be necessary to fit up this, and sell the rest, and there to quietly exist upon what would remain after paying the rent. For my part, I was more ambitious and less contented. I thought of all the things by which a woman, past middle age, and with the education common to ladies fifty years ago, could earn or add to a living without materially losing caste; but at length I put even this last clause on one side, and wondered what in the world Miss Matty could do.

Teaching was, of course, the first thing that suggested itself. If Miss Matty could teach children anything, it would throw her among the little elves in whom her soul delighted. I ran over her accomplishments. Once upon a time I had heard her say she could play "Ah! vous dirai-je, maman?" on the piano, but that was long, long ago; that faint shadow of musical acquirement had died out years before. She had also once been able to trace out patterns very nicely for muslin embroidery, by dint of placing a piece of silver paper over the design to be copied, and holding both against the window-pane while she marked the scollop and eyelet-holes. But that was her nearest approach to the accomplishment of drawing, and I did not think it would go very far. Then again, as to the branches of a solid English education—fancy work and the use of the globes—such as the mistress of the Ladies' Seminary, to which all the trades people in Cranford sent their daughters, professed to teach; Miss Matty's eyes were failing her, and I doubted if she could discover the number of threads in a worsted-work pattern, or rightly appreciate the different shades required for Queen Adelaide's face in the loyal wool-work now fashionable in Cranford. As for the use of the globes, I had never been able to find it out myself, so perhaps I was not a good judge of Miss Matty's capability of instructing in this branch of education; but it struck me that equators and tropics, and such mystical circles, were very imaginary lines indeed to her, and that she looked upon the signs of the zodiac as so many remnants of the black art.

What she piqued herself upon, as arts in which she excelled, was making candle-lighters, or "spills" (as she preferred calling them), of coloured paper, cut so as to resemble feathers, and knitting garters in a variety of dainty stitches. I had once said, on receiving a present of an elaborate pair, that I should feel quite tempted to drop one of them in the street, in order to have it admired; but I found this little joke (and it was a very little one) was such a distress to her sense of propriety, and was taken with such anxious, earnest alarm, lest the temptation might some day prove too strong for me, that I quite regretted having ventured upon it. A present of these delicately-wrought garters, a bunch of gay "spills," or a set of cards on which sewing-silk was wound in a mystical manner, were the well-known tokens of Miss Matty's favour. But would any one pay to have their children taught these arts? or, indeed, would Miss Matty sell for filthy lucre the knack and the skill with which she made trifles of value to those who loved her?

I had to come down to reading, writing, and arithmetic; and, in reading the chapter every morning, she always coughed before coming to long words. I doubted her power of getting through a genealogical chapter, with any number of coughs. Writing she did well and delicately—but spelling! She seemed to think that the more out-of the-way this was, and the more trouble it cost her, the greater the compliment she paid to her correspondent; and words that she would spell quite correctly in her letters to me became perfect enigmas when she wrote to my father.

No! there was nothing she could teach to the rising generation of Cranford, unless they had been quick learners and ready imitators of her patience, her humility, her sweetness, her quiet contentment with all that she could not do. I pondered and pondered until dinner was announced by Martha, with a face all blubbered and swollen with crying.

Miss Matty had a few little peculiarities which Martha was apt to regard as whims below her attention, and appeared to consider as childish fancies of which an old lady of fifty-eight should try to cure herself. But today everything was attended to with the most careful regard. The bread was cut to the imaginary pattern of excellence that existed in Miss Matty's mind, as being the way which her mother had preferred, the curtain was drawn so as to exclude the dead brick-wall of a neighbour's stables, and yet left so as to show every tender leaf of the poplar which was bursting into spring beauty. Martha's tone to Miss Matty was just such as that good, rough-spoken servant usually kept sacred for little children, and which I had never heard her use to any grown-up person.

I had forgotten to tell Miss Matty about the pudding, and I was afraid she might not do justice to it, for she had evidently very little appetite this day; so I seized the opportunity of letting her into the secret while Martha took away the meat. Miss Matty's eyes filled with tears, and she could not speak, either to express surprise or delight, when Martha returned bearing it aloft, made in the most wonderful representation of a lion *couchant* that ever was moulded. Martha's face gleamed with triumph as she set it down before Miss Matty with an exultant "There!" Miss Matty wanted to speak her thanks, but could not; so she took Martha's hand and shook it warmly, which set Martha off crying, and I myself could hardly keep up the necessary composure. Martha burst out of the room, and Miss Matty had to clear her voice once or twice before she could speak. At last she said, "I should like to keep this pudding under a glass shade, my dear!" and the notion of the lion *couchant*, with his currant eyes, being hoisted up to the place of honour on a mantel-piece, tickled my hysterical fancy, and I began to laugh, which rather surprised Miss Matty.

"I am sure, dear, I have seen uglier things under a glass shade before now," said she.

So had I, many a time and oft, and I accordingly composed my countenance (and now I could hardly keep from crying), and we both fell to upon the pudding, which was indeed excellent—only every morsel seemed to choke us, our hearts were so full.

We had too much to think about to talk much that afternoon. It passed over very tranquilly. But when the tea-urn was brought in a new thought came into my head. Why should not Miss Matty sell tea—be an agent to the East India Tea Company which then existed? I could see no objection to this plan, while the advantages were many—always supposing that Miss Matty could get over the degradation of condescending to anything like trade. Tea was neither greasy nor sticky—grease and stickiness being two of the qualities which Miss Matty could not endure. No shop window would be required. A small, genteel notification of her being licensed to sell tea would, it is true, be necessary, but I hoped that it could be placed where no one would see it. Neither was tea a heavy article, so as to tax Miss Matty's fragile strength. The only thing against my plan was the buying and selling involved.

While I was giving but absent answers to the questions Miss Matty was putting—almost as absently—we heard a clumping sound on the stairs, and a whispering outside the door, which, indeed, once opened and shut as if by some invisible agency. After a little while Martha came in, dragging after her a great tall young man, all crimson with shyness, and finding his only relief in perpetually sleeking down his hair.

"Please, ma'am, he's only Jem Hearn," said Martha, by way of an introduction; and so out of breath was she that I imagine she had had some bodily struggle before she could overcome his reluctance to be presented on the courtly scene of Miss Matilda Jenkyns's drawing-room.

"And, please, ma'am, he wants to marry me off-hand. And please, ma'am, we want to take a lodger—just one quiet lodger, to make our two ends meet; and we'd take any house conformable; and, oh, dear Miss Matty, if I may be so bold, would you have any objections to lodging with us? Jem wants it as much as I do." [To Jem:] "You great oaf! why can't you back me?—But he does want it all the same, very bad—don't you, Jem?—only, you see, he's dazed at being called on to speak before quality."

"It's not that," broke in Jem. "It's that you've taken me all on a sudden, and I didn't think for to get married so soon— and such quick work does flabbergast a man. It's not that I'm against it, ma'am" (addressing Miss Matty), "only Martha has such quick ways with her when once she takes a thing into her head; and marriage, ma'am—marriage nails a man, as one may say. I dare say I shan't mind it after it's once over."

"Please, ma'am," said Martha, who had plucked at his sleeve, and nudged him with her elbow, and otherwise tried to interrupt him all the time he had been speaking, "don't mind him, he'll come to; 'twas only last night he was an-axing me, and an-axing me, and all the more because I said I could not think of it for years to come, and now he's only taken aback with the suddenness of the joy; but you know, Jem, you are just as full as me about wanting a lodger." (Another great nudge.)

"Ay! if Miss Matty would lodge with us—otherwise I've no mind to be cumbered with strange folk in the house," said Jem, with a want of tact which I could see enraged Martha, who was trying to represent a lodger as the great object they wished to obtain, and that, in fact, Miss Matty would be smoothing their path and conferring a favour, if she would only come and live with them.

Miss Matty herself was bewildered by the pair. Their, or rather Martha's, sudden resolution in favour of matrimony staggered her, and stood between her and the contemplation of the plan which Martha had at heart. Miss Matty began:

"Marriage is a very solemn thing, Martha."

"It is indeed, ma'am," quoth Jem. "Not that I've no objections to Martha."

"You've never let me a-be for asking me for to fix when I would be married," said Martha, her face all a-fire, and ready to cry with vexation, "and now you're shaming me before my missus and all."

"Nay, now! Martha, don't ee! don't ee! only a man likes to have breathing-time," said Jem, trying to possess himself of her hand, but in vain. Then, seeing that she was more seriously hurt than he had imagined, he seemed to try to rally his scattered faculties, and with more straightforward dignity than, ten minutes before, I should have thought it possible for him to assume, he turned to Miss Matty, and said, "I hope, ma'am, you know that I am bound to respect every one who has been kind to Martha. I always looked on her as to be my wife—some time; and she has often and often spoken of you as the kindest lady that ever was; and though the plain truth is, I would not like to be troubled with lodgers of the common run, yet if, ma'am, you'd honour us by living with us, I'm sure Martha would do her best to make you comfortable; and I'd keep out of your way as much as I could, which I reckon would be the best kindness such an awkward chap as me could do."

Miss Matty had been very busy with taking off her spectacles, wiping them, and replacing them; but all she could say was, "Don't let any thought of me hurry you into marriage; pray don't! Marriage is such a very solemn thing!"

"But Miss Matilda will think of your plan, Martha," said I, struck with the advantages that it offered, and unwilling to lose the opportunity of considering about it. "And I'm sure neither she nor I can ever forget your kindness; nor yours either, Jem."

"Why, yes, ma'am! I'm sure I mean kindly, though I'm a bit fluttered by being pushed straight ahead into matrimony, as it were, and mayn't express myself conformable. But I'm sure I'm willing enough, and give me time to get accustomed; so, Martha, wench, what's the use of crying so, and slapping me if I come near?"

This last was *sotto voce*, and had the effect of making Martha bounce out of the room, to be followed and soothed by her lover. Whereupon Miss Matty sat down and cried very heartily, and accounted for it by saying that the thought of Martha being married so soon gave her quite a shock, and that she should never forgive herself if she thought she was hurrying the poor creature. I think my pity was more for Jem, of the two; but both Miss Matty and I appreciated to the full the kindness of the honest couple, although we said little about this, and a good deal about the chances and dangers of matrimony.

The next morning, very early, I received a note from Miss Pole, so mysteriously wrapped up, and with so many seals on it to secure secrecy, that I had to tear the paper before I could unfold it. And when I came to the writing I could hardly understand the meaning, it was so involved and oracular. I made out, however, that I was to go to Miss Pole's at eleven o'clock; the number *eleven* being written in full length as well as in numerals, and *A.M.* twice dashed under, as if I were very likely to come at eleven at night, when all Cranford was usually a-bed and asleep by ten. There was no signature except Miss Pole's initials reversed, P.E.; but, as Martha had given me the note "with Miss Pole's kind regards," it needed no wizard to find out who sent it; and, if the writer's name was to be kept secret, it was very well that I was alone when Martha delivered it.

I went as requested to Miss Pole's. The door was opened to me by her little maid, Lizzy, in Sunday trim, as if some grand event was impending over this work-day. And the drawing-room upstairs was arranged in accordance with this idea. The table was set out with the best green card-cloth, and writing materials upon it. On the little chiffonier was a tray with a newly decanted bottle of cowslip wine, and some ladies'-finger biscuits. Miss Pole herself was in solemn array, as if to receive visitors, although it was only eleven o'clock. Mrs. Forrester was there, crying quietly and sadly, and my arrival seemed only to call forth fresh tears. Before we had finished our greetings, performed with lugubrious mystery of demeanour, there was another rat-tat-tat, and Mrs. Fitz-Adam appeared, crimson with walking and excitement. It seemed as if this was all the company expected; for now Miss Pole made several demonstrations of being about to open the business of the meeting, by stirring the fire, opening and shutting the door, and coughing and blowing her nose. Then she arranged us all round the table, taking care to place me opposite to her; and last of all, she inquired of me if the sad report was true, as she feared it was, that Miss Matty had lost all her fortune?

Of course, I had but one answer to make; and I never saw more unaffected sorrow depicted on any countenances than I did there on the three before me.

"I wish Mrs. Jamieson was here!" said Mrs. Forrester at last; but to judge from Mrs. Fitz-Adam's face, she could not second the wish.

"But without Mrs. Jamieson," said Miss Pole, with just a sound of offended merit in her voice, "we, the ladies of Cranford, in my drawing-room assembled, can resolve upon something. I imagine we are none of us what may be called rich, though we all possess a genteel competency, sufficient for tastes that are elegant and refined, and would not, if they could, be vulgarly ostentatious." (Here I observed Miss Pole refer to a small card concealed in her hand, on which I imagine she had put down a few notes.)

"Miss Smith," she continued, addressing me (familiarly known as "Mary" to all the company assembled, but this was a state occasion), "I have conversed in private—I made it my business to do so yesterday afternoon—with these ladies on the misfortune which has happened to our friend, and one and all of us have agreed that, while we have a superfluity, it is not only a duty, but a pleasure—a true pleasure, Mary!"— her voice was rather choked just here, and she had to wipe her spectacles before she could go on—"to give what we can to assist her—Miss Matilda Jenkyns. Only in consideration of the feelings of delicate independence existing in the mind of every refined female"—I was sure she had got back to the card now—"we wish to contribute our mites in a secret and concealed manner, so as not to hurt the feelings I have referred to. And our object in requesting you to meet us this morning is that, believing you are the daughter—that your father is, in fact, her confidential adviser in all pecuniary matters, we imagined that, by consulting with him, you might devise some mode in which our contribution could be made to appear the legal due which Miss Matilda Jenkyns ought to receive from—Probably your father, knowing her investments, can fill up the blank."

Miss Pole concluded her address, and looked round for approval and agreement.

"I have expressed your meaning, ladies, have I not? And while Miss Smith considers what reply to make, allow me to offer you some little refreshment."

I had no great reply to make; I had more thankfulness at my heart for their kind thoughts than I cared to put into words; and so I only mumbled out something to the effect "that I would name what Miss Pole had said to my father, and that if anything could be arranged for dear Miss Matty"—and here I broke down utterly, and had to be refreshed with a glass of cowslip wine before I could check the crying which had been repressed for the last two or three days. The worst was, all the ladies cried in concert. Even Miss Pole cried, who had said a hundred times that to betray emotion before any one was a sign of weakness and want of self-control. She recovered herself into a slight degree of impatient anger, directed against me, as having set them all off; and, moreover, I think she was vexed that I could not make a speech back in return for hers; and if I had known beforehand what was to be said, and had a card on which to express the probable feelings that would rise in my heart, I would have tried to gratify her. As it was, Mrs. Forrester was the person to speak when we had recovered our composure.

"I don't mind, among friends, stating that I—no! I'm not poor exactly, but I don't think I'm what you may call rich; I wish I were, for dear Miss Matty's sake—but, if you please, I'll write down in a sealed paper what I can give. I only wish it was more; my dear Mary, I do indeed."

Now I saw why paper, pens, and ink were provided. Every lady wrote down the sum she could give annually, signed the paper, and sealed it mysteriously. If their proposal was acceded to, my father was to be allowed to open the papers, under pledge of secrecy. If not, they were to be returned to their writers.

When this ceremony had been gone through, I rose to depart; but each lady seemed to wish to have a private conference with me. Miss Pole kept me in the drawing-room to explain why, in Mrs. Jamieson's absence, she had taken the lead in this "movement," as she was pleased to call it, and also to inform me that she had heard from good sources that Mrs. Jamieson was coming home directly in a state of high displeasure against her sister-in-law, who was forthwith to leave her house, and was, she believed, to return to Edinburgh that very afternoon. Of course, this piece of intelligence could not be communicated before Mrs. Fitz-Adam, more especially as Miss Pole was inclined to think that Lady Glenmire's engagement to Mr. Hoggins could not possibly hold against the blaze of Mrs. Jamieson's displeasure. A few hearty inquiries after Miss Matty's health concluded my interview with Miss Pole.

On coming downstairs I found Mrs. Forrester waiting for me at the entrance to the dining-parlour; she drew me in, and, when the door was shut, she tried two or three times to begin on some subject, which was so unapproachable apparently, that I began to despair of our ever getting to a clear under-standing. At last out it came; the poor old lady trembling all the time as if it were a great crime which she was exposing to daylight, in telling me how very, very little she had to live upon; a confession which she was brought to make from a dread lest we should think that the small contribution named in her paper bore any proportion to her love and regard for Miss Matty. And yet that sum which she so eagerly relinquished was, in truth, more than a twentieth part of what she had to live upon, and keep house, and a little serving-maid, all as became one born a Tyrrell. And when the whole income does not nearly amount to a hundred pounds, to give up a twentieth of it will necessitate many careful economies, and many pieces of self-denial, small and insignificant in the world's account, but bearing a different value in another account-book that I have heard of. She did so wish she was rich, she said, and this wish she kept repeating, with no thought of herself in it, only with a longing, yearning desire to be able to heap up Miss Matty's measure of comforts.

It was some time before I could console her enough to leave her; and then, on quitting the house, I was waylaid by Mrs. Fitz-Adam, who had also her confidence to make of pretty nearly the opposite description. She had not liked to put down all that she could afford and was ready to give. She told me she thought she never could look Miss Matty in the face again if she presumed to be giving her so much as she should like to do. "Miss Matty!" continued she, "that I thought was such a fine young lady when I was nothing but a country girl, coming to market with eggs and butter and such like things. For my father, though well-to-do, would always make me go on as my mother had done before me, and I had to come into Cranford every Saturday, and see after sales, and prices, and what not. And one day, I remember, I met Miss Matty in the lane that leads to Combehurst; she was walking on the footpath, which, you know, is raised a good way above the road, and a gentleman rode beside her, and was talking to her, and she was looking down at some primroses she had gathered, and pulling them all to pieces, and I do believe she was crying. But after she had passed, she turned round and ran after me to ask—oh, so kindly—about my poor mother, who lay on her death-bed; and when I cried she took hold of my hand to comfort me— and the gentleman waiting for her all the time—and her poor heart very full of something, I am sure; and I thought it such an honour to be spoken to in that pretty way by the Rector's daughter, who visited at Arley Hall. I have loved her ever since, though perhaps I'd no right to do it; but if you can think of any way in which I might be allowed to give a little more without any one knowing it I should be so much obliged to you, my dear. And my brother would be delighted to doctor her for nothing—medicines, leeches, and all. I know that he and her ladyship (my dear, I little thought in the days I was telling you of that I should ever come to be sister-in-law to a ladyship!) would do anything for her. We all would."

I told her I was quite sure of it, and promised all sorts of things in my anxiety to get home to Miss Matty, who might well be wondering what had become of me—absent from her two hours without being able to account for it. She had taken very little note of time, however, as she had been occupied in numberless little arrangements preparatory to the great step of giving up her house. It was evidently a relief to her to be doing something in the way of retrenchment; for, as she said, whenever she paused to think, the recollection of the poor fellow with his bad five-pound note came over her, and she felt quite dishonest; only if it made her so uncomfortable, what must it not be doing to the directors of the bank, who must know so much more of the misery consequent upon this failure? She almost made me angry by dividing her sympathy between these directors (whom she imagined overwhelmed by self-reproach for the mismanagement of other people's affairs) and those who were suffering like her. Indeed, of the two, she seemed to think poverty a lighter burden than self-reproach; but I privately doubted if the directors would agree with her.

Old hoards were taken out and examined as to their money value, which luckily was small, or else I don't know how Miss Matty would have prevailed upon herself to part with such things as her mother's wedding-ring, the strange, uncouth brooch with which her father had disfigured his shirt-frill, etc. However, we arranged things a little in order as to their pecuniary estimation, and were all ready for my father when he came the next morning.

I am not going to weary you with the details of all the business we went through; and one reason for not telling about them is, that I did not understand what we were doing at the time, and cannot recollect it now. Miss Matty and I sat assenting to accounts, and schemes, and reports, and documents, of which I do not believe we either of us understood a word; for my father was clear-headed and decisive, and a capital man of business, and, if we made the slightest inquiry, or expressed the slightest want of comprehension, he had a sharp way of saying, "Eh? eh? it's as clear as daylight. What's your objection?" And as we had not comprehended anything of what he had proposed, we found it rather difficult to shape our objections; in fact, we never were sure if we had any. So presently Miss Matty got into a nervously acquiescent state, and said "Yes" and "Certainly" at every pause, whether required or not; but when I once joined in as chorus to a "Decidedly," pronounced by Miss Matty in a tremblingly dubious tone, my father fired round at me and asked me "What there was to decide?" And I am sure to this day I have never known. But, in justice to him, I must say he had come over from Drumble to help Miss Matty when he could ill spare the time, and when his own affairs were in a very anxious state.

While Miss Matty was out of the room giving orders for luncheon—and sadly perplexed between her desire of honouring my father by a delicate, dainty meal, and her conviction that she had no right, now that all her money was gone, to indulge this desire—I told him of the meeting of the Cranford ladies at Miss Pole's the day before. He kept brushing his hand before his eyes as I spoke; and when I went back to Martha's offer the evening before, of receiving Miss Matty as a lodger, he fairly walked away from me to the window, and began drumming with his fingers upon it. Then he turned abruptly round, and said, "See, Mary, how a good innocent life makes friends all around. Confound it! I could make a good lesson out of it if I were a parson; but, as it is, I can't get a tail to my sentences—only I'm sure you feel what I want to say. You and I will have a walk after lunch and talk a bit more about these plans."

The lunch—a hot, savoury mutton-chop, and a little of the cold loin sliced and fried—was now brought in. Every morsel of this last dish was finished, to Martha's great gratification. Then my father bluntly told Miss Matty he wanted to talk to me alone, and that he would stroll out and see some of the old places, and then I could tell her what plan we thought desirable. Just before we went out, she called me back and said, "Remember, dear, I'm the only one left—I mean, there's no one to be hurt by what I do. I'm willing to do anything that's right and honest; and I don't think, if Deborah knows where she is, she'll care so very much if I'm not genteel; because, you see, she'll know all, dear. Only let me see what I can do, and pay the poor people as far as I'm able."

I gave her a hearty kiss, and ran after my father. The result of our conversation was this. If all parties were agreeable, Martha and Jem were to be married with as little delay as possible, and they were to live on in Miss Matty's present abode; the sum which the Cranford ladies had agreed to contribute annually being sufficient to meet the greater part of the rent, and leaving Martha free to appropriate what Miss Matty should pay for her lodgings to any little extra comforts required. About the sale, my father was dubious at first. He said the old rectory furniture, however carefully used and reverently treated, would fetch very little; and that little would be but as a drop in the sea of the debts of the Town and County Bank. But when I represented how Miss Matty's tender conscience would be soothed by feeling that she had done what she could, he gave way; especially after I had told him the five-pound note adventure, and he had scolded me well for allowing it. I then alluded to my idea that she might add to her small income by selling tea; and, to my surprise (for I had nearly given up the plan), my father grasped at it with all the energy of a tradesman. I think he reckoned his chickens before they were hatched, for he immediately ran up the profits of the sales that she could effect in Cranford to more than twenty pounds a year. The small dining parlour was to be converted into a shop, without any of its degrading characteristics; a table was to be the counter, one window was to be retained unaltered, and the other changed into a glass door. I evidently rose in his estimation for having made his bright suggestion. I only hoped we should not both fall in Miss Matty's.

But she was patient and content with all our arrangements. She knew, she said, that we should do the best we could for her; and she only hoped, only stipulated, that she should pay every farthing that she could be said to owe, for her father's sake, who had been so respected in Cranford. My father and I had agreed to say as little as possible about the bank, indeed never to mention it again, if it could be helped. Some of the plans were evidently a little perplexing to her; but she had seen me sufficiently snubbed in the morning for want of comprehension to venture on too many inquiries now; and all passed over well, with a hope on her part that no one would be hurried into marriage on her account. When we came to the proposal that she should sell tea, I could see it was rather a shock to her; not on account of any personal loss of gentility involved, but only because she distrusted her own powers of action in a new line of life, and would timidly have preferred a little more privation to any exertion for which she feared she was unfitted. However, when she saw my father was bent upon it, she sighed, and said she would try; and, if she did not do well, of course she might give it up. One good thing about it was, she did not think men ever brought tea; and it was of men particularly she was afraid. They had such sharp, loud ways with them; and did up accounts, and counted their change so quickly! Now, if she might only sell comfits to children, she was sure she could please them!

CHAPTER 15

A Happy Return

Before I left Miss Matty at Cranford everything had been comfortably arranged for her. Even Mrs. Jamieson's approval of her selling tea had been gained. That oracle had taken a few days to consider whether by so doing Miss Matty would forfeit her right to the privileges of society in Cranford. I think she had some little idea of mortifying Lady Glenmire by the decision she gave at last; which was to this effect: that, whereas a married woman takes her husband's rank by the strict laws of precedence, an unmarried woman retains the station her father occupied. So Cranford was allowed to visit Miss Matty; and, whether allowed or not, it intended to visit Lady Glenmire.

But what was our surprise—our dismay—when we learned that Mr. and *Mrs. Hoggins* were returning on the following Tuesday. Mrs. Hoggins! Had she absolutely dropped her title, and so, in a spirit of bravado, cut the aristocracy to become a Hoggins! She, who might have been called Lady Glenmire to her dying day! Mrs. Jamieson was pleased. She said it only convinced her of what she had known from the first, that the creature had a low taste. But "the creature" looked very happy on Sunday at church; nor did we see it necessary to keep our veils down on that side of our bonnets on which Mr. and Mrs. Hoggins sat, as Mrs. Jamieson did; thereby missing all the smiling glory of his face, and all the becoming blushes of hers.

I am not sure if Martha and Jem looked more radiant in the afternoon, when they, too, made their first appearance. Mrs. Jamieson soothed the turbulence of her soul by having the blinds of her windows drawn down, as if for a funeral, on the day when Mr. and Mrs. Hoggins received callers; and it was with some difficulty that she was prevailed upon to continue *The St. James's Chronicle*, so indignant was she with its having inserted the announcement of the marriage.

Miss Matty's sale went off famously. She retained the furniture of her sitting-room and bedroom; the former of which she was to occupy till Martha could meet with a lodger who might wish to take it; and into this sitting-room and bedroom she had to cram all sorts of things, which were (the auctioneer assured her) brought in for her at the sale by an unknown friend. I always suspected Mrs. Fitz-Adam of this; but she must have had an accessory, who knew what articles were particularly regarded by Miss Matty on account of their associations with her early days. The rest of the house looked rather bare, to be sure; all except one tiny bedroom, of which my father allowed me to purchase the furniture for my occasional use in case of Miss Matty's illness.

I had expended my own small store in buying all manner of comfits and lozenges, in order to tempt the little people whom Miss Matty loved so much to come about her. Tea in bright green canisters, and comfits in tumblers—Miss Matty and I felt quite proud as we looked round us on the evening before the shop was to be opened. Martha had scoured the boarded floor to a white cleanness, and it was adorned with a brilliant piece of oil-cloth, on which customers were to stand before the table-counter. The wholesome smell of plaster and whitewash pervaded the apartment. A very small "Matilda Jenkyns, licensed to sell tea," was hidden under the lintel of the new door, and two boxes of tea, with cabalistic inscriptions all over them, stood ready to disgorge their contents into the canisters.

Miss Matty, as I ought to have mentioned before, had had some scruples of conscience at selling tea when there was already Mr. Johnson in the town, who included it among his numerous commodities; and, before she could quite reconcile herself to the adoption of her new business, she had trotted down to his shop, unknown to me, to tell him of the project that was entertained, and to inquire if it was likely to injure his business. My father called this idea of hers "great nonsense," and "wondered how trades people were to get on if there was to be a continual consulting of each other's interests, which would put a stop to all competition directly." And, perhaps, it would not have done in Drumble, but in Cranford it answered very well; for, not only did Mr. Johnson kindly put at rest all Miss Matty's scruples and fear of injuring his business, but I have reason to know he repeatedly sent customers to her, saying that the teas he kept were of a common kind, but that Miss Jenkyns had all the choice sorts. And expensive tea is a very favourite luxury with well-to-do trades-people and rich farmers' wives, who turn up their noses at the Congou and Souchong prevalent at many tables of gentility, and will have nothing else than Gunpowder and Pekoe for themselves.

But to return to Miss Matty. It was really very pleasant to see how her unselfishness and simple sense of justice called out the same good qualities in others. She never seemed to think any one would impose upon her, because she should be so grieved to do it to them. I have heard her put a stop to the asseverations of the man who brought her coals by quietly saying, "I am sure you would be sorry to bring me wrong weight;" and if the coals were short measure that time, I don't believe they ever were again. People would have felt as much ashamed of presuming on her good faith as they would have done on that of a child. But my father says "such simplicity might be very well in Cranford, but would never do in the world." And I fancy the world must be very bad, for with all my father's suspicions of every one with whom he has dealings, and in spite of all his many precautions, he lost upwards of a thousand pounds by roguery only last year.

I just stayed long enough to establish Miss Matty in her new mode of life, and to pack up the library, which the Rector had purchased. He had written a very kind letter to Miss Matty, saying "how glad he should be to take a library, so well selected as he knew that the late Mr. Jenkyns's must have been, at any valuation put upon them." And when she agreed to this, with a touch of sorrowful gladness that they would go back to the rectory and be arranged on the accustomed walls once more, he sent word that he feared that he had not room for them all, and perhaps Miss Matty would kindly allow him to leave some volumes on her shelves. But Miss Matty said that she had her Bible and Johnson's Dictionary, and should not have much time for reading, she was afraid; still, I retained a few books out of consideration for the Rector's kindness.

The money which he had paid, and that produced by the sale, was partly expended in the stock of tea, and part of it was invested against a rainy day—*i.e.*, old age or illness. It was but a small sum, it is true; and it occasioned a few evasions of truth and white lies (all of which I think very wrong indeed—in theory—and would rather not put in practice), for we knew Miss Matty would be perplexed as to her duty if she were aware of any little reserve-fund being made for her while the debts of the bank remained unpaid. Moreover, she had never been told of the way in which her friends were contributing to pay the rent. I should have liked to tell her this, but the mystery of the affair gave a piquancy to their deed of kindness which the ladies were unwilling to give up; and at first Martha had to shirk many a perplexed question as to her ways and means of living in such a house, but by and by Miss Matty's prudent uneasiness sank down into acquiescence with the existing arrangement.

I left Miss Matty with a good heart. Her sales of tea during the first two days had surpassed my most sanguine expectations. The whole country round seemed to be all out of tea at once. The only alteration I could have desired in Miss Matty's way of doing business was, that she should not have so plaintively entreated some of her customers not to buy green tea—running it down as slow poison, sure to destroy the nerves, and produce all manner of evil. Their pertinacity in taking it, in spite of all her warnings, distressed her so much that I really thought she would relinquish the sale of it, and so lose half her custom; and I was driven to my wits' end for instances of longevity entirely attributable to a persevering use of green tea. But the final argument, which settled the question, was a happy reference of mine to the train-oil and tallow candles which the Esquimaux not only enjoy but digest. After that she acknowledged that "one man's meat might be another man's poison," and contented herself thenceforward with an occasional remonstrance when she thought the purchaser was too young and innocent to be acquainted with the evil effects green tea produced on some constitutions, and an habitual sigh when people old enough to choose more wisely would prefer it.

I went over from Drumble once a quarter at least to settle the accounts, and see after the necessary business letters. And, speaking of letters, I began to be very much ashamed of remembering my letter to the Aga Jenkyns, and very glad I had never named my writing to any one. I only hoped the letter was lost. No answer came. No sign was made.

About a year after Miss Matty set up shop, I received one of Martha's hieroglyphics, begging me to come to Cranford very soon. I was afraid that Miss Matty was ill, and went off that very afternoon, and took Martha by surprise when she saw me on opening the door. We went into the kitchen, as usual, to have our confidential conference, and then Martha told me she was expecting her confinement very soon—in a week or two; and she did not think Miss Matty was aware of it, and she wanted me to break the news to her, "for indeed, miss," continued Martha, crying hysterically, "I'm afraid she won't approve of it, and I'm sure I don't know who is to take care of her as she should be taken care of when I am laid up."

I comforted Martha by telling her I would remain till she was about again, and only wished she had told me her reason for this sudden summons, as then I would have brought the requisite stock of clothes. But Martha was so tearful and tender-spirited, and unlike her usual self, that I said as little as possible about myself, and endeavoured rather to comfort Martha under all the probable and possible misfortunes which came crowding upon her imagination.

I then stole out of the house door, and made my appearance as if I were a customer in the shop, just to take Miss Matty by surprise, and gain an idea of how she looked in her new situation. It was warm May weather, so only the little half-door was closed; and Miss Matty sat behind her counter knitting an elaborate pair of garters; elaborate they seemed to me, but the difficult stitch was no weight upon her mind, for she was singing in a low voice to herself as her needles went rapidly in and out. I call it singing, but I dare say a musician would not use that word to the tuneless yet sweet humming of the low worn voice. I found out from the words, far more than from the attempt at the tune, that it was the Old Hundredth she was crooning to herself; but the quiet, continuous sound told of content, and gave me a pleasant feeling, as I stood in the street just outside the door, quite in harmony with that soft May morning. I went in. At first she did not catch who it was, and stood up as if to serve me; but in another minute watchful pussy had clutched her knitting, which was dropped in eager joy at seeing me. I found, after we had had a little conversation, that it was as Martha said, and that Miss Matty had no idea of the approaching household event. So I thought I would let things take their course, secure that when I went to her with the baby in my arms, I should obtain that forgiveness for Martha which she was needlessly frightening herself into believing that Miss Matty would with-hold, under some notion that the new claimant would require attentions from its mother that it would be faithless treason to Miss Matty to render.

But I was right. I think that must be an hereditary quality, for my father says he is scarcely ever wrong. One morning, within a week after I arrived, I went to call Miss Matty, with a little bundle of flannel in my arms. She was very much awe-struck when I showed her what it was, and asked for her spectacles off the dressing-table, and looked at it curiously, with a sort of tender wonder at its small perfec-tion of parts. She could not banish the thought of the surprise all day, but went about on tiptoe, and was very silent. But she stole up to see Martha, and they both cried with joy, and she got into a complimentary speech to Jem, and did not know how to get out of it again, and was only extricated from her dilemma by the sound of the shop-bell, which was an equal relief to the shy, proud, honest Jem, who shook my hand so vigorously when I congratulated him, that I think I feel the pain of it yet.

I had a busy life while Martha was laid up. I attended on Miss Matty, and prepared her meals; I cast up her accounts, and examined into the state of her canisters and tumblers. I helped her, too, occasionally, in the shop; and it gave me no small amusement, and sometimes a little uneasiness, to watch her ways there. If a little child came in to ask for an ounce of almond-comfits (and four of the large kind which Miss Matty sold weighed that much), she always added one more by "way of make weight," as she called it, although the scale was handsomely turned before; and when I remonstrated against this, her reply was, "The little things like it so much!" There was no use in telling her that the fifth comfit weighed a quarter of an ounce, and made every sale into a loss to her pocket. So I remembered the green tea, and winged my shaft with a feather out of her own plumage. I told her how unwholesome almond-comfits were, and how ill excess in them might make the little children. This argument produced some effect; for, henceforward, instead of the fifth comfit, she always told them to hold out their tiny palms, into which she shook either peppermint or ginger lozenges, as a preventive to the dangers that might arise from the previous sale. Altogether, the lozenge trade, conducted on these principles, did not promise to be remunerative; but I was happy to find she had made more than twenty pounds during the last year by her sales of tea; and, moreover, that now she was accustomed to it, she did not dislike the employment, which brought her into kindly intercourse with many of the people round about. If she gave them good weight, they, in their turn, brought many a little country present to the "old Rector's daughter"; a cream cheese, a few new-laid eggs, a little fresh ripe fruit, a bunch of flowers. The counter was quite loaded with these offerings sometimes, as she told me.

As for Cranford in general, it was going on much as usual. The Jamieson and Hoggins feud still raged, if a feud it could be called, when only one side cared much about it. Mr. and Mrs. Hoggins were very happy together, and, like most very happy people, quite ready to be friendly; indeed, Mrs. Hoggins was really desirous to be restored to Mrs. Jamieson's good graces, because of the former intimacy. But Mrs. Jamieson considered their very happiness an insult to the Glenmire family, to which she had still the honour to belong, and she doggedly refused and rejected every advance. Mr. Mulliner, like a faithful clansman, espoused his mistress's side with ardour. If he saw either Mr. or Mrs. Hoggins, he would cross the street, and appear absorbed in the contemplation of life in general, and his own path in particular, until he had passed them by. Miss Pole used to amuse herself with wondering what in the world Mrs. Jamieson would do, if either she, or Mr. Mulliner, or any other member of her household was taken ill; she could hardly have the face to call in Mr. Hoggins after the way she had behaved to them. Miss Pole grew quite impatient for some indisposition or accident to befall Mrs. Jamieson or her dependents, in order that Cranford might see how she would act under the perplexing circumstances.

Martha was beginning to go about again, and I had already fixed a limit, not very far distant, to my visit, when one afternoon, as I was sitting in the shop-parlour with Miss Matty—I remember the weather was colder now than it had been in May, three weeks before, and we had a fire and kept the door fully closed—we saw a gentleman go slowly past the window, and then stand opposite to the door, as if looking out for the name which we had so carefully hidden. He took out a double eye-glass and peered about for some time before he could discover it. Then he came in. And, all on a sudden, it flashed across me that it was the Aga himself! For his clothes had an out-of-the-way foreign cut about them, and his face was deep brown, as if tanned and re-tanned by the sun. His complexion contrasted oddly with his plentiful snow-white hair, his eyes were dark and piercing, and he had an odd way of contracting them and puckering up his cheeks into innumerable wrinkles when he looked earnestly at objects. He did so to Miss Matty when he first came in. His glance had first caught and lingered a little upon me, but then turned, with the peculiar searching look I have described, to Miss Matty. She was a little fluttered and nervous, but no more so than she always was when any man came into her shop. She thought that he would probably have a note, or a sovereign at least, for which she would have to give change, which was an operation she very much disliked to perform. But the present customer stood opposite to her, without asking for anything, only looking fixedly at her as he drummed upon the table with his fingers, just for all the world as Miss Jenkyns used to do. Miss Matty was on the point of asking him what he wanted (as she told me afterwards), when he turned sharp to me: "Is your name Mary Smith?"

"Yes!" said I.

All my doubts as to his identity were set at rest, and I only wondered what he would say or do next, and how Miss Matty would stand the joyful shock of what he had to reveal. Apparently he was at a loss how to announce himself, for he looked round at last in search of something to buy, so as to gain time, and, as it happened, his eye caught on the almond comfits, and he boldly asked for a pound of "those things." I doubt if Miss Matty had a whole pound in the shop, and, besides the unusual magnitude of the order, she was distressed with the idea of the indigestion they would produce, taken in such unlimited quantities. She looked up to remonstrate. Something of tender relaxation in his face struck home to her heart. She said, "It is—oh, sir! can you be Peter?" and trembled from head to foot. In a moment he was round the table and had her in his arms, sobbing the tearless cries of old age. I brought her a glass of wine, for indeed her colour had changed so as to alarm me and Mr. Peter too. He kept saying, "I have been too sudden for you, Matty—I have, my little girl."

I proposed that she should go at once up into the drawing-room and lie down on the sofa there. She looked wistfully at her brother, whose hand she had held tight, even when nearly fainting; but, on his assuring her that he would not leave her, she allowed him to carry her upstairs.

I thought that the best I could do was to run and put the kettle on the fire for early tea, and then to attend to the shop, leaving the brother and sister to exchange some of the many thousand things they must have to say. I had also to break the news to Martha, who received it with a burst of tears which nearly infected me. She kept recovering herself to ask me if I was sure it was indeed Miss Matty's brother, for I had mentioned that he had gray hair, and she had always heard that he was a very handsome young man. Something of the same kind perplexed Miss Matty at tea-time, when she was installed in the great easy-chair opposite to Mr. Jenkyns's in order to gaze her fill. She could hardly drink for looking at him, and as for eating, that was out of the question.

"I suppose hot climates age people very quickly," said she, almost to herself. "When you left Cranford you had not a gray hair in your head."

"But how many years ago is that?" said Mr. Peter, smiling.

"Ah, true! yes, I suppose you and I are getting old. But still I did not think we were so very old! But white hair is very becoming to you, Peter," she continued—a little afraid lest she had hurt him by revealing how his appearance had impressed her.

"I suppose I forgot dates too, Matty, for what do you think I have brought for you from India? I have an Indian muslin gown and a pearl necklace for you somewhere in my chest at Portsmouth." He smiled as if amused at the idea of the incongruity of his presents with the appearance of his sister; but this did not strike her all at once, while the elegance of the articles did. I could see that for a moment her imagination dwelt complacently on the idea of herself thus attired; and instinctively she put her hand up to her throat—that little delicate throat which (as Miss Pole had told me) had been one of her youthful charms; but the hand met the touch of folds of soft muslin in which she was always swathed up to her chin, and the sensation recalled a sense of the unsuitableness of a pearl necklace to her age. She said, "I'm afraid I'm too old; but it was very kind of you to think of it. They are just what I should have liked years ago—when I was young."

"So I thought, my little Matty. I remembered your tastes; they were so like my dear mother's." At the mention of that name the brother and sister clasped each other's hands yet more fondly, and, although they were perfectly silent, I fancied they might have something to say if they were unchecked by my presence, and I got up to arrange my room for Mr. Peter's occupation that night, intending myself to share Miss Matty's bed. But at my movement he started up. "I must go and settle about a room at the George. My carpet-bag is there too."

"No!" said Miss Matty, in great distress; "you must not go; please, dear Peter—pray, Mary!—oh! you must not go!"

She was so much agitated that we both promised everything she wished. Peter sat down again and gave her his hand, which for better security she held in both of hers, and I left the room to accomplish my arrangements.

Long, long into the night, far, far into the morning did Miss Matty and I talk. She had much to tell me of her brother's life and adventures, which he had communicated to her as they had sat alone. She said all was thoroughly clear to her; but I never quite understood the whole story; and, when in after days I lost my awe of Mr. Peter enough to question him myself, he laughed at my curiosity, and told me stories that sounded so very much like Baron Münchausen's that I was sure he was making fun of me. What I heard from Miss Matty was that he had been a volunteer at the siege of Rangoon; had been taken prisoner by the Burmese; had somehow obtained favour and eventual freedom from knowing how to bleed the chief of the small tribe in some case of dangerous illness; that on his release from years of captivity he had his letters returned from England with the ominous word "Dead" marked upon them; and believing himself to be the last of his race, he had settled down as an indigo planter, and had proposed to spend the remainder of his life in the country to whose inhabitants and modes of life he had become habituated, when my letter had reached him; and, with the odd vehemence which characterised him in age as it had done in youth, he had sold his land and all his possessions to the first purchaser, and come home to the poor old sister, who was more glad and rich than any princess when she looked at him. She talked me to sleep at last, and then I was awakened by a slight sound at the door, for which she begged my pardon as she crept penitently into bed; but it seems that when I could no longer confirm her belief that the long-lost was really here—under the same roof—she had begun to fear lest it was only a waking dream of hers; that there never had been a Peter sitting by her all that blessed evening—but that the real Peter lay dead far away beneath some wild sea-wave, or under some strange eastern tree. And so strong had this nervous feeling of hers become, that she was fain to get up and go and convince herself that he was really there by listening through the door to his even, regular breathing. I don't like to call it snoring, but I heard it myself through two closed doors—and by and by it soothed Miss Matty to sleep.

I don't believe Mr. Peter came home from India as rich as a nabob; he even considered himself poor, but neither he nor Miss Matty cared much about that. At any rate, he had enough to live upon "very genteelly" at Cranford; he and Miss Matty together. And a day or two after his arrival, the shop was closed, while troops of little urchins gleefully awaited the shower of comfits and lozenges that came from time to time down upon their faces as they stood up-gazing at Miss Matty's drawing-room windows. Occasionally Miss Matty would say to them (half-hidden behind the curtain), "My dear children, don't make yourselves ill;" but a strong arm pulled her back, and a more rattling shower than ever succeeded. A part of the tea was sent in presents to the Cranford ladies; and some of it was distributed among the old people who remembered Mr. Peter in the days of his frolicsome youth. The Indian muslin gown was reserved for darling Flora Gordon (Miss Jessie Brown's daughter). The Gordons had been on the continent for the last few years, but were now expected to return very soon; and Miss Matty, in her sisterly pride, anticipated great delight in the joy of showing them Mr. Peter. The pearl necklace disappeared; and about that time many handsome and useful presents made their appearance in the households of Miss Pole and Mrs. Forrester; and some rare and delicate Indian ornaments graced the drawing-rooms of Mrs. Jamieson and Mrs. Fitz-Adam. I myself was not forgotten. Among other things, I had the handsomest-bound and best edition of Dr. Johnson's works that could be procured; and dear Miss Matty, with tears in her eyes, begged me to consider it as a present from her sister as well as herself. In short, no one was forgotten; and, what was more, every one, however insignificant, who had shown kindness to Miss Matty at any time, was sure of Mr. Peter's cordial regard.

CHAPTER 16

Peace to Cranford

It was not surprising that Mr. Peter became such a favourite at Cranford. The ladies vied with each other who should admire him most; and no wonder, for their quiet lives were astonishingly stirred up by the arrival from India—especially as the person arrived told more wonderful stories than Sinbad the Sailor; and, as Miss Pole said, was quite as good as an Arabian night any evening. For my own part, I had vibrated all my life between Drumble and Cranford, and I thought it was quite possible that all Mr. Peter's stories might be true, although wonderful; but when I found that, if we swallowed an anecdote of tolerable magnitude one week, we had the dose considerably increased the next, I began to have my doubts; especially as I noticed that when his sister was present the accounts of Indian life were comparatively tame; not that she knew more than we did, perhaps less. I noticed also that when the rector came to call, Mr. Peter talked in a different way about the countries he had been in. But I don't think the ladies in Cranford would have considered him such a wonderful traveller if they had only heard him talk in the quiet way he did to him. They liked him the better, indeed, for being what they called "so very Oriental."

One day, at a select party in his honour, which Miss Pole gave, and from which, as Mrs. Jamieson honoured it with her presence, and had even offered to send Mr. Mulliner to wait, Mr. and Mrs. Hoggins and Mrs. Fitz-Adam were necessarily excluded—one day at Miss Pole's, Mr. Peter said he was tired of sitting upright against the hard-backed, uneasy chairs, and asked if he might not indulge himself in sitting cross-legged. Miss Pole's consent was eagerly given, and down he went with the utmost gravity. But when Miss Pole asked me, in an audible whisper, "if he did not remind me of the Father of the Faithful" I could not help thinking of poor Simon Jones, the lame tailor; and while Mrs. Jamieson slowly commented on the elegance and convenience of the attitude, I remembered how we had all followed that lady's lead in condemning Mr. Hoggins for vulgarity because he simply crossed his legs as he sat still on his chair. Many of Mr. Peter's ways of eating were a little strange amongst such ladies as Miss Pole, and Miss Matty, and Mrs. Jamieson, especially when I recollected the untasted green peas and two-pronged forks at poor Mr. Holbrook's dinner.

The mention of that gentleman's name recalls to my mind a conversation between Mr. Peter and Miss Matty one evening in the summer after he returned to Cranford. The day had been very hot, and Miss Matty had been much oppressed by the weather, in the heat of which her brother revelled. I remember that she had been unable to nurse Martha's baby, which had become her favourite employment of late, and which was as much at home in her arms as in its mother's, as long as it remained a light-weight, portable by one so fragile as Miss Matty. This day to which I refer, Miss Matty had seemed more than usually feeble and languid, and only revived when the sun went down, and her sofa was wheeled to the open window, through which, although it looked into the neighbouring street of Cranford, the fragrant smell of the neighbouring hayfields came in every now and then, borne by the soft breezes that stirred the dull air of the summer twilight, and then died away. The silence of the sultry atmosphere was lost in the murmuring noises which came in from many an open window and door; even the children were abroad in the street, late as it was (between ten and eleven), enjoying the game of play for which they had not had spirits during the heat of the day. It was a source of satisfaction to Miss Matty to see how few candles were lighted, even in the apartments of those houses from which issued the greatest signs of life. Mr. Peter, Miss Matty, and I had all been quiet, each with a separate reverie, for some little time, when Mr. Peter broke in:

"Do you know, little Matty, I could have sworn you were on the high-road to matrimony when I left England that last time! If anybody had told me you would have lived and died an old maid then, I should have laughed in their faces."

Miss Matty made no reply, and I tried in vain to think of some subject which should effectually turn the conversation; but I was very stupid; and before I spoke he went on:

"It was Holbrook, that fine manly fellow who lived at Woodley, that I used to think would carry off my little Matty. You would not think it now, I dare say, Mary; but this sister of mine was once a very pretty girl—at least, I thought so, and so I've a notion did poor Holbrook. What business had he to die before I came home to thank him for all his kindness to a good-for-nothing cub as I was? It was that that made me first think he cared for you; for in all our fishing expeditions it was Matty, Matty, we talked about. Poor Deborah! What a lecture she read me on having asked him home to lunch one day, when she had seen the Arley carriage in the town, and thought that my lady might call. Well, that's long years ago; more than half a life-time, and yet it seems like yesterday! I don't know a fellow I should have liked better as a brother-in-law. You must have played your cards badly, my little Matty, somehow or another—wanted your brother to be a good go-between, eh, little one?" said he, putting out his hand to take hold of hers as she lay on the sofa. "Why, what's this?

you're shivering and shaking, Matty, with that confounded open window. Shut it, Mary, this minute!"

I did so, and then stooped down to kiss Miss Matty, and see if she really were chilled. She caught at my hand, and gave it a hard squeeze—but unconsciously, I think—for in a minute or two she spoke to us quite in her usual voice, and smiled our uneasiness away, although she patiently submitted to the prescriptions we enforced of a warm bed and a glass of weak negus. I was to leave Cranford the next day, and before I went I saw that all the effects of the open window had quite vanished. I had superintended most of the alterations necessary in the house and household during the latter weeks of my stay. The shop was once more a parlour; the empty, resounding rooms again furnished up to the very garrets.

There had been some talk of establishing Martha and Jem in another house, but Miss Matty would not hear of this. Indeed, I never saw her so much roused as when Miss Pole had assumed it to be the most desirable arrangement. As long as Martha would remain with Miss Matty, Miss Matty was only too thankful to have her about her; yes, and Jem too, who was a very pleasant man to have in the house, for she never saw him from week's end to week's end. And as for the probable children, if they would all turn out such little darlings as her god-daughter, Matilda, she should not mind the number, if Martha didn't. Besides, the next was to be called Deborah—a point which Miss Matty had reluctantly yielded to Martha's stubborn determination that her first-born was to be Matilda. So Miss Pole had to lower her colours, and even her voice, as she said to me that, as Mr. and Mrs. Hearn were still to go on living in the same house with Miss Matty, we had certainly done a wise thing in hiring Martha's niece as an auxiliary.

I left Miss Matty and Mr. Peter most comfortable and contented; the only subject for regret to the tender heart of the one, and the social friendly nature of the other, being the unfortunate quarrel between Mrs. Jamieson and the plebeian Hogginses and their following. In joke, I prophesied one day that this would only last until Mrs. Jamieson or Mr. Mulliner were ill, in which case they would only be too glad to be friends with Mr. Hoggins; but Miss Matty did not like my looking forward to anything like illness in so light a manner, and before the year was out all had come round in a far more satisfactory way.

I received two Cranford letters on one auspicious October morning. Both Miss Pole and Miss Matty wrote to ask me to come over to meet the Gordons, who had returned to England alive and well with their two children, now almost grown up. Dear Jessie Brown had kept her old kind nature, although she had changed her name and station; and she wrote to say that she and Major Gordon expected to be in Cranford on the fourteenth, and she hoped and begged to be remembered to Mrs. Jamieson (named first, as became her honourable station), Miss Pole, and Miss Matty—could she ever forget their kindness to her poor father and sister?—Mrs. Forrester, Mr. Hoggins (and here again came in an allusion to kindness shown to the dead long ago), his new wife, who, as such, must allow Mrs. Gordon to desire to make her acquaintance, and who was, moreover, an old Scotch friend of her husband's. In short, every one was named, from the rector—who had been appointed to Cranford in the interim between Captain Brown's death and Miss Jessie's marriage, and was now associated with the latter event—down to Miss Betty Barker. All were asked to the luncheon; all except Mrs. Fitz-Adam, who had come to live in Cranford since Miss Jessie Brown's days, and whom I found rather moping on account of the omission. People wondered at Miss Betty Barker's being included in the honourable list; but, then, as Miss Pole said, we must remember the disregard of the genteel proprieties of life in which the poor Captain had educated his girls, and for his sake we swallowed our pride. Indeed, Mrs. Jamieson rather took it as a compliment, as putting Miss Betty (formerly *her* maid) on a level with "those Hogginses."

But when I arrived in Cranford, nothing was as yet ascertained of Mrs. Jamieson's own intentions; would the honourable lady go, or would she not? Mr. Peter declared that she should and she would; Miss Pole shook her head and desponded. But Mr. Peter was a man of resources. In the first place, he persuaded Miss Matty to write to Mrs. Gordon, and to tell her of Mrs. Fitz-Adam's existence, and to beg that one so kind, and cordial, and generous, might be included in the pleasant invitation. An answer came back by return of post, with a pretty little note for Mrs. Fitz-Adam, and a request that Miss Matty would deliver it herself and explain the previous omission. Mrs. Fitz-Adam was as pleased as could be, and thanked Miss Matty over and over again. Mr. Peter had said, "Leave Mrs. Jamieson to me;" so we did; especially as we knew nothing that we could do to alter her determination if once formed.

I did not know, nor did Miss Matty, how things were going on, until Miss Pole asked me, just the day before Mrs. Gordon came, if I thought there was anything between Mr. Peter and Mrs. Jamieson in the matrimonial line, for that Mrs. Jamieson was really going to the lunch at the "George." She had sent Mr. Mulliner down to desire that there might be a footstool put to the warmest seat in the room, as she meant to come, and knew that their chairs were very high. Miss Pole had picked this piece of news up, and from it she conjectured all sorts of things, and bemoaned yet more. "If Peter should marry, what would become of poor dear Miss Matty? And Mrs. Jamieson, of all people!" Miss Pole seemed to think there were other ladies in Cranford who would have done more credit to his choice, and I think she must have had some one who was unmarried in her head, for she kept saying "It was so wanting in delicacy in a widow to think of such a thing."

When I got back to Miss Matty's I really did begin to

think that Mr. Peter might be thinking of Mrs. Jamieson for a wife, and I was as unhappy as Miss Pole about it. He had the proof sheet of a great placard in his hand. "Signor Brunoni, Magician to the King of Delhi, the Rajah of Oude, and the Great Lama of Thibet," etc., etc., was going to "perform in Cranford for one night only," the very next night; and Miss Matty, exultant, showed me a letter from the Gordons, promising to remain over this gaiety, which Miss Matty said was entirely Peter's doing. He had written to ask the signor to come, and was to be at all the expenses of the affair. Tickets were to be sent gratis to as many as the room would hold. In short, Miss Matty was charmed with the plan, and said that tomorrow Cranford would remind her of the Preston Guild, to which she had been in her youth—a luncheon at the George, with the dear Gordons, and the Signor in the assembly room in the evening. But I—I looked only at the fatal words—

"*Under the Patronage of the* Honourable Mrs. Jamieson."

She, then, was chosen to preside over this entertainment of Mr. Peter's; she was perhaps going to displace my dear Miss Matty in his heart, and make her life lonely once more. I could not look forward to the morrow with any pleasure; and every innocent anticipation of Miss Matty's only served to add to my annoyance.

So, angry and irritated, and exaggerating every little incident which could add to my irritation, I went on till we were all assembled in the great parlour at the "George." Major and Mrs. Gordon and pretty Flora and Mr. Ludovic were all as bright and handsome and friendly as could be; but I could hardly attend to them for watching Mr. Peter, and I saw that Miss Pole was equally busy. I had never seen Mrs. Jamieson so roused and animated before; her face looked full of interest in what Mr. Peter was saying. I drew near to listen. My relief was great when I caught that his words were not words of love, but that, for all his grave face, he was at his old tricks. He was telling her of his travels in India, and describing the wonderful height of the Himalaya mountains; one touch after another added to their size, and each exceeded the former in absurdity; but Mrs. Jamieson really enjoyed all in perfect good faith. I supposed she required strong stimulants to excite her to come out of her apathy. Mr. Peter wound up his account by saying that, of course, at that altitude there were none of the animals to be found that existed in the lower regions; the game—everything was different. Firing one day at some flying creature, he was very much dismayed, when it fell, to find that he had shot a cherubim! Mr. Peter caught my eye at this moment, and gave me such a funny twinkle, that I felt sure he had no thoughts of Mrs. Jamieson as a wife from that time. She looked uncomfortably amazed.

"But, Mr. Peter, shooting a cherubim—don't you think—I am afraid that was sacrilege!"

Mr. Peter composed his countenance in a moment, and appeared shocked at the idea, which, as he said truly enough, was now presented to him for the first time; but then Mrs. Jamieson must remember that he had been living for a long time among savages—all of whom were heathens—some of them, he was afraid, were downright Dissenters. Then, seeing Miss Matty draw near, he hastily changed the conversation, and, after a little while, turning to me, he said, "Don't be shocked, prim little Mary, at all my wonderful stories. I consider Mrs. Jamieson fair game, and besides I am bent on propitiating her, and the first step towards it is keeping her well awake. I bribed her here by asking her to let me have her name as patroness for my poor conjurer this evening; and I don't want to give her time enough to get up her rancour against the Hogginses, who are just coming in. I want every-body to be friends, for it harasses Matty so much to hear of these quarrels. I shall go at it again by and by, so you need not look shocked. I intend to enter the assembly room tonight with Mrs. Jamieson on one side, and my lady, Mrs. Hoggins, on the other. You see if I don't."

Somehow or another he did; and fairly got them into conversation together. Major and Mrs. Gordon helped at the good work with their perfect ignorance of any existing coolness between any of the inhabitants of Cranford.

Ever since that day there has been the old friendly sociability in Cranford society; which I am thankful for, because of my dear Miss Matty's love of peace and kindliness. We all love Miss Matty, and I somehow think we are all of us better when she is near us.

Classic Literature: Words and Phrases
adapted from the Collins English Dictionary

Accoucheur NOUN a male midwife or doctor ❑ *I think my sister must have had some general idea that I was a young offender whom an Accoucheur Policemen had taken up (on my birthday) and delivered over to her* (*Great Expectations* by Charles Dickens)

addled ADJ confused and unable to think properly ❑ *But she counted and counted till she got that addled* (*The Adventures of Huckleberry Finn* by Mark Twain)

admiration NOUN amazement or wonder ❑ *lifting up his hands and eyes by way of admiration* (*Gulliver's Travels* by Jonathan Swift)

afeard ADJ afeard means afraid ❑ *shake it – and don't be afeard* (*The Adventures of Huckleberry Finn* by Mark Twain)

affected VERB affected means followed ❑ *Hadst thou affected sweet divinity* (*Doctor Faustus 5.2* by Christopher Marlowe)

aground ADV when a boat runs aground, it touches the ground in a shallow part of the water and gets stuck ❑ *what kep' you? – boat get aground?* (*The Adventures of Huckleberry Finn* by Mark Twain)

ague NOUN a fever in which the patient has alternate hot and cold shivering fits ❑ *his exposure to the wet and cold had brought on fever and ague* (*Oliver Twist* by Charles Dickens)

alchemy ADJ false or worthless ❑ *all wealth alchemy* (*The Sun Rising* by John Donne)

all alike PHRASE the same all the time ❑ *Love, all alike* (*The Sun Rising* by John Donne)

alow and aloft PHRASE alow means in the lower part or bottom, and aloft means on the top, so alow and aloft means on the top and in the bottom or throughout ❑ *Someone's turned the chest out alow and aloft* (*Treasure Island* by Robert Louis Stevenson)

ambuscade NOUN ambuscade is not a proper word. Tom means an ambush, which is when a group of people attack their enemies, after hiding and waiting for them ❑ *and so we would lie in ambuscade, as he called it* (*The Adventures of Huckleberry Finn* by Mark Twain)

amiable ADJ likeable or pleasant ❑ *Such amiable qualities must speak for themselves* (*Pride and Prejudice* by Jane Austen)

amulet NOUN an amulet is a charm thought to drive away evil spirits. ❑ *uttered phrases at once occult and familiar, like the amulet worn on the heart* (*Silas Marner* by George Eliot)

amusement NOUN here amusement means a strange and disturbing puzzle ❑ *this was an amusement the other way* (*Robinson Crusoe* by Daniel Defoe)

ancient NOUN an ancient was the flag displayed on a ship to show which country it belongs to. It is also called the ensign ❑ *her ancient and pendants out* (*Robinson Crusoe* by Daniel Defoe)

antic ADJ here antic means horrible or grotesque ❑ *armed and dressed after a very antic manner* (*Gulliver's Travels* by Jonathan Swift)

antics NOUN antics is an old word meaning clowns, or people who do silly things to make other people laugh ❑ *And point like antics at his triple crown* (*Doctor Faustus 3.2* by Christopher Marlowe)

appanage NOUN an appanage is a living allowance ❑ *As if loveliness were not the special prerogative of woman – her legitimate appanage and heritage!* (*Jane Eyre* by Charlotte Brontë)

appended VERB appended means attached or added to ❑ *and these words appended* (*Treasure Island* by Robert Louis Stevenson)

approver NOUN an approver is someone who gives evidence against someone he used to work with ❑ *Mr. Noah Claypole: receiving a free pardon from the Crown in consequence of being admitted approver against Fagin* (*Oliver Twist* by Charles Dickens)

areas NOUN the areas is the space, below street level, in front of the basement of a house ❑ *The Dodger had a vicious propensity, too, of pulling the caps from the heads of small boys and tossing them down areas* (*Oliver Twist* by Charles Dickens)

argument NOUN theme or important idea or subject which runs through a piece of writing ❑ *Thrice needful to the argument which now* (*The Prelude* by William Wordsworth) .

artificially ADJ artfully or cleverly ❑ *and he with a sharp flint sharpened very artificially* (*Gulliver's Travels* by Jonathan Swift)

artist NOUN here artist means a skilled workman ❑ *This man was a most ingenious artist* (*Gulliver's Travels* by Jonathan Swift)

assizes NOUN assizes were regular court sessions which a visiting judge was in charge of ❑ *you shall hang at the next assizes* (*Treasure Island* by Robert Louis Stevenson)

attraction NOUN gravitation, or Newton's theory of gravitation ❑ *he predicted the same fate to attraction* (*Gulliver's Travels* by Jonathan Swift)

aver VERB to aver is to claim something strongly ❑ *for Jem Rodney,*

the mole catcher, averred that one evening as he was returning homeward (*Silas Marner* by George Eliot)

baby NOUN here baby means doll, which is a child's toy that looks like a small person ❑ *and skilful dressing her baby* (*Gulliver's Travels* by Jonathan Swift)

bagatelle NOUN bagatelle is a game rather like billiards and pool ❑ *Breakfast had been ordered at a pleasant little tavern, a mile or so away upon the rising ground beyond the green; and there was a bagatelle board in the room, in case we should desire to unbend our minds after the solemnity.* (*Great Expectations* by Charles Dickens)

bah EXCLAM Bah is an exclamation of frustration or anger ❑ *"Bah," said Scrooge.* (*A Christmas Carol* by Charles Dickens)

bairn NOUN a northern word for child ❑ *Who has taught you those fine words, my bairn?* (*Wuthering Heights* by Emily Brontë)

bait VERB to bait means to stop on a journey to take refreshment ❑ *So, when they stopped to bait the horse, and ate and drank and enjoyed themselves, I could touch nothing that they touched, but kept my fast unbroken.* (*David Copperfield* by Charles Dickens)

balustrade NOUN a balustrade is a row of vertical columns that form railings ❑ *but I mean to say you might have got a hearse up that staircase, and taken it broadwise, with the splinter-bar towards the wall, and the door towards the balustrades: and done it easy* (*A Christmas Carol* by Charles Dickens)

bandbox NOUN a large lightweight box for carrying bonnets or hats ❑ *I am glad I bought my bonnet, if it is only for the fun of having another bandbox* (*Pride and Prejudice* by Jane Austen)

barren NOUN a barren here is a stretch or expanse of barren land ❑ *a line* of upright stones, continued the length of the barren (*Wuthering Heights* by Emily Brontë)

basin NOUN a basin was a cup without a handle ❑ *who is drinking his tea out of a basin* (*Wuthering Heights* by Emily Brontë)

battalia NOUN the order of battle ❑ *till I saw part of his army in battalia* (*Gulliver's Travels* by Jonathan Swift)

battery NOUN a Battery is a fort or a place where guns are positioned ❑ *You bring the lot to me, at that old Battery over yonder* (*Great Expectations* by Charles Dickens)

battledore and shuttlecock NOUN The game battledore and shuttlecock was an early version of the game now known as badminton. The aim of the early game was simply to keep the shuttlecock from hitting the ground. ❑ *Battledore and shuttlecock's a wery good game vhen you an't the shuttlecock and two lawyers the battledores, in which case it gets too excitin' to be pleasant* (*Pickwick Papers* by Charles Dickens)

beadle NOUN a beadle was a local official who had power over the poor ❑ *But these impertinences were speedily checked by the evidence of the surgeon, and the testimony of the beadle* (*Oliver Twist* by Charles Dickens)

bearings NOUN the bearings of a place are the measurements or directions that are used to find or locate it ❑ *the bearings of the island* (*Treasure Island* by Robert Louis Stevenson)

beaufet NOUN a beaufet was a sideboard ❑ *and sweet-cake from the beaufet* (*Emma* by Jane Austen)

beck NOUN a beck is a small stream ❑ *a beck which follows the bend of the glen* (*Wuthering Heights* by Emily Brontë)

bedight VERB decorated ❑ *and bedight with Christmas holly stuck into the top.* (*A Christmas Carol* by Charles Dickens)

Bedlam NOUN Bedlam was a lunatic asylum in London which had statues carved by Caius Gabriel Cibber at its entrance ❑ *Bedlam, and those carved maniacs at the gates* (*The Prelude* by William Wordsworth)

beeves NOUN oxen or castrated bulls which are animals used for pulling vehicles or carrying things ❑ *to deliver in every morning six beeves* (*Gulliver's Travels* by Jonathan Swift)

begot VERB created or caused ❑ *Begot in thee* (*On His Mistress* by John Donne)

behoof NOUN behoof means benefit ❑ *"Yes, young man," said he, releasing the handle of the article in question, retiring a step or two from my table, and speaking for the behoof of the landlord and waiter at the door* (*Great Expectations* by Charles Dickens)

berth NOUN a berth is a bed on a boat ❑ *this is the berth for me* (*Treasure Island* by Robert Louis Stevenson)

bevers NOUN a bever was a snack, or small portion of food, eaten between main meals ❑ *that buys me thirty meals a day and ten bevers* (*Doctor Faustus 2.1* by Christopher Marlowe)

bilge water NOUN the bilge is the widest part of a ship's bottom, and the bilge water is the dirty water that collects there ❑ *no gush of bilge-water had turned it to fetid puddle* (*Jane Eyre* by Charlotte Brontë)

bills NOUN bills is an old term meaning prescription. A prescription is the piece of paper on which your doctor writes an order for medicine and which you give to a chemist to get the medicine ❑ *Are not thy bills hung up as monuments* (*Doctor Faustus 1.1* by Christopher Marlowe)

black cap NOUN a judge wore a black cap when he was about to sentence a prisoner to death ❑ *The judge* assumed the black cap, and the prisoner still stood with the same air and gesture. (*Oliver Twist* by Charles Dickens)

black gentleman NOUN this was another word for the devil ❑ *for she is as impatient as the black gentleman* (*Emma* by Jane Austen)

boot-jack NOUN a wooden device to help take boots off ❑ *The speaker appeared to throw a boot-jack, or some such article, at the person he addressed* (*Oliver Twist* by Charles Dickens)

booty NOUN booty means treasure or prizes ❑ *would be inclined to give up their booty in payment of the dead man's debts* (*Treasure Island* by Robert Louis Stevenson)

Bow Street runner PHRASE Bow Street runners were the first British police force, set up by the author Henry Fielding in the eighteenth century ❑ *as would have convinced a judge or a Bow Street runner* (*Treasure Island* by Robert Louis Stevenson)

brawn NOUN brawn is a dish of meat which is set in jelly ❑ *Heaped up upon the floor, to form a kind of throne, were turkeys, geese, game, poultry, brawn, great joints of meat, sucking-pigs* (*A Christmas Carol* by Charles Dickens)

bray VERB when a donkey brays, it makes a loud, harsh sound ❑ *and she doesn't bray like a jackass* (*The Adventures of Huckleberry Finn* by Mark Twain)

break VERB in order to train a horse you first have to break it ❑*"If a high-mettled creature like this," said he, "can't be broken by fair means, she will never be good for anything"* (*Black Beauty* by Anna Sewell)

bullyragging VERB bullyragging is an old word which means bullying. To bullyrag someone is to threaten or force someone to do something they don't want to do ❑ *and a lot of loafers bullyragging him for sport* (*The Adventures of Huckleberry Finn* by Mark Twain)

but PREP except for (this) ❑ *but this, all pleasures fancies be* (*The Good-Morrow* by John Donne)

by hand PHRASE by hand was a common expression of the time meaning that baby had been fed either using a spoon or a bottle rather than by breast-feeding ❑ *My sister, Mrs. Joe Gargery, was more than twenty years older than I, and had established a great reputation with herself . . . because she had bought me up 'by hand'* (*Great Expectations* by Charles Dickens)

bye-spots NOUN bye-spots are lonely places ❑ *and bye-spots of tales rich with indigenous produce* (*The Prelude* by William Wordsworth)

calico NOUN calico is plain white fabric made from cotton ❑ *There was two old dirty calico dresses* (*The Adventures of Huckleberry Finn* by Mark Twain)

camp-fever NOUN camp-fever was another word for the disease typhus ❑ *during a severe camp-fever* (*Emma* by Jane Austen)

cant NOUN cant is insincere or empty talk ❑ *"Man," said the Ghost, "if man you be in heart, not adamant, forbear that wicked cant until you have discovered What the surplus is, and Where it is."* (*A Christmas Carol* by Charles Dickens)

canty ADJ canty means lively, full of life ❑ *My mother lived til eighty, a canty dame to the last* (*Wuthering Heights* by Emily Brontë)

canvas VERB to canvas is to discuss ❑ *We think so very differently on this point Mr Knightley, that there can be no use in canvassing it* (*Emma* by Jane Austen)

capital ADJ capital means excellent or extremely good ❑ *for it's capital, so shady, light, and big* (*Little Women* by Louisa May Alcott)

capstan NOUN a capstan is a device used on a ship to lift sails and anchors ❑ *capstans going, ships going out to sea, and unintelligible sea creatures* *roaring curses over the bulwarks at respondent lightermen* (*Great Expectations* by Charles Dickens)

case-bottle NOUN a square bottle designed to fit with others into a case ❑ *The spirit being set before him in a huge case-bottle, which had originally come out of some ship's locker* (*The Old Curiosity Shop* by Charles Dickens)

casement NOUN casement is a word meaning window. The teacher in Nicholas Nickleby misspells window showing what a bad teacher he is ❑ *W-i-n, win, d-e-r, der, winder, a casement.'* (*Nicholas Nickleby* by Charles Dickens)

cataleptic ADJ a cataleptic fit is one in which the victim goes into a trance-like state and remains still for a long time ❑ *It was at this point in their history that Silas's cataleptic fit occurred during the prayer-meeting* (*Silas Marner* by George Eliot)

cauldron NOUN a cauldron is a large cooking pot made of metal ❑ *stirring a large cauldron which seemed to be full of soup* (*Alice's Adventures in Wonderland* by Lewis Carroll)

cephalic ADJ cephalic means to do with the head ❑ *with ink composed of a cephalic tincture* (*Gulliver's Travels* by Jonathan Swift)

chaise and four NOUN a closed four-wheel carriage pulled by four horses ❑ *he came down on Monday in a chaise and four to see the place* (*Pride and Prejudice* by Jane Austen)

chamberlain NOUN the main servant in a household ❑ *In those times a bed was always to be got there at any hour of the night, and the chamberlain, letting me in at his ready wicket, lighted the candle next in order on his shelf* (*Great Expectations* by Charles Dickens)

characters NOUN distinguishing marks ❑ *Impressed upon all forms the characters* (*The Prelude* by William Wordsworth)

chary ADJ cautious ❑ *I should have been chary of discussing my guardian too freely even with her* (*Great Expectations* by Charles Dickens)

cherishes VERB here cherishes means cheers or brightens ❑ *some philosophic song of Truth that cherishes our daily life* (*The Prelude* by William Wordsworth)

chickens' meat PHRASE chickens' meat is an old term which means chickens' feed or food ❑ *I had shook a bag of chickens' meat out in that place* (*Robinson Crusoe* by Daniel Defoe)

chimeras NOUN a chimera is an unrealistic idea or a wish which is unlikely to be fulfilled ❑ *with many other wild impossible chimeras* (*Gulliver's Travels* by Jonathan Swift)

chines NOUN chine is a cut of meat that includes part or all of the backbone of the animal ❑ *and they found hams and chines uncut* (*Silas Marner* by George Eliot)

chits NOUN chits is a slang word which means girls ❑ *I hate affected, niminy-piminy chits!* (*Little Women* by Louisa May Alcott)

chopped VERB chopped means come suddenly or accidentally ❑ *if I had chopped upon them* (*Robinson Crusoe* by Daniel Defoe)

chute NOUN a narrow channel ❑ *One morning about day-break, I found a canoe and crossed over a chute to the main shore* (*The Adventures of Huckleberry Finn* by Mark Twain)

circumspection NOUN careful observation of events and circumstances; caution ❑ *I honour your circumspection* (*Pride and Prejudice* by Jane Austen)

clambered VERB clambered means to climb somewhere with difficulty, usually using your hands and your feet ❑ *he clambered up and down stairs* (*Treasure Island* by Robert Louis Stevenson)

clime NOUN climate ❑ *no season knows nor clime* (*The Sun Rising* by John Donne)

clinched VERB clenched ❑ *the tops whereof I could but just reach with my fist clinched* (*Gulliver's Travels* by Jonathan Swift)

close chair NOUN a close chair is a sedan chair, which is an covered chair which has room for one person. The sedan chair is carried on two poles by two men, one in front and one behind ❑ *persuaded even the Empress herself to let me hold her in her close chair* (*Gulliver's Travels* by Jonathan Swift)

clown NOUN clown here means peasant or person who lives off the land ❑ *In ancient days by emperor and clown* (*Ode on a Nightingale* by John Keats)

coalheaver NOUN a coalheaver loaded coal onto ships using a spade ❑ *Good, strong, wholesome medicine, as was given with great success to two Irish labourers and a coalheaver* (*Oliver Twist* by Charles Dickens)

coal-whippers NOUN men who worked at docks using machines to load coal onto ships ❑ *here, were colliers by the score and score, with the coal-whippers plunging off stages on deck* (*Great Expectations* by Charles Dickens)

cobweb NOUN a cobweb is the net which a spider makes for catching insects ❑ *the walls and ceilings were all hung round with cobwebs* (*Gulliver's Travels* by Jonathan Swift)

coddling VERB coddling means to treat someone too kindly or protect them too much ❑ *and I've been coddling the fellow as if I'd been his grandmother* (*Little Women* by Louisa May Alcott)

coil NOUN coil means noise or fuss or disturbance ❑ *What a coil is there?* (*Doctor Faustus 4.7* by Christopher Marlowe)

collared VERB to collar something is a slang term which means to capture. In this sentence, it means he stole it [the money] ❑ *he collared it* (*The Adventures of Huckleberry Finn* by Mark Twain)

colling VERB colling is an old word which means to embrace and kiss ❑ *and no clasping and colling at all* (*Tess of the D'Urbervilles* by Thomas Hardy)

colloquies NOUN colloquy is a formal conversation or dialogue ❑ *Such colloquies have occupied many a pair of pale-faced weavers* (*Silas Marner* by George Eliot)

comfit NOUN sugar-covered pieces of fruit or nut eaten as sweets ❑ *and pulled out a box of comfits* (*Alice's Adventures in Wonderland* by Lewis Carroll)

coming out VERB when a girl came out in society it meant she was of marriageable age. In order to 'come out' girls were expecting to attend balls and other parties during a season ❑ *The younger girls formed hopes of coming out a year or two sooner than they might otherwise have done* (*Pride and Prejudice* by Jane Austen)

commit VERB commit means arrest or stop ❑ *Commit the rascals* (*Doctor Faustus 4.7* by Christopher Marlowe)

commodious ADJ commodious means convenient ❑ *the most commodious and effectual ways* (*Gulliver's Travels* by Jonathan Swift)

commons NOUN commons is an old term meaning food shared with others ❑ *his pauper assistants ranged themselves behind him; the gruel was served out; and a long grace was said over the short commons.* (*Oliver Twist* by Charles Dickens)

complacency NOUN here complacency means a desire to please others. Today complacency means feeling pleased with oneself without good reason. ❑ *Twas thy power that raised the first complacency in me* (*The Prelude* by William Wordsworth)

complaisance NOUN complaisance was eagerness to please ❑ *we cannot wonder at his complaisance* (*Pride and Prejudice* by Jane Austen)

complaisant ADJ complaisant means polite ❑ *extremely cheerful and complaisant to their guest* (*Gulliver's Travels* by Jonathan Swift)

conning VERB conning means learning by heart ❑ *Or conning more* (*The Prelude* by William Wordsworth)

consequent NOUN consequence ❑ *as avarice is the necessary consequent of old age* (*Gulliver's Travels* by Jonathan Swift)

consorts NOUN concerts ❑ *The King, who delighted in music, had frequent consorts at Court* (*Gulliver's Travels* by Jonathan Swift)

conversible ADJ conversible meant easy to talk to, companionable ❑ *He can be a conversible companion* (*Pride and Prejudice* by Jane Austen)

copper NOUN a copper is a large pot that can be heated directly over a fire ❑ *He gazed in stupefied astonishment on the small rebel for some seconds, and then clung for support to the copper* (*Oliver Twist* by Charles Dickens)

copper-stick NOUN a copper-stick is the long piece of wood used to stir washing in the copper (or boiler) which was usually the biggest cooking pot in the house ❑ *It was Christmas Eve, and I had to stir the pudding for next day, with a copper-stick, from seven to eight by the Dutch clock* (*Great Expectations* by Charles Dickens)

counting-house NOUN a counting house is a place where accountants work ❑ *Once upon a time – of all the good days in the year, on Christmas Eve – old Scrooge sat busy in his countinghouse* (*A Christmas Carol* by Charles Dickens)

courtier NOUN a courtier is someone who attends the king or queen – a member of the court ❑ *next the ten courtiers;* (*Alice's Adventures in Wonderland* by Lewis Carroll)

covies NOUN covies were flocks of partridges ❑ *and will save all of the best covies for you* (*Pride and Prejudice* by Jane Austen)

cowed VERB cowed means frightened or intimidated ❑ *it cowed me more than the pain* (*Treasure Island* by Robert Louis Stevenson)

cozened VERB cozened means tricked or deceived ❑ *Do you remember, sir, how you cozened me* (*Doctor Faustus* 4.7 by Christopher Marlowe)

cravats NOUN a cravat is a folded cloth that a man wears wrapped around his neck as a decorative item of clothing ❑ *we'd a' slept in our cravats to-night* (*The Adventures of Huckleberry Finn* by Mark Twain)

crock and dirt PHRASE crock and dirt is an old expression meaning soot and dirt ❑ *and the mare catching cold at the door, and the boy grimed with crock and dirt* (*Great Expectations* by Charles Dickens)

crockery NOUN here crockery means pottery ❑ *By one of the parrots was a cat made of crockery* (*The Adventures of Huckleberry Finn* by Mark Twain)

crooked sixpence PHRASE it was considered unlucky to have a bent sixpence ❑ *You've got the beauty, you see, and I've got the luck, so you must keep me by you for your crooked sixpence* (*Silas Marner* by George Eliot)

croquet NOUN croquet is a traditional English summer game in which players try to hit wooden balls through hoops ❑ *and once she remembered trying to box her own ears for having cheated herself in a game of croquet* (*Alice's Adventures in Wonderland* by Lewis Carroll)

cross PREP across ❑ *The two great streets, which run cross and divide it into four quarters* (*Gulliver's Travels* by Jonathan Swift)

culpable ADJ if you are culpable for something it means you are to blame ❑ *deep are the sorrows that spring from false ideas for which no man is culpable.* (*Silas Marner* by George Eliot)

cultured ADJ cultivated ❑ *Nor less when spring had warmed the cultured Vale* (*The Prelude* by William Wordsworth)

cupidity NOUN cupidity is greed ❑ *These people hated me with the hatred of cupidity and disappointment.* (*Great Expectations* by Charles Dickens)

curricle NOUN an open two-wheeled carriage with one seat for the driver and space for a single passenger ❑ *and they saw a lady and a gentleman in a curricle* (*Pride and Prejudice* by Jane Austen)

cynosure NOUN a cynosure is something that strongly attracts attention or admiration ❑ *Then I thought of Eliza and Georgiana; I beheld one the cynosure of a ballroom, the other the inmate of a convent cell* (*Jane Eyre* by Charlotte Brontë)

dalliance NOUN someone's dalliance with something is a brief involvement with it ❑ *nor sporting in the dalliance of love* (*Doctor Faustus Chorus* by Christopher Marlowe)

darkling ADV darkling is an archaic way of saying in the dark ❑ *Darkling I listen* (*Ode on a Nightingale* by John Keats)

delf-case NOUN a sideboard for holding dishes and crockery ❑ *at the pewter dishes and delf-case* (*Wuthering Heights* by Emily Brontë)

determined ■ VERB here determined means ended ❑ *and be out of vogue when that was determined* (*Gulliver's Travels* by Jonathan Swift) ■ VERB determined can mean to have been learned or found especially by investigation or experience ❑ *All the sensitive feelings it wounded so cruelly, all the shame and misery it kept alive within my breast, became more poignant as I*

thought of this; and I determined that the life was unendurable (*David Copperfield* by Charles Dickens)

Deuce NOUN a slang term for the Devil ❑ *Ah, I dare say I did. Deuce take me, he added suddenly, I know I did. I find I am not quite unscrewed yet.* (*Great Expectations* by Charles Dickens)

diabolical ADJ diabolical means devilish or evil ❑ *and with a thousand diabolical expressions* (*Treasure Island* by Robert Louis Stevenson)

direction NOUN here direction means address ❑ *Elizabeth was not surprised at it, as Jane had written the direction remarkably ill* (*Pride and Prejudice* by Jane Austen)

discover VERB to make known or announce ❑ *the Emperor would discover the secret while I was out of his power* (*Gulliver's Travels* by Jonathan Swift)

dissemble VERB hide or conceal ❑ *Dissemble nothing* (*On His Mistress* by John Donne)

dissolve VERB dissolve here means to release from life, to die ❑ *Fade far away, dissolve, and quite forget* (*Ode on a Nightingale* by John Keats)

distrain VERB to distrain is to seize the property of someone who is in debt in compensation for the money owed ❑ *for he's threatening to distrain for it* (*Silas Marner* by George Eliot)

Divan NOUN a Divan was originally a Turkish council of state – the name was transferred to the couches they sat on and is used to mean this in English ❑ *Mr Brass applauded this picture very much, and the bed being soft and comfortable, Mr Quilp determined to use it, both as a sleeping place by night and as a kind of Divan by day.* (*The Old Curiosity Shop* by Charles Dickens)

divorcement NOUN separation ❑ *By all pains which want and divorcement* *hath* (*On His Mistress* by John Donne)

dog in the manger, PHRASE this phrase describes someone who prevents you from enjoying something that they themselves have no need for ❑ *You are a dog in the manger, Cathy, and desire no one to be loved but yourself* (*Wuthering Heights* by Emily Brontë)

dolorifuge NOUN dolorifuge is a word which Thomas Hardy invented. It means pain-killer or comfort ❑ *as a species of dolorifuge* (*Tess of the D'Urbervilles* by Thomas Hardy)

dome NOUN building ❑ *that river and that mouldering dome* (*The Prelude* by William Wordsworth)

domestic PHRASE here domestic means a person's management of the house ❑ *to give some account of my domestic* (*Gulliver's Travels* by Jonathan Swift)

dunce NOUN a dunce is another word for idiot ❑ *Do you take me for a dunce? Go on?* (*Alice's Adventures in Wonderland* by Lewis Carroll)

Ecod EXCLAM a slang exclamation meaning 'oh God!' ❑ *"Ecod," replied Wemmick, shaking his head, "that's not my trade."* (*Great Expectations* by Charles Dickens)

egg-hot NOUN an egg-hot (see also 'flip' and 'negus') was a hot drink made from beer and eggs, sweetened with nutmeg ❑ *She fainted when she saw me return, and made a little jug of egg-hot afterwards to console us while we talked it over.* (*David Copperfield* by Charles Dickens)

encores NOUN an encore is a short extra performance at the end of a longer one, which the entertainer gives because the audience has enthusiastically asked for it ❑ *we want a little something to answer encores with, anyway* (*The Adventures of Huckleberry Finn* by Mark Twain)

equipage NOUN an elegant and impressive carriage ❑ *and besides, the equipage did not answer to any of*

their neighbours (*Pride and Prejudice* by Jane Austen)

exordium NOUN an exordium is the opening part of a speech ❑ *"Now, Handel," as if it were the grave beginning of a portentous business exordium, he had suddenly given up that tone* (*Great Expectations* by Charles Dickens)

expect VERB here expect means to wait for ❑ *to expect his farther commands* (*Gulliver's Travels* by Jonathan Swift)

familiars NOUN familiars means spirits or devils who come to someone when they are called ❑ *I'll turn all the lice about thee into familiars* (*Doctor Faustus* 1.4 by Christopher Marlowe)

fantods NOUN a fantod is a person who fidgets or can't stop moving nervously ❑ *It most give me the fantods* (*The Adventures of Huckleberry Finn* by Mark Twain)

farthing NOUN a farthing is an old unit of British currency which was worth a quarter of a penny ❑ *Not a farthing less. A great many back-payments are included in it, I assure you.* (*A Christmas Carol* by Charles Dickens)

farthingale NOUN a hoop worn under a skirt to extend it ❑ *A bell with an old voice – which I dare say in its time had often said to the house, Here is the green farthingale* (*Great Expectations* by Charles Dickens)

favours NOUN here favours is an old word which means ribbons ❑ *A group of humble mourners entered the gate: wearing white favours* (*Oliver Twist* by Charles Dickens)

feigned VERB pretend or pretending ❑ *not my feigned page* (*On His Mistress* by John Donne)

fence ■ NOUN a fence is someone who receives and sells stolen goods ❑ *What are you up to? Ill-treating the boys, you covetous, avaricious, in-sa-ti-a-ble old fence?* (*Oliver Twist* by

Charles Dickens) ■ NOUN defence or protection ❑ *but honesty hath no fence against superior cunning* (*Gulliver's Travels* by Jonathan Swift)

fess ADJ fess is an old word which means pleased or proud ❑ *You'll be fess enough, my poppet* (*Tess of the D'Urbervilles* by Thomas Hardy)

fettered ADJ fettered means bound in chains or chained ❑ *"You are fettered," said Scrooge, trembling. "Tell me why?"* (*A Christmas Carol* by Charles Dickens)

fidges VERB fidges means fidgets, which is to keep moving your hands slightly because you are nervous or excited ❑ *Look, Jim, how my fingers fidges* (*Treasure Island* by Robert Louis Stevenson)

finger-post NOUN a finger-post is a sign-post showing the direction to different places ❑ *"The gallows," continued Fagin, "the gallows, my dear, is an ugly finger-post, which points out a very short and sharp turning that has stopped many a bold fellow's career on the broad highway."* (*Oliver Twist* by Charles Dickens)

fire-irons NOUN fire-irons are tools kept by the side of the fire to either cook with or look after the fire ❑ *the fire-irons came first* (*Alice's Adventures in Wonderland* by Lewis Carroll)

fire-plug NOUN a fire-plug is another word for a fire hydrant ❑ *The pony looked with great attention into a fire-plug, which was near him, and appeared to be quite absorbed in contemplating it* (*The Old Curiosity Shop* by Charles Dickens)

flank NOUN flank is the side of an animal ❑ *And all her silken flanks with garlands dressed* (*Ode on a Grecian Urn* by John Keats)

flip NOUN a flip is a drink made from warmed ale, sugar, spice and beaten egg ❑ *The events of the day, in combination with the twins, if not with the flip, had made Mrs. Micawber hysterical, and she shed tears as she replied* (*David Copperfield* by Charles Dickens)

flit VERB flit means to move quickly ❑ *and if he had meant to flit to Thrushcross Grange* (*Wuthering Heights* by Emily Brontë)

floorcloth NOUN a floorcloth was a hard-wearing piece of canvas used instead of carpet ❑ *This avenging phantom was ordered to be on duty at eight on Tuesday morning in the hall (it was two feet square, as charged for floorcloth)* (*Great Expectations* by Charles Dickens)

fly-driver NOUN a fly-driver is a carriage drawn by a single horse ❑ *The fly-drivers, among whom I inquired next, were equally jocose and equally disrespectful* (*David Copperfield* by Charles Dickens)

fob NOUN a small pocket in which a watch is kept ❑ *"Certain," replied the man, drawing a gold watch from his fob* (*Oliver Twist* by Charles Dickens)

folly NOUN folly means foolishness or stupidity ❑ *the folly of beginning a work* (*Robinson Crusoe* by Daniel Defoe)

fond ADJ fond means foolish ❑ *Fond worldling* (*Doctor Faustus 5.2* by Christopher Marlowe)

fondness NOUN silly or foolish affection ❑ *They have no fondness for their colts or foals* (*Gulliver's Travels* by Jonathan Swift)

for his fancy PHRASE for his fancy means for his liking or as he wanted ❑ *and as I did not obey quick enough for his fancy* (*Treasure Island* by Robert Louis Stevenson)

forlorn ADJ lost or very upset ❑ *you are from that day forlorn* (*Gulliver's Travels* by Jonathan Swift)

foster-sister NOUN a foster-sister was someone brought up by the same nurse or in the same household ❑ *I had been his foster-sister* (*Wuthering Heights* by Emily Brontë)

fox-fire NOUN fox-fire is a weak glow that is given off by decaying, rotten wood ❏ *what we must have was a lot of them rotten chunks that's called fox-fire* (*The Adventures of Huckleberry Finn* by Mark Twain)

frozen sea PHRASE the Arctic Ocean ❏ *into the frozen sea* (*Gulliver's Travels* by Jonathan Swift)

gainsay VERB to gainsay something is to say it isn't true or to deny it ❏ *"So she had," cried Scrooge. "You're right. I'll not gainsay it, Spirit. God forbid!"* (*A Christmas Carol* by Charles Dickens)

gaiters NOUN gaiters were leggings made of a cloth or piece of leather which covered the leg from the knee to the ankle ❏ *Mr Knightley was hard at work upon the lower buttons of his thick leather gaiters* (*Emma* by Jane Austen)

galluses NOUN galluses is an old spelling of gallows, and here means suspenders. Suspenders are straps worn over someone's shoulders and fastened to their trousers to prevent the trousers falling down ❏ *and home-knit galluses* (*The Adventures of Huckleberry Finn* by Mark Twain)

galoot NOUN a sailor but also a clumsy person ❏ *and maybe a galoot on it chopping* (*The Adventures of Huckleberry Finn* by Mark Twain)

gayest ADJ gayest means the most lively and bright or merry ❏ *Beth played her gayest march* (*Little Women* by Louisa May Alcott)

gem NOUN here gem means jewellery ❏ *the mountain shook off turf and flower, had only heath for raiment and crag for gem* (*Jane Eyre* by Charlotte Brontë)

giddy ADJ giddy means dizzy ❏ *and I wish you wouldn't keep appearing and vanishing so suddenly; you make one quite giddy.* (Alice's Adventures in Wonderland by Lewis Carroll)

gig NOUN a light two-wheeled carriage ❏ *when a gig drove up to the garden gate: out of which there jumped a*

fat gentleman (*Oliver Twist* by Charles Dickens)

gladsome ADJ gladsome is an old word meaning glad or happy ❏ *Nobody ever stopped him in the street to say, with gladsome looks* (*A Christmas Carol* by Charles Dickens)

glen NOUN a glen is a small valley; the word is used commonly in Scotland ❏ *a beck which follows the bend of the glen* (*Wuthering Heights* by Emily Brontë)

gravelled VERB gravelled is an old term which means to baffle or defeat someone ❏ *Gravelled the pastors of the German Church* (*Doctor Faustus 1.1* by Christopher Marlowe)

grinder NOUN a grinder was a private tutor ❏ *but that when he had had the happiness of marrying Mrs Pocket very early in his life, he had impaired his prospects and taken up the calling of a Grinder* (*Great Expectations* by Charles Dickens)

gruel NOUN gruel is a thin, watery corn-meal or oatmeal soup ❏ *and the little saucepan of gruel (Scrooge had a cold in his head) upon the hob.* (*A Christmas Carol* by Charles Dickens)

guinea, half a NOUN a half guinea was ten shillings and sixpence ❏ *but lay out half a guinea at Ford's* (*Emma* by Jane Austen)

gull VERB gull is an old term which means to fool or deceive someone ❏ *Hush, I'll gull him supernaturally* (*Doctor Faustus 3.4* by Christopher Marlowe)

gunnel NOUN the gunnel, or gunwhale, is the upper edge of a boat's side ❏ *But he put his foot on the gunnel and rocked her* (*The Adventures of Huckleberry Finn* by Mark Twain)

gunwale NOUN the side of a ship ❏ *He dipped his hand in the water over the boat's gunwale* (*Great Expectations* by Charles Dickens)

Gytrash NOUN a Gytrash is an omen of misfortune to the superstitious, usually taking the form of a hound

❑ *I remembered certain of Bessie's tales, wherein figured a North-of-England spirit, called a 'Gytrash'* (*Jane Eyre* by Charlotte Brontë)

hackney-cabriolet NOUN a two-wheeled carriage with four seats for hire and pulled by a horse ❑ *A hackney-cabriolet was in waiting; with the same vehemence which she had exhibited in addressing Oliver, the girl pulled him in with her, and drew the curtains close.* (*Oliver Twist* by Charles Dickens)

hackney-coach NOUN a four-wheeled horse-drawn vehicle for hire ❑ *The twilight was beginning to close in, when Mr. Brownlow alighted from a hackney-coach at his own door, and knocked softly.* (*Oliver Twist* by Charles Dickens)

haggler NOUN a haggler is someone who travels from place to place selling small goods and items ❑ *when I be plain Jack Durbeyfield, the haggler* (*Tess of the D'Urbervilles* by Thomas Hardy)

halter NOUN a halter is a rope or strap used to lead an animal or to tie it up ❑ *I had of course long been used to a halter and a headstall* (*Black Beauty* by Anna Sewell)

hamlet NOUN a hamlet is a small village or a group of houses in the countryside ❑ *down from the hamlet* (*Treasure Island* by Robert Louis Stevenson)

hand-barrow NOUN a hand-barrow is a device for carrying heavy objects. It is like a wheelbarrow except that it has handles, rather than wheels, for moving the barrow ❑ *his sea chest following behind him in a hand-barrow* (*Treasure Island* by Robert Louis Stevenson)

handspike NOUN a handspike was a stick which was used as a lever ❑ *a bit of stick like a handspike* (*Treasure Island* by Robert Louis Stevenson)

haply ADV haply means by chance or perhaps ❑ *And haply the Queen-Moon is on her throne* (*Ode on a Nightingale* by John Keats)

harem NOUN the harem was the part of the house where the women lived ❑ *mostly they hang round the harem* (*The Adventures of Huckleberry Finn* by Mark Twain)

hautboys NOUN hautboys are oboes ❑ *sausages and puddings resembling flutes and hautboys* (*Gulliver's Travels* by Jonathan Swift)

hawker NOUN a hawker is someone who sells goods to people as he travels rather than from a fixed place like a shop ❑ *to buy some stockings from a hawker* (*Treasure Island* by Robert Louis Stevenson)

hawser NOUN a hawser is a rope used to tie up or tow a ship or boat ❑ *Again among the tiers of shipping, in and out, avoiding rusty chain-cables, frayed hempen hawsers* (*Great Expectations* by Charles Dickens)

headstall NOUN the headstall is the part of the bridle or halter that goes around a horse's head ❑ *I had of course long been used to a halter and a headstall* (*Black Beauty* by Anna Sewell)

hearken VERB hearken means to listen ❑ *though we sometimes stopped to lay hold of each other and hearken* (*Treasure Island* by Robert Louis Stevenson)

heartless ADJ here heartless means without heart or dejected ❑ *I am not heartless* (*The Prelude* by William Wordsworth)

hebdomadal ADJ hebdomadal means weekly ❑ *It was the hebdomadal treat to which we all looked forward from Sabbath to Sabbath* (*Jane Eyre* by Charlotte Brontë)

highwaymen NOUN highwaymen were people who stopped travellers and robbed them ❑ *We are highwaymen* (*The Adventures of Huckleberry Finn* by Mark Twain)

hinds NOUN hinds means farm hands, or people who work on a farm ❑ *He called his hinds about him* (*Gulliver's Travels* by Jonathan Swift)

histrionic ADJ if you refer to someone's behaviour as histrionic, you are being critical of it because it is dramatic and exaggerated ❑ *But the histrionic muse is the darling* (*The Adventures of Huckleberry Finn* by Mark Twain)

hogs NOUN hogs is another word for pigs ❑ *Tom called the hogs 'ingots'* (*The Adventures of Huckleberry Finn* by Mark Twain)

horrors NOUN the horrors are a fit, called delirium tremens, which is caused by drinking too much alcohol ❑ *I'll have the horrors* (*Treasure Island* by Robert Louis Stevenson)

huffy ADJ huffy means to be obviously annoyed or offended about something ❑ *They will feel that more than angry speeches or huffy actions* (*Little Women* by Louisa May Alcott)

hulks NOUN hulks were prison-ships ❑ *The miserable companion of thieves and ruffians, the fallen outcast of low haunts, the associate of the scourings of the jails and hulks* (*Oliver Twist* by Charles Dickens)

humbug NOUN humbug means nonsense or rubbish ❑ *"Bah," said Scrooge. "Humbug!"* (*A Christmas Carol* by Charles Dickens)

humours NOUN it was believed that there were four fluids in the body called humours which decided the temperament of a person depending on how much of each fluid was present ❑ *other peccant humours* (*Gulliver's Travels* by Jonathan Swift)

husbandry NOUN husbandry is farming animals ❑ *bad husbandry were plentifully anointing their wheels* (*Silas Marner* by George Eliot)

huswife NOUN a huswife was a small sewing kit ❑ *but I had put my huswife on it* (*Emma* by Jane Austen)

ideal ADJ ideal in this context means imaginary ❑ *I discovered the yell was not ideal* (*Wuthering Heights* by Emily Brontë)

If our two PHRASE if both our ❑ *If our two loves be one* (*The Good-Morrow* by John Donne)

ignis-fatuus NOUN ignis-fatuus is the light given out by burning marsh gases, which lead careless travellers into danger ❑ *it is madness in all women to let a secret love kindle within them, which, if unreturned and unknown, must devour the life that feeds it; and, if discovered and responded to, must lead ignis-fatuus-like, into miry wilds whence there is no extrication.* (*Jane Eyre* by Charlotte Brontë)

imaginations NOUN here imaginations means schemes or plans ❑ *soon drove out those imaginations* (*Gulliver's Travels* by Jonathan Swift)

impressible ADJ impressible means open or impressionable ❑ *for Marner had one of those impressible, self-doubting natures* (*Silas Marner* by George Eliot)

in good intelligence PHRASE friendly with each other ❑ *that these two persons were in good intelligence with each other* (*Gulliver's Travels* by Jonathan Swift)

inanity NOUN inanity is sillyness or dull stupidity ❑ *Do we not wile away moments of inanity* (*Silas Marner* by George Eliot)

incivility NOUN incivility means rudeness or impoliteness ❑ *if it's only for a piece of incivility like to-night's* (*Treasure Island* by Robert Louis Stevenson)

indigenae NOUN indigenae means natives or people from that area ❑ *an exotic that the surly indigenae will not recognise for kin* (*Wuthering Heights* by Emily Brontë)

indocible ADJ unteachable ❑ *so they were the most restive and indocible* (*Gulliver's Travels* by Jonathan Swift)

ingenuity NOUN inventiveness ❑ *entreated me to give him something as an encouragement to ingenuity*

(*Gulliver's Travels* by Jonathan Swift)

ingots NOUN an ingot is a lump of a valuable metal like gold, usually shaped like a brick ❑ *Tom called the hogs 'ingots'* (*The Adventures of Huckleberry Finn* by Mark Twain)

inkstand NOUN an inkstand is a pot which was put on a desk to contain either ink or pencils and pens ❑ *throwing an inkstand at the Lizard as she spoke* (*Alice's Adventures in Wonderland* by Lewis Carroll)

inordinate ADJ without order. Today inordinate means 'excessive'. ❑ *Though yet untutored and inordinate* (*The Prelude* by William Wordsworth)

intellectuals NOUN here intellectuals means the minds (of the workmen) ❑ *those instructions they give being too refined for the intellectuals of their workmen* (*Gulliver's Travels* by Jonathan Swift)

interview NOUN meeting ❑ *By our first strange and fatal interview* (*On His Mistress* by John Donne)

jacks NOUN jacks are rods for turning a spit over a fire ❑ *It was a small bit of pork suspended from the kettle hanger by a string passed through a large door key, in a way known to primitive housekeepers unpossessed of jacks* (*Silas Marner* by George Eliot)

jews-harp NOUN a jews-harp is a small, metal, musical instrument that is played by the mouth ❑ *A jews-harp's plenty good enough for a rat* (*The Adventures of Huckleberry Finn* by Mark Twain)

jorum NOUN a large bowl ❑ *while Miss Skiffins brewed such a jorum of tea, that the pig in the back premises became strongly excited* (*Great Expectations* by Charles Dickens)

jostled VERB jostled means bumped or pushed by someone or some people ❑ *being jostled himself into the kennel* (*Gulliver's Travels* by Jonathan Swift)

keepsake NOUN a keepsake is a gift which reminds someone of an event or of the person who gave it to them. ❑ *books and ornaments they had in their boudoirs at home: keepsakes that different relations had presented to them* (*Jane Eyre* by Charlotte Brontë)

kenned VERB kenned means knew ❑ *though little kenned the lamplighter that he had any company but Christmas!* (*A Christmas Carol* by Charles Dickens)

kennel NOUN kennel means gutter, which is the edge of a road next to the pavement, where rain water collects and flows away ❑ *being jostled himself into the kennel* (*Gulliver's Travels* by Jonathan Swift)

knock-knee ADJ knock-knee means slanted, at an angle. ❑ *LOT 1 was marked in whitewashed knock-knee letters on the brewhouse* (*Great Expectations* by Charles Dickens)

ladylike ADJ to be ladylike is to behave in a polite, dignified and graceful way ❑ *No, winking isn't ladylike* (*Little Women* by Louisa May Alcott)

lapse NOUN flow ❑ *Stealing with silent lapse to join the brook* (*The Prelude* by William Wordsworth)

larry NOUN larry is an old word which means commotion or noisy celebration ❑ *That was all a part of the larry!* (*Tess of the D'Urbervilles* by Thomas Hardy)

laths NOUN laths are strips of wood ❑ *The panels shrunk, the windows cracked; fragments of plaster fell out of the ceiling, and the naked laths were shown instead* (*A Christmas Carol* by Charles Dickens)

leer NOUN a leer is an unpleasant smile ❑ *with a kind of leer* (*Treasure Island* by Robert Louis Stevenson)

lenities NOUN these are different kinds of drugs or medicines: lenities and palliatives were pain relievers; aperitives were laxatives;

abstersives caused vomiting; corrosives destroyed human tissue; restringents caused constipation; cephalalgics stopped headaches; icterics were used as medicine for jaundice; apophlegmatics were cough medicine, and acoustics were cures for the loss of hearing ❑ *lenitives, aperitives, abstersives, corrosives, restringents, palliatives, laxatives, cephalalgics, icterics, apophlegmatics, acoustics* (*Gulliver's Travels* by Jonathan Swift)

lest CONJ in case. If you do something lest something (usually) unpleasant happens you do it to try to prevent it happening ❑ *She went in without knocking, and hurried upstairs, in great fear lest she should meet the real Mary Ann* (*Alice's Adventures in Wonderland* by Lewis Carroll)

levee NOUN a levee is an old term for a meeting held in the morning, shortly after the person holding the meeting has got out of bed ❑ *I used to attend the King's levee once or twice a week* (*Gulliver's Travels* by Jonathan Swift)

life-preserver NOUN a club which had lead inside it to make it heavier and therefore more dangerous ❑ *and with no more suspicious articles displayed to view than two or three heavy bludgeons which stood in a corner, and a 'life-preserver' that hung over the chimney-piece.* (*Oliver Twist* by Charles Dickens)

lighterman NOUN a lighterman is another word for sailor ❑ *in and out, hammers going in ship-builders' yards, saws going at timber, clashing engines going at things unknown, pumps going in leaky ships, capstans going, ships going out to sea, and unintelligible sea creatures roaring curses over the bulwarks at respondent lightermen* (*Great Expectations* by Charles Dickens)

livery NOUN servants often wore a uniform known as a livery ❑ *suddenly a footman in livery came running out of the wood* (*Alice's Adventures in Wonderland* by Lewis Carroll)

livid ADJ livid means pale or ash coloured. Livid also means very angry ❑ *a dirty, livid white* (*Treasure Island* by Robert Louis Stevenson)

lottery-tickets NOUN a popular card game ❑ *and Mrs. Philips protested that they would have a nice comfortable noisy game of lottery tickets* (*Pride and Prejudice* by Jane Austen)

lower and upper world PHRASE the earth and the heavens are the lower and upper worlds ❑ *the changes in the lower and upper world* (*Gulliver's Travels* by Jonathan Swift)

lustres NOUN lustres are chandeliers. A chandelier is a large, decorative frame which holds light bulbs or candles and hangs from the ceiling ❑ *the lustres, lights, the carving and the guilding* (*The Prelude* by William Wordsworth)

lynched VERB killed without a criminal trial by a crowd of people ❑ *He'll never know how nigh he come to getting lynched* (*The Adventures of Huckleberry Finn* by Mark Twain)

malingering VERB if someone is malingering they are pretending to be ill to avoid working ❑ *And you stand there malingering* (*Treasure Island* by Robert Louis Stevenson)

managing PHRASE treating with consideration ❑ *to think the honour of my own kind not worth managing* (*Gulliver's Travels* by Jonathan Swift)

manhood PHRASE manhood means human nature ❑ *concerning the nature of manhood* (*Gulliver's Travels* by Jonathan Swift)

man-trap NOUN a man-trap is a set of steel jaws that snap shut when trodden on and trap a person's leg ❑ *"Don't go to him," I called out of the window, "he's an assassin! A* *man-trap!"* (*Oliver Twist* by Charles Dickens)

maps NOUN charts of the night sky ❏ *Let maps to others, worlds on worlds have shown* (*The Good-Morrow* by John Donne)

mark VERB look at or notice ❏ *Mark but this flea, and mark in this* (*The Flea* by John Donne)

maroons NOUN A maroon is someone who has been left in a place which it is difficult for them to escape from, like a small island ❏ *if schooners, islands, and maroons* (*Treasure Island* by Robert Louis Stevenson)

mast NOUN here mast means the fruit of forest trees ❏ *a quantity of acorns, dates, chestnuts, and other mast* (*Gulliver's Travels* by Jonathan Swift)

mate VERB defeat ❏ *Where Mars did mate the warlike Carthigens* (*Doctor Faustus Chorus* by Christopher Marlowe)

mealy ADJ Mealy when used to describe a face meant palid, pale or colourless ❏ *I only know two sorts of boys. Mealy boys, and beef-faced boys* (*Oliver Twist* by Charles Dickens)

middling ADJ fairly or moderately ❏ *she worked me middling hard for about an hour* (*The Adventures of Huckleberry Finn* by Mark Twain)

mill NOUN a mill, or treadmill, was a device for hard labour or punishment in prison ❏ *Was you never on the mill?* (*Oliver Twist* by Charles Dickens)

milliner's shop NOUN a milliner's sold fabrics, clothing, lace and accessories; as time went on they specialized more and more in hats ❏ *to pay their duty to their aunt and to a milliner's shop just over the way* (*Pride and Prejudice* by Jane Austen)

minching un' munching PHRASE how people in the north of England used to describe the way people from the south speak ❏ *Minching*

un' munching! (*Wuthering Heights* by Emily Brontë)

mine NOUN gold ❏ *Whether both th'Indias of spice and mine* (*The Sun Rising* by John Donne)

mire NOUN mud ❏ *Tis my fate to be always ground into the mire under the iron heel of oppression* (*The Adventures of Huckleberry Finn* by Mark Twain)

miscellany NOUN a miscellany is a collection of many different kinds of things ❏ *under that, the miscellany began* (*Treasure Island* by Robert Louis Stevenson)

mistarshers NOUN mistarshers means moustache, which is the hair that grows on a man's upper lip ❏ *when he put his hand up to his mistarshers* (*Tess of the D'Urbervilles* by Thomas Hardy)

morrow NOUN here good-morrow means tomorrow and a new and better life ❏ *And now good-morrow to our waking souls* (*The Good-Morrow* by John Donne)

mortification NOUN mortification is an old word for gangrene which is when part of the body decays or 'dies' because of disease ❏ *Yes, it was a mortification – that was it* (*The Adventures of Huckleberry Finn* by Mark Twain)

mought PARTICIPLE mought is an old spelling of might ❏ *what you mought call me? You mought call me captain* (*Treasure Island* by Robert Louis Stevenson)

move VERB move me not means do not make me angry ❏ *Move me not, Faustus* (*Doctor Faustus 2.1* by Christopher Marlowe)

muffin-cap NOUN a muffin cap is a flat cap made from wool ❏ *the old one, remained stationary in the muffin-cap and leathers* (*Oliver Twist* by Charles Dickens)

mulatter NOUN a mulatter was another word for mulatto, which is a person with parents who are from different races ❏ *a mulatter, most as white as* a white man (*The Adventures of Huckleberry Finn* by Mark Twain)

mummery NOUN mummery is an old word that meant meaningless (or pretentious) ceremony ❏ *When they were all gone, and when Trabb and his men – but not his boy: I looked for him – had crammed their mummery into bags, and were gone too, the house felt wholesomer.* (*Great Expectations* by Charles Dickens)

nap NOUN the nap is the woolly surface on a new item of clothing. Here the surface has been worn away so it looks bare ❏ *like an old hat with the nap rubbed off* (*The Adventures of Huckleberry Finn* by Mark Twain)

natural ◼ NOUN a natural is a person born with learning difficulties ❏ *though he had been left to his particular care by their deceased father, who thought him almost a natural.* (*David Copperfield* by Charles Dickens) ◼ ADJ natural meant illegitimate ❏ *Harriet Smith was the natural daughter of somebody* (*Emma* by Jane Austen)

navigator NOUN a navigator was originally someone employed to dig canals. It is the origin of the word 'navvy' meaning a labourer ❏ *She ascertained from me in a few words what it was all about, comforted Dora, and gradually convinced her that I was not a labourer – from my manner of stating the case I believe Dora concluded that I was a navigator, and went balancing myself up and down a plank all day with a wheelbarrow – and so brought us together in peace.* (*David Copperfield* by Charles Dickens)

necromancy NOUN necromancy means a kind of magic where the magician speaks to spirits or ghosts to find out what will happen in the future ❏ *He surfeits upon cursed necromancy* (*Doctor Faustus chorus* by Christopher Marlowe)

negus NOUN a negus is a hot drink made from sweetened wine and water ❏ *He sat placidly perusing the newspaper, with his little head on one side, and a glass of warm sherry negus at his elbow.* (*David Copperfield* by Charles Dickens)

nice ADJ discriminating. Able to make good judgements or choices ❏ *consequently a claim to be nice* (*Emma* by Jane Austen)

nigh ADV nigh means near ❏ *He'll never know how nigh he come to getting lynched* (*The Adventures of Huckleberry Finn* by Mark Twain)

nimbleness NOUN nimbleness means being able to move very quickly or skillfully ❏ *and with incredible accuracy and nimbleness* (*Treasure Island* by Robert Louis Stevenson)

noggin NOUN a noggin is a small mug or a wooden cup ❏ *you'll bring me one noggin of rum* (*Treasure Island* by Robert Louis Stevenson)

none ADJ neither ❏ *none can die* (*The Good-Morrow* by John Donne)

notices NOUN observations ❏ *Arch are his notices* (*The Prelude* by William Wordsworth)

occiput NOUN occiput means the back of the head ❏ *saw off the occiput of each couple* (*Gulliver's Travels* by Jonathan Swift)

officiously ADJ kindly ❏ *the governess who attended Glumdalclitch very officiously lifted me up* (*Gulliver's Travels* by Jonathan Swift)

old salt PHRASE old salt is a slang term for an experienced sailor ❏ *a 'true sea-dog', and a 'real old salt'* (*Treasure Island* by Robert Louis Stevenson)

or ere PHRASE before ❏ *or ere the Hall was built* (*The Prelude* by William Wordsworth)

ostler NOUN one who looks after horses at an inn ❏ *The bill paid, and the waiter remembered, and the ostler not forgotten, and the chambermaid taken into consideration* (*Great Expectations* by Charles Dickens)

ostry NOUN an ostry is an old word for a pub or hotel ❑ *lest I send you into the ostry with a vengeance* (*Doctor Faustus 2.2* by Christopher Marlowe)

outrunning the constable PHRASE outrunning the constable meant spending more than you earn ❑ *but I shall by this means be able to check your bills and to pull you up if I find you outrunning the constable.* (*Great Expectations* by Charles Dickens)

over ADJ across ❑ *It is in length six yards, and in the thickest part at least three yards over* (*Gulliver's Travels* by Jonathan Swift)

over the broomstick PHRASE this is a phrase meaning 'getting married without a formal ceremony' ❑ *They both led tramping lives, and this woman in Gerrard-street here, had been married very young, over the broomstick (as we say), to a tramping man, and was a perfect fury in point of jealousy.* (*Great Expectations* by Charles Dickens)

own VERB own means to admit or to acknowledge ❑ *It's my old girl that advises. She has the head. But I never own to it before her. Discipline must be maintained* (*Bleak House* by Charles Dickens)

page NOUN here page means a boy employed to run errands ❑ *not my feigned page* (*On His Mistress* by John Donne)

paid pretty dear PHRASE paid pretty dear means paid a high price or suffered quite a lot ❑ *I paid pretty dear for my monthly fourpenny piece* (*Treasure Island* by Robert Louis Stevenson)

pannikins NOUN pannikins were small tin cups ❑ *of lifting light glasses and cups to his lips, as if they were clumsy pannikins* (*Great Expectations* by Charles Dickens)

pards NOUN pards are leopards ❑ *Not charioted by Bacchus and his pards* (*Ode on a Nightingale* by John Keats)

parlour boarder NOUN a pupil who lived with the family and somebody had lately raised her from the condition of scholar to parlour boarder (*Emma* by Jane Austen)

particular, a London PHRASE London in Victorian times and up to the 1950s was famous for having very dense fog – which was a combination of real fog and the smog of pollution from factories ❑ *This is a London particular . . . A fog, miss'* (*Bleak House* by Charles Dickens)

patten NOUN pattens were wooden soles which were fixed to shoes by straps to protect the shoes in wet weather ❑ *carrying a basket like the Great Seal of England in plaited straw, a pair of pattens, a spare shawl, and an umbrella, though it was a fine bright day* (*Great Expectations* by Charles Dickens)

paviour NOUN a paviour was a labourer who worked on the street pavement ❑ *the paviour his pickaxe* (*Oliver Twist* by Charles Dickens)

peccant ADJ peccant means unhealthy ❑ *other peccant humours* (*Gulliver's Travels* by Jonathan Swift)

penetralium NOUN penetralium is a word used to describe the inner rooms of the house ❑ *and I had no desire to aggravate his impatience previous to inspecting the penetralium* (*Wuthering Heights* by Emily Brontë)

pensive ADV pensive means deep in thought or thinking seriously about something ❑ *and she was leaning pensive on a tomb-stone with her right elbow* (*The Adventures of Huckleberry Finn* by Mark Twain)

penury NOUN penury is the state of being extremely poor ❑ *Distress, if not penury, loomed in the distance* (*Tess of the D'Urbervilles* by Thomas Hardy)

perspective NOUN telescope ❑ *a pocket perspective* (*Gulliver's Travels* by Jonathan Swift)

phaeton NOUN a phaeton was an open carriage for four people ❑ *often* *condescends to drive by my humble abode in her little phaeton and ponies* (*Pride and Prejudice* by Jane Austen)

phantasm NOUN a phantasm is an illusion, something that is not real. It is sometimes used to mean ghost ❑ *Experience had bred no fancies in him that could raise the phantasm of appetite* (*Silas Marner* by George Eliot)

physic NOUN here physic means medicine ❑ *there I studied physic two years and seven months* (*Gulliver's Travels* by Jonathan Swift)

pinioned VERB to pinion is to hold both arms so that a person cannot move them ❑ *But the relentless Ghost pinioned him in both his arms, and forced him to observe what happened next.* (*A Christmas Carol* by Charles Dickens)

piquet NOUN piquet was a popular card game in the C18th ❑ *Mr Hurst and Mr Bingley were at piquet* (*Pride and Prejudice* by Jane Austen)

plaister NOUN a plaister is a piece of cloth on which an apothecary (or pharmacist) would spread ointment. The cloth is then applied to wounds or bruises to treat them ❑ *Then, she gave the knife a final smart wipe on the edge of the plaister, and then sawed a very thick round off the loaf: which she finally, before separating from the loaf, hewed into two halves, of which Joe got one, and I the other.* (*Great Expectations* by Charles Dickens)

plantations NOUN here plantations means colonies, which are countries controlled by a more powerful country ❑ *besides our plantations in America* (*Gulliver's Travels* by Jonathan Swift)

plastic ADV here plastic is an old term meaning shaping or a power that was forming ❑ *A plastic power abode with me* (*The Prelude* by William Wordsworth)

players NOUN actors ❑ *of players which upon the world's stage be* (*On His Mistress* by John Donne)

plump ADV all at once, suddenly ❑ *But it took a bit of time to get it well round, the change come so uncommon plump, didn't it?* (*Great Expectations* by Charles Dickens)

plundered VERB to plunder is to rob or steal from ❑ *These crosses stand for the names of ships or towns that they sank or plundered* (*Treasure Island* by Robert Louis Stevenson)

pommel ■ VERB to pommel someone is to hit them repeatedly with your fists ❑ *hug him round the neck, pommel his back, and kick his legs in irrepressible affection!* (*A Christmas Carol* by Charles Dickens) ■ NOUN a pommel is the part of a saddle that rises up at the front ❑ *He had his gun across his pommel* (*The Adventures of Huckleberry Finn* by Mark Twain)

poor's rates NOUN poor's rates were property taxes which were used to support the poor ❑ *"Oh!" replied the undertaker; "why, you know, Mr. Bumble, I pay a good deal towards the poor's rates."* (*Oliver Twist* by Charles Dickens)

popular ADJ popular means ruled by the people, or Republican, rather than ruled by a monarch ❑ *With those of Greece compared and popular Rome* (*The Prelude* by William Wordsworth)

porringer NOUN a porringer is a small bowl ❑ *Of this festive composition each boy had one porringer, and no more* (*Oliver Twist* by Charles Dickens)

postboy NOUN a postboy was the driver of a horse-drawn carriage ❑ *He spoke to a postboy who was dozing under the gateway* (*Oliver Twist* by Charles Dickens)

post-chaise NOUN a fast carriage for two or four passengers ❑ *Looking round, he saw that it was a post-chaise, driven at great speed* (*Oliver Twist* by Charles Dickens)

postern NOUN a small gate usually at the back of a building ❑ *The little servant happening to be entering the fortress with two hot rolls, I passed through the postern and crossed the drawbridge, in her company* (*Great Expectations* by Charles Dickens)

pottle NOUN a pottle was a small basket ❑ *He had a paper-bag under each arm and a pottle of strawberries in one hand . . .* (*Great Expectations* by Charles Dickens)

pounce NOUN pounce is a fine powder used to prevent ink spreading on untreated paper ❑ *in that grim atmosphere of pounce and parchment, red-tape, dusty wafers, ink-jars, brief and draft paper, law reports, writs, declarations, and bills of costs* (*David Copperfield* by Charles Dickens)

pox NOUN pox means sexually transmitted diseases like syphilis ❑ *how the pox in all its consequences and denominations* (*Gulliver's Travels* by Jonathan Swift)

prelibation NOUN prelibation means a foretaste of or an example of something to come ❑ *A prelibation to the mower's scythe* (*The Prelude* by William Wordsworth)

prentice NOUN an apprentice ❑ *and Joe, sitting on an old gun, had told me that when I was 'prentice to him regularly bound, we would have such Larks there!* (*Great Expectations* by Charles Dickens)

presently ADV immediately ❑ *I presently knew what they meant* (*Gulliver's Travels* by Jonathan Swift)

pumpion NOUN pumpkin ❑ *for it was almost as large as a small pumpion* (*Gulliver's Travels* by Jonathan Swift)

punctual ADJ kept in one place ❑ *was not a punctual presence, but a spirit* (*The Prelude* by William Wordsworth)

quadrille ■ NOUN a quadrille is a dance invented in France which is usually performed by four couples ❑ *However, Mr Swiveller had Miss Sophy's hand for the first quadrille (country-dances being low, were utterly proscribed)* (*The Old Curiosity Shop* by Charles Dickens) ■ NOUN quadrille was a card game for four people ❑ *to make up her pool of quadrille in the evening* (*Pride and Prejudice* by Jane Austen)

quality NOUN gentry or upper-class people ❑ *if you are with the quality* (*The Adventures of Huckleberry Finn* by Mark Twain)

quick parts PHRASE quick-witted ❑ *Mr Bennet was so odd a mixture of quick parts* (*Pride and Prejudice* by Jane Austen)

quid NOUN a quid is something chewed or kept in the mouth, like a piece of tobacco ❑ *rolling his quid* (*Treasure Island* by Robert Louis Stevenson)

quit VERB quit means to avenge or to make even ❑ *But Faustus's death shall quit my infamy* (*Doctor Faustus 4.3* by Christopher Marlowe)

rags NOUN divisions ❑ *Nor hours, days, months, which are the rags of time* (*The Sun Rising* by John Donne)

raiment NOUN raiment means clothing ❑ *the mountain shook off turf and flower, had only heath for raiment and crag for gem* (*Jane Eyre* by Charlotte Brontë)

rain cats and dogs PHRASE an expression meaning rain heavily. The origin of the expression is unclear ❑ *But it'll perhaps rain cats and dogs to-morrow* (*Silas Marner* by George Eliot)

raised Cain PHRASE raised Cain means caused a lot of trouble. Cain is a character in the Bible who killed his brother Abel ❑ *and every time he got drunk he raised Cain around town* (*The Adventures of Huckleberry Finn* by Mark Twain)

rambling ADJ rambling means confused and not very clear ❑ *my* *head began to be filled very early with rambling thoughts* (*Robinson Crusoe* by Daniel Defoe)

raree-show NOUN a raree-show is an old term for a peep-show or a fairground entertainment ❏ *A raree-show is here, with children gathered round* (*The Prelude* by William Wordsworth)

recusants NOUN people who resisted authority ❏ *hardy recusants* (*The Prelude* by William Wordsworth)

redounding VERB eddying. An eddy is a movement in water or air which goes round and round instead of flowing in one direction ❏ *mists and steam-like fogs redounding everywhere* (*The Prelude* by William Wordsworth)

redundant ADJ here redundant means overflowing but Wordsworth also uses it to mean excessively large or too big ❏ *A tempest, a redundant energy* (*The Prelude* by William Wordsworth)

reflex NOUN reflex is a shortened version of reflexion, which is an alternative spelling of reflection ❏ *To cut across the reflex of a star* (*The Prelude* by William Wordsworth)

Reformatory NOUN a prison for young offenders/criminals ❏ *Even when I was taken to have a new suit of clothes, the tailor had orders to make them like a kind of Reformatory, and on no account to let me have the free use of my limbs.* (*Great Expectations* by Charles Dickens)

remorse NOUN pity or compassion ❏ *by that remorse* (*On His Mistress* by John Donne)

render VERB in this context render means give. ❏ *and Sarah could render no reason that would be sanctioned by the feeling of the community.* (*Silas Marner* by George Eliot)

repeater NOUN a repeater was a watch that chimed the last hour when a button was pressed – as a result it was useful in the dark ❏ *And his watch is a gold repeater, and worth a hundred pound if it's worth a penny.* (*Great Expectations* by Charles Dickens)

repugnance NOUN repugnance means a strong dislike of something or someone ❏ *overcoming a strong repugnance* (*Treasure Island* by Robert Louis Stevenson)

reverence NOUN reverence means bow. When you bow to someone, you briefly bend your body towards them as a formal way of showing them respect ❏ *made my reverence* (*Gulliver's Travels* by Jonathan Swift)

reverie NOUN a reverie is a day dream ❏ *I can guess the subject of your reverie* (*Pride and Prejudice* by Jane Austen)

revival NOUN a religious meeting held in public ❏ *well I'd ben a-running' a little temperance revival thar' bout a week* (*The Adventures of Huckleberry Finn* by Mark Twain)

revolt VERB revolt means turn back or stop your present course of action and go back to what you were doing before ❏ *Revolt, or I'll in piecemeal tear thy flesh* (*Doctor Faustus 5.1* by Christopher Marlowe)

rheumatics/rheumatism NOUN rheumatics [rheumatism] is an illness that makes your joints or muscles stiff and painful ❏ *a new cure for the rheumatics* (*Treasure Island* by Robert Louis Stevenson)

riddance NOUN riddance is usually used in the form good riddance which you say when you are pleased that something has gone or been left behind ❏ *I'd better go into the house, and die and be a riddance* (*David Copperfield* by Charles Dickens)

rimy ADJ rimy is an ADJECTIVE which means covered in ice or frost ❏ *It was a rimy morning, and very damp* (*Great Expectations* by Charles Dickens)

riper ADJ riper means more mature or older ❑ *At riper years to Wittenberg he went* (*Doctor Faustus chorus* by Christopher Marlowe)

rubber NOUN a set of games in whist or backgammon ❑ *her father was sure of his rubber* (*Emma* by Jane Austen)

ruffian NOUN a ruffian is a person who behaves violently ❑ *and when the ruffian had told him* (*Treasure Island* by Robert Louis Stevenson)

sadness NOUN sadness is an old term meaning seriousness ❑ *But I prithee tell me, in good sadness* (*Doctor Faustus 2.2* by Christopher Marlowe)

sailed before the mast PHRASE this phrase meant someone who did not look like a sailor ❑ *he had none of the appearance of a man that sailed before the mast* (*Treasure Island* by Robert Louis Stevenson)

scabbard NOUN a scabbard is the covering for a sword or dagger ❑ *Girded round its middle was an antique scabbard; but no sword was in it, and the ancient sheath was eaten up with rust* (*A Christmas Carol* by Charles Dickens)

schooners NOUN A schooner is a fast, medium-sized sailing ship ❑ *if schooners, islands, and maroons* (*Treasure Island* by Robert Louis Stevenson)

science NOUN learning or knowledge ❑ *Even Science, too, at hand* (*The Prelude* by William Wordsworth)

scrouge VERB to scrouge means to squeeze or to crowd ❑ *to scrouge in and get a sight* (*The Adventures of Huckleberry Finn* by Mark Twain)

scrutore NOUN a scrutore, or escritoire, was a writing table ❑ *set me gently on my feet upon the scrutore* (*Gulliver's Travels* by Jonathan Swift)

scutcheon/escutcheon NOUN an escutcheon is a shield with a coat of arms, or the symbols of a family name, engraved on it ❑ *On the*

scutcheon we'll have a bend (*The Adventures of Huckleberry Finn* by Mark Twain)

sea-dog PHRASE sea-dog is a slang term for an experienced sailor or pirate ❑ *a 'true sea-dog', and a 'real old salt,'* (*Treasure Island* by Robert Louis Stevenson)

see the lions PHRASE to see the lions was to go and see the sights of London. Originally the phrase referred to the menagerie in the Tower of London and later in Regent's Park ❑ *We will go and see the lions for an hour or two – it's something to have a fresh fellow like you to show them to, Copperfield* (*David Copperfield* by Charles Dickens)

self-conceit NOUN self-conceit is an old term which means having too high an opinion of oneself, or deceiving yourself ❑ *Till swollen with cunning, of a self-conceit* (*Doctor Faustus chorus* by Christopher Marlowe)

seneschal NOUN a steward ❑ *where a grey-headed seneschal sings a funny chorus with a funnier body of vassals* (*Oliver Twist* by Charles Dickens)

sensible ADJ if you were sensible of something you are aware or conscious of something ❑ *If my children are silly I must hope to be always sensible of it* (*Pride and Prejudice* by Jane Austen)

sessions NOUN court cases were heard at specific times of the year called sessions ❑ *He lay in prison very ill, during the whole interval between his committal for trial, and the coming round of the Sessions.* (*Great Expectations* by Charles Dickens)

shabby ADJ shabby places look old and in bad condition ❑ *a little bit of a shabby village named Pikesville* (*The Adventures of Huckleberry Finn* by Mark Twain)

shay-cart NOUN a shay-cart was a small cart drawn by one horse ❑ *"I were at the Bargemen t'other night, Pip;"*

whenever he subsided into affection, he called me Pip, and whenever he relapsed into politeness he called me Sir; "when there come up in his shay-cart Pumblechook." (Great Expectations by Charles Dickens)

shilling NOUN a shilling is an old unit of currency. There were twenty shillings in every British pound ❑ *"Ten shillings too much," said the gentleman in the white waistcoat.* (*Oliver Twist* by Charles Dickens)

shines NOUN tricks or games ❑ *well, it would make a cow laugh to see the shines that old idiot cut* (*The Adventures of Huckleberry Finn* by Mark Twain)

shirking VERB shirking means not doing what you are meant to be doing, or evading your duties ❑ *some of you shirking lubbers* (*Treasure Island* by Robert Louis Stevenson)

shiver my timbers PHRASE shiver my timbers is an expression which was used by sailors and pirates to express surprise ❑ *why, shiver my timbers, if I hadn't forgotten my score!* (*Treasure Island* by Robert Louis Stevenson)

shoe-roses NOUN shoe-roses were roses made from ribbons which were stuck on to shoes as decoration ❑ *the very shoe-roses for Netherfield were got by proxy* (*Pride and Prejudice* by Jane Austen)

singular ADJ singular means very great and remarkable or strange ❑ *"Singular dream," he says* (*The Adventures of Huckleberry Finn* by Mark Twain)

sire NOUN sire is an old word which means lord or master or elder ❑ *She also defied her sire* (*Little Women* by Louisa May Alcott)

sixpence NOUN a sixpence was half of a shilling ❑ *if she had only a shilling in the world, she would be very lilkely to give away sixpence of it* (*Emma* by Jane Austen)

slavey NOUN the word slavey was used when there was only one servant in a house or boarding-house – so she had to perform all the duties of a larger staff ❑ *Two distinct knocks, sir, will produce the slavey at any time* (*The Old Curiosity Shop* by Charles Dickens)

slender ADJ weak ❑ *In slender accents of sweet verse* (*The Prelude* by William Wordsworth)

slop-shops NOUN slop-shops were shops where cheap ready-made clothes were sold. They mainly sold clothes to sailors ❑ *Accordingly, I took the jacket off, that I might learn to do without it; and carrying it under my arm, began a tour of inspection of the various slop-shops.* (*David Copperfield* by Charles Dickens)

sluggard NOUN a lazy person ❑ *"Stand up and repeat 'Tis the voice of the sluggard,'" said the Gryphon.* (*Alice's Adventures in Wonderland* by Lewis Carroll)

smallpox NOUN smallpox is a serious infectious disease ❑ *by telling the men we had smallpox aboard* (*The Adventures of Huckleberry Finn* by Mark Twain)

smalls NOUN smalls are short trousers ❑ *It is difficult for a large-headed, small-eyed youth, of lumbering make and heavy countenance, to look dignified under any circum-stances; but it is more especially so, when superadded to these personal attractions are a red nose and yellow smalls* (*Oliver Twist* by Charles Dickens)

sneeze-box NOUN a box for snuff was called a sneeze-box because sniffing snuff makes the user sneeze ❑ *To think of Jack Dawkins — lummy Jack — the Dodger — the Artful Dodger — going abroad for a common twopenny-halfpenny sneeze-box!* (*Oliver Twist* by Charles Dickens)

snorted VERB slept ❑ *Or snorted we in the Seven Sleepers' den?* (*The Good-Morrow* by John Donne)

snuff NOUN snuff is tobacco in powder form which is taken by sniffing ❑

as he thrust his thumb and forefinger into the proffered snuff-box of the undertaker: which was an ingenious little model of a patent coffin. (*Oliver Twist* by Charles Dickens)

soliloquized VERB to soliloquize is when an actor in a play speaks to himself or herself rather than to another actor ❏ *"A new servitude! There is something in that," I soliloquized (mentally, be it understood; I did not talk aloud) (Jane Eyre* by Charlotte Brontë)

sough NOUN a sough is a drain or a ditch ❏ *as you may have noticed the sough that runs from the marshes* (*Wuthering Heights* by Emily Brontë)

spirits NOUN a spirit is the nonphysical part of a person which is believed to remain alive after their death ❏ *that I might raise up spirits when I please* (*Doctor Faustus 1.5* by Christopher Marlowe)

spleen ◼ NOUN here spleen means a type of sadness or depression which was thought to only affect the wealthy ❏ *yet here I could plainly discover the true seeds of spleen* (*Gulliver's Travels* by Jonathan Swift) ◼ NOUN irritability and low spirits ❏ *Adieu to disappointment and spleen* (*Pride and Prejudice* by Jane Austen)

spondulicks NOUN spondulicks is a slang word which means money ❏ *not for all his spondulicks and as much more on top of it* (*The Adventures of Huckleberry Finn* by Mark Twain)

stalled of VERB to be stalled of something is to be bored with it ❏ *I'm stalled of doing naught* (*Wuthering Heights* by Emily Brontë)

stanchion NOUN a stanchion is a pole or bar that stands upright and is used as a buidling support ❏ *and slid down a stanchion* (*The Adventures of Huckleberry Finn* by Mark Twain)

stang NOUN stang is another word for pole which was an old measurement ❏ *These fields were intermingled with woods of half a stang* (*Gulliver's Travels* by Jonathan Swift)

starlings NOUN a starling is a wall built around the pillars that support a bridge to protect the pillars ❏ *There were states of the tide when, having been down the river, I could not get back through the eddy-chafed arches and starlings of old London Bridge* (*Great Expectations* by Charles Dickens)

startings NOUN twitching or night-time movements of the body ❏ *with midnight's startings* (*On His Mistress* by John Donne)

stomacher NOUN a panel at the front of a dress ❏ *but send her aunt the pattern of a stomacher* (*Emma* by Jane Austen)

stoop VERB swoop ❏ *Once a kite hovering over the garden made a swoop at me* (*Gulliver's Travels* by Jonathan Swift)

succedaneum NOUN a succedaneum is a substitute ❏ *But as a succedaneum* (*The Prelude* by William Wordsworth)

suet NOUN a hard animal fat used in cooking ❏ *and your jaws are too weak For anything tougher than suet* (*Alice's Adventures in Wonderland* by Lewis Carroll)

sultry ADJ sultry weather is hot and damp. Here sultry means unpleasant or risky ❏ *for it was getting pretty sultry for us* (*The Adventures of Huckleberry Finn* by Mark Twain)

summerset NOUN summerset is an old spelling of somersault. If someone does a somersault, they turn over completely in the air ❏ *I have seen him do the summerset* (*Gulliver's Travels* by Jonathan Swift)

supper NOUN supper was a light meal taken late in the evening. The main meal was dinner which was eaten at four or five in the afternoon ❏ *and the supper table was all set out* (*Emma* by Jane Austen)

surfeits VERB to surfeit in something is to have far too much of it, or to overindulge in it to an unhealthy degree ❑ *He surfeits upon cursed necromancy* (*Doctor Faustus chorus* by Christopher Marlowe)

surtout NOUN a surtout is a long close-fitting overcoat ❑ *He wore a long black surtout reaching nearly to his ankles* (*The Old Curiosity Shop* by Charles Dickens)

swath NOUN swath is the width of corn cut by a scythe ❑ *while thy hook Spares the next swath* (*Ode to Autumn* by John Keats)

sylvan ADJ sylvan means belonging to the woods ❑ *Sylvan historian* (*Ode on a Grecian Urn* by John Keats)

taction NOUN taction means touch. This means that the people had to be touched on the mouth or the ears to get their attention ❑ *without being roused by some external taction upon the organs of speech and hearing* (*Gulliver's Travels* by Jonathan Swift)

Tag and Rag and Bobtail PHRASE the riff-raff, or lower classes. Used in an insulting way ❑ *"No," said he; "not till it got about that there was no protection on the premises, and it come to be considered dangerous, with convicts and Tag and Rag and Bobtail going up and down."* (*Great Expectations* by Charles Dickens)

tallow NOUN tallow is hard animal fat that is used to make candles and soap ❑ *and a lot of tallow candles* (*The Adventures of Huckleberry Finn* by Mark Twain)

tan VERB to tan means to beat or whip ❑ *and if I catch you about that school I'll tan you good* (*The Adventures of Huckleberry Finn* by Mark Twain)

tanyard NOUN the tanyard is part of a tannery, which is a place where leather is made from animal skins ❑ *hid in the old tanyard* (*The Adventures of Huckleberry Finn* by Mark Twain)

tarry ADJ tarry means the colour of tar or black ❑ *his tarry pig-tail* (*Treasure Island* by Robert Louis Stevenson)

thereof PHRASE from there ❑ *By all desires which thereof did ensue* (*On His Mistress* by John Donne)

thick with, be PHRASE if you are 'thick with someone' you are very close, sharing secrets – it is often used to describe people who are planning something secret ❑ *Hasn't he been thick with Mr Heathcliff lately?* (*Wuthering Heights* by Emily Brontë)

thimble NOUN a thimble is a small cover used to protect the finger while sewing ❑ *The paper had been sealed in several places by a thimble* (*Treasure Island* by Robert Louis Stevenson)

thirtover ADJ thirtover is an old word which means obstinate or that someone is very determined to do want they want and can not be persuaded to do something in another way ❑ *I have been living on in a thirtover, lackadaisical way* (*Tess of the D'Urbervilles* by Thomas Hardy)

timbrel NOUN timbrel is a tambourine ❑ *What pipes and timbrels?* (*Ode on a Grecian Urn* by John Keats)

tin NOUN tin is slang for money/cash ❑ *Then the plain question is, an't it a pity that this state of things should continue, and how much better would it be for the old gentleman to hand over a reasonable amount of tin, and make it all right and comfortable* (*The Old Curiosity Shop* by Charles Dickens)

tincture NOUN a tincture is a medicine made with alcohol and a small amount of a drug ❑ *with ink composed of a cephalic tincture* (*Gulliver's Travels* by Jonathan Swift)

tithe NOUN a tithe is a tax paid to the church ❑ *and held farms which, speaking from a spiritual point of view, paid highly-desirable tithes* (*Silas Marner* by George Eliot)

towardly ADJ a towardly child is dutiful or obedient ❑ *and a towardly child* (*Gulliver's Travels* by Jonathan Swift)

toys NOUN trifles are things which are considered to have little importance, value, or significance ❑ *purchase my life from them by some bracelets, glass rings, and other toys* (*Gulliver's Travels* by Jonathan Swift)

tract NOUN a tract is a religious pamphlet or leaflet ❑ *and Joe Harper got a hymn-book and a tract* (*The Adventures of Huckleberry Finn* by Mark Twain)

train-oil NOUN train-oil is oil from whale blubber ❑ *The train-oil and gunpowder were shoved out of sight in a minute* (*Wuthering Heights* by Emily Brontë)

tribulation NOUN tribulation means the suffering or difficulty you experience in a particular situation ❑ *Amy was learning this distinction through much tribulation* (*Little Women* by Louisa May Alcott)

trivet NOUN a trivet is a three-legged stand for resting a pot or kettle ❑ *a pocket-knife in his right; and a pewter pot on the trivet* (*Oliver Twist* by Charles Dickens)

trot line NOUN a trot line is a fishing line to which a row of smaller fishing lines are attached ❑ *when he got along I was hard at it taking up a trot line* (*The Adventures of Huckleberry Finn* by Mark Twain)

troth NOUN oath or pledge ❑ *I wonder, by my troth* (*The Good-Morrow* by John Donne)

truckle NOUN a truckle bedstead is a bed that is on wheels and can be slid under another bed to save space ❑ *It rose under my hand, and the door yielded. Looking in, I saw a lighted candle on a table, a bench, and a mattress on a truckle bedstead.* (*Great Expectations* by Charles Dickens)

trump NOUN a trump is a good, reliable person wo can be trusted ❑ *This lad Hawkins is a trump, I perceive* (*Treasure Island* by Robert Louis Stevenson)

tucker NOUN a tucker is a frilly lace collar which is worn around the neck ❑ *Whereat Scrooge's niece's sister the plump one with the lace tucker: not the one with the roses blushed.* (*A Christmas Carol* by Charles Dickens)

tureen NOUN a large bowl with a lid from which soup or vegetables are served ❑ *Waiting in a hot tureen!* (*Alice's Adventures in Wonderland* by Lewis Carroll)

turnkey NOUN a prison officer; jailer ❑ *As we came out of the prison through the lodge, I found that the great importance of my guardian was appreciated by the turnkeys, no less than by those whom they held in charge.* (*Great Expectations* by Charles Dickens)

turnpike NOUN the upkeep of many roads of the time was paid for by tolls (fees) collected at posts along the road. There was a gate to prevent people travelling further along the road until the toll had been paid. ❑ *Traddles, whom I have taken up by appointment at the turnpike, presents a dazzling combination of cream colour and light blue; and both he and Mr. Dick have a general effect about them of being all gloves.* (*David Copperfield* by Charles Dickens)

twas PHRASE it was ❑ *twas but a dream of thee* (*The Good-Morrow* by John Donne)

tyrannized VERB tyrannized means bullied or forced to do things against their will ❑ *for people would soon cease coming there to be tyrannized over and put down* (*Treasure Island* by Robert Louis Stevenson)

'un NOUN 'un is a slang term for one – usually used to refer to a person ❑ *She's been thinking the old 'un* (*David Copperfield* by Charles Dickens)

undistinguished ADJ undiscriminating or incapable of making a distinction between good and bad things ❑ *their undistinguished appetite to devour everything* (*Gulliver's Travels* by Jonathan Swift)

use NOUN habit ❑ *Though use make you apt to kill me* (*The Flea* by John Donne)

vacant ADJ vacant usually means empty, but here Wordsworth uses it to mean carefree ❑ *To vacant musing, unreproved neglect* (*The Prelude* by William Wordsworth)

valetudinarian NOUN one too concerned with his or her own health. ❑ *for having been a valetudinarian all his life* (*Emma* by Jane Austen)

vamp VERB vamp means to walk or tramp to somewhere ❑ *Well, vamp on to Marlott, will 'ee* (*Tess of the D'Urbervilles* by Thomas Hardy)

vapours NOUN the vapours is an old term which means unpleasant and strange thoughts, which make the person feel nervous and unhappy ❑ *and my head was full of vapours* (*Robinson Crusoe* by Daniel Defoe)

vegetables NOUN here vegetables means plants ❑ *the other vegetables are in the same proportion* (*Gulliver's Travels* by Jonathan Swift)

venturesome ADJ if you are venturesome you are willing to take risks ❑ *he must be either hopelessly stupid or a venturesome fool* (*Wuthering Heights* by Emily Brontë)

verily ADJ verily means really or truly ❑ *though I believe verily* (*Robinson Crusoe* by Daniel Defoe)

vicinage NOUN vicinage is an area or the residents of an area ❑ *and to his thought the whole vicinage was haunted by her.* (*Silas Marner* by George Eliot)

victuals NOUN victuals means food ❑ *grumble a little over the victuals* (*The Adventures of Huckleberry Finn* by Mark Twain)

vintage NOUN vintage in this context means wine ❑ *Oh, for a draught of vintage!* (*Ode on a Nightingale* by John Keats)

virtual ADJ here virtual means powerful or strong ❑ *had virtual faith* (*The Prelude* by William Wordsworth)

vittles NOUN vittles is a slang word which means food ❑ *There never was such a woman for givin' away vittles and drink* (*Little Women* by Louisa May Alcott)

voided straight PHRASE voided straight is an old expression which means emptied immediately ❑ *see the rooms be voided straight* (*Doctor Faustus 4.1* by Christopher Marlowe)

wainscot NOUN wainscot is wood panel lining in a room so wainscoted means a room lined with wooden panels ❑ *in the dark wainscoted parlor* (*Silas Marner* by George Eliot)

walking the plank PHRASE walking the plank was a punishment in which a prisoner would be made to walk along a plank on the side of the ship and fall into the sea, where they would be abandoned ❑ *about hanging, and walking the plank* (*Treasure Island* by Robert Louis Stevenson)

want VERB want means to be lacking or short of ❑ *The next thing wanted was to get the picture framed* (*Emma* by Jane Austen)

wanting ADJ wanting means lacking or missing ❑ *wanting two fingers of the left hand* (*Treasure Island* by Robert Louis Stevenson)

wanting, I was not PHRASE I was not wanting means I did not fail ❑ *I was not wanting to lay a foundation of religious knowledge in his mind* (*Robinson Crusoe* by Daniel Defoe)

ward NOUN a ward is, usually, a child who has been put under the protection of the court or a guardian for his or her protection ❑

I call the Wards in Jarndcye. The are caged with all the others. (*Bleak House* by Charles Dickens)

waylay VERB to waylay someone is to lie in wait for them or to intercept them ❏ *I must go up the road and waylay him* (*The Adventures of Huckleberry Finn* by Mark Twain)

weazen NOUN weazen is a slang word for throat. It actually means shrivelled ❏ *You with a uncle too! Why, I knowed you at Gargery's when you was so small a wolf that I could have took your weazen betwixt this finger and thumb and chucked you away dead* (*Great Expectations* by Charles Dickens)

wery ■ ADV very ❏ *Be wery careful o' vidders all your life* (*Pickwick Papers* by Charles Dickens) ■ *See* wibrated

wherry NOUN wherry is a small swift rowing boat for one person ❏ *It was flood tide when Daniel Quilp sat himself down in the wherry to cross to the opposite shore.* (*The Old Curiosity Shop* by Charles Dickens)

whether PREP whether means which of the two in this example ❏ *we came in full view of a great island or continent (for we knew not whether)* (*Gulliver's Travels* by Jonathan Swift)

whetstone NOUN a whetstone is a stone used to sharpen knives and other tools ❏ *I dropped pap's whetstone there too* (*The Adventures of Huckleberry Finn* by Mark Twain)

wibrated VERB in Dickens's use of the English language 'w' often replaces 'v' when he is reporting speech. So here 'wibrated' means 'vibrated'. In Pickwick Papers a judge asks Sam Weller (who constantly confuses the two letters) 'Do you spell is with a 'v' or a 'w'?' to which Weller replies 'That depends upon the taste and fancy of the speller, my Lord' ❏ *There are strings . . . in the human heart that had better not be wibrated'* (*Barnaby Rudge* by Charles Dickens)

wicket NOUN a wicket is a little door in a larger entrance ❏ *Having rested here, for a minute or so, to collect a good burst of sobs and an imposing show of tears and terror, he knocked loudly at the wicket;* (*Oliver Twist* by Charles Dickens)

without CONJ without means unless ❏ *You don't know about me, without you have read a book by the name of The Adventures of Tom Sawyer* (*The Adventures of Huckleberry Finn* by Mark Twain)

wittles ■ NOUN vittles is a slang word which means food ❏ *I live on broken wittles – and I sleep on the coals* (*David Copperfield* by Charles Dickens) ■ *See* wibrated

woo VERB courts or forms a proper relationship with ❏ *before it woo* (*The Flea* by John Donne)

words, to have PHRASE if you have words with someone you have a disagreement or an argument ❏ *I do not want to have words with a young thing like you.* (*Black Beauty* by Emily Brontë)

workhouse NOUN workhouses were places where the homeless were given food and a place to live in return for doing very hard work ❏ *And the Union workhouses? demanded Scrooge. Are they still in operation?* (*A Christmas Carol* by Charles Dickens)

yawl NOUN a yawl is a small boat kept on a bigger boat for short trips. Yawl is also the name for a small fishing boat ❏ *She sent out her yawl, and we went aboard* (*The Adventures of Huckleberry Finn* by Mark Twain)

yeomanry NOUN the yeomanry was a collective term for the middle classes involved in agriculture ❏ *The yeomanry are precisely the order of people with whom I feel I can have nothing to do* (*Emma* by Jane Austen)

yonder ADV yonder means over there ❏ *all in the same second we seem to hear low voices in yonder!* (*The Adventures of Huckleberry Finn* by Mark Twain)